THE LAST SUNSET

I0460552

A Novel Written By

REECE HEWITT

www.thelastsunset.co.nz

Ark House Press
PO Box 1722, Port Orchard, WA 98366 USA
PO Box 1321, Mona Vale NSW 1660 Australia
PO Box 318 334, West Harbour, Auckland 0661 New Zealand
arkhousepress.com

Cataloguing in Publication Data:
Title: The Last Sunset
ISBN: 9780994596888 (pbk.)
Subjects: Fiction, Christian
Other Authors/Contributors: Hewitt, Reece

Cover Design: Jeremy Hay
Layout by initiateagency.com

Disclaimer

This is a work of fiction. Names, characters, businesses, places, events and incidents are either the products of the author's imagination or used in a fictitious manner. Any resemblance to actual persons, living or dead, or actual events is purely coincidental.

I would like to expressly convey to you (the reader) that were I to accidentally offend anyone due to the content contained in this book it is entirely unintentional of me to do so. Verses quoted from the Bible are often out of context and I have no theological qualifications. I have provided references to where you can read the rest of the surrounding material should the reader wish to.

Thanks to:
God
My loving wife
My awesome Beta Readers
My family and friends
Without all your support this book would not be possible.
high fives on me!

Cover art:
Jeremy Hay

I hope you enjoy the read!
- Reece Hewitt

TABLE OF CONTENTS

Chapter 1

Aisle Seven

A man in his late fifties walks through a supermarket. The man's name is Eric Peterson. He picks up a small green cardboard box from one of the shelves. He reads it.

"Please note: This product *may* contain all necessary vitamins and minerals for your daily needs."

Eric read aloud to himself in jest.

"Are they not sure what they put in these or something?"

The small supermarket was crammed but tidy. Typical easy listening music was playing quietly in the background. There were not many other shoppers this early in the morning, just the way Eric liked it.

After a brief thought he put the box of muesli bars back on to the shelf. Eric was wearing his comfortable black track pants and a well used green T-shirt. His balding head was bordered with light brown hair and he had a kind face.

He wandered a little further down aisle four of his local supermarket. Eric was a true family man, always happy to spend time at home. He thought of his loving wife Claire-Anne and his two children often. However, recently he couldn't help but feel a little lonely. His children had grown up and moved out of home and his wife was frequently away on business trips.

Eric ignored the escalating violence and disease all over the front page of the local papers on display. He'd been avoiding nearly all the news for months now; he found it too depressing. Eric noticed one solitary box of his favorite cereal remaining on the top-most shelf of the breakfast aisle.

"Thank you God for making me tall," He prayed silently.

Eric had shopped at this supermarket hundreds of times before over the years and it now felt quite homely. He recognized all the staff that worked there, and smiled at them whenever he paid for his groceries. He couldn't remember their names but was thankful for the helpful invention of nametags. Not that he would be expected to know their names; he just liked knowing that if he wanted to use their names he could.

Eric pushed his lightly squeaking trolley slowly along. His mind started to slip into another day dream. A vision of greatness and bright lights started to enter his mind. Vague images of crowds and cheering. There were hundreds of faces all looking to him.

Another shopper walking into view at the end of the aisle jolted Eric back to reality. His favorite cereal 'Mighty-pops' had been selling fast and he wanted to make sure he got the last box. The other shopper started down the aisle towards him from the opposite end. Eric quickened his pace just in case they were after his box of cereal. Eric walked quickly, but not so fast that he embarrassed himself. He arrived before the other shopper, who continued past to another section.

Relaxing somewhat, Eric turned to peruse the breakfast foods. 'Wacky-Wheaties' on the next shelf down seemed to pop out at him. Eric dismissed it as the bright blue packaging doing its job. Definitely a more healthy option, but at that price he thought he could always get that one next time.

Eric reached up towards the last red box of Mighty-pops. Eric was tall and he still needed to stretch to reach it. He smiled as his fingertips touched the side of the box. No wonder this was the only one left. He began to read the back of the box as he pulled it down.

"Contains vitamins! 95% fat free! Great tasting…."

Eric's skull fragments tore into the cardboard box he was holding. The surrounding shelves were drenched in blood and bone. Eric collapsed to the floor; he was not surprisingly, dead. He never got to finish reading the cereal box that was still clutched in his hand. Eric died before he felt any pain, and had no knowledge of what killed him. If he had chosen any other cereal the high caliber bullet would have flown straight past his head and been harmlessly lodged in the shelving. If he had the chance, he wished he told his family how much he loved them.

The other few people in the supermarket were initially oblivious to Eric's death, and continued on with their shopping. Steve Jenkinson was the duty manager of the supermarket on that fateful day. He had been pleaded with by another manager to cover his early shift. Steve was not a morning person but he eventually accepted the shift swap.

Steve heard what he thought was another clumsy customer dropping a glass jar onto the floor. He put down his paperwork on to the desk in his office at the back of the supermarket and began to walk towards the source of the sound. Steve was planning on how he would scold his newest employee if the mess wasn't cleaned up by the time he arrived on the scene. Shrieks and crying pierced the air and Steve began to run.

Steve was greeted by the most horrific mess in aisle seven to date. Eric's dead body lay on the floor in the middle of the aisle with a growing crowd of onlookers standing around him. This was not the attention Eric was daydreaming of.

But this is not Eric's story; it is the story of his killer.

Chapter 2

Light winds

Bishop Kephas picked up his Bible and walked over to his favorite leather armchair. He was clad in his comfy white fluffy slippers and a faded blue dressing gown. He had a head of short grey hair and short stubbled beard. There was a soft light in his study and a familiar smell of home.

Kephas lowered himself slowly to sit. He wasn't as young as he used to be and was feeling his age a little more than usual today.

"Seventy seven years young," he would often assure himself.

Just as he sat down, the Bible he was holding slipped out of his hand and landed on the carpeted floor. It opened, but not to the page he had bookmarked. His eyes were drawn to read a certain verse as he picked it up off the ground.

Zephaniah 1

[14] The great day of the LORD is near—
near and coming quickly.
The cry on the day of the LORD is bitter;
the Mighty Warrior shouts his battle cry.
[15] That day will be a day of wrath—
a day of distress and anguish,
a day of trouble and ruin,
a day of darkness and gloom,
a day of clouds and blackness—

Kephas wondered what this could mean.

…

In the great expanse of the deep blue ocean there was a small yacht. Onboard, Zackary Michaels let out a relaxed sigh. This trip is just what he needed, time to relax, take things slowly and forget all his worries. Of which there were many. He felt like his life had just sped past him. The last couple of years especially felt like a dream. He had short brown hair; and his holiday outfit consisted of beige cargo shorts and a loose fitting pale grey t-shirt. He stretched out and made himself comfortable. He closed his eyes.

"What was the weather forecast Zacky?" a familiar voice called.

Zack considered for a moment pretending to fall back to sleep.

"Just a second Graham," he replied.

Zack could hear the soothing sound of the waves rolling all around him. He felt the gentle up and down of the boat beneath him and the cold sea air caressing his face. He reluctantly opened his eyes. The bright blue sky above shined in, causing him to squint. He put his hand up to shield his eyes and wondered where he put his sunglasses. Zack slowly sat up and looked around. He could see Graham looking at him from the back of the yacht expectantly.

"Yip, I'm getting there man."

Zack stood up from his comfortable spot lying on the front of the yacht and made his way to where Graham was.

"Um, light winds and a few clouds, was all I could remember it saying. Why?"

"Just checking."

He only now noticed that Graham wore a confused look and was counting on his fingers like he was trying to work something out. Graham had messy black hair and wore a blue t-shirt with an indistinguishable logo covering the back. He wore faded jeans with the legs rolled up showing his bare feet. Graham had one hand on the steering wheel that was rocking back and forth slowly trying to keep 'The Champion' on its course.

The forty foot pleasure yacht that the four early twenty-something-year-olds had rented for the week was slowly making its way further from shore.

Zack thought this cruise would take his mind off things. So far it wasn't working. Zack had a lot of emotional baggage and he had not found the courage to tell his best friend Graham. Zack wondered if he should mention it now.

"What's up?" Beth asked as she and Mindy climbed out of the cabin.

Beth had long dark hair with dark brown eyes. She wore scruffy faded jeans and a dressy silver blouse. Mindy had bright green eyes and had short rusty red hair. Mindy always had her hair tied up with a yellow ribbon. Today she wore a well-matched summer outfit consisting of a pale-red skirt and a white top with a flower pictured on it. Zack always had liked Mindy but hadn't yet had the nerve to tell her. They both sat down in the helm behind Graham.

"Oh nothing, just me being paranoid," Graham assured.

"Then why are we turning around?" Mindy pointed towards the wheel as Graham had inadvertently started turning the yacht in a slow left turn.

"Whoops! Silly me." He regained control and corrected course out towards the island in the distance.

"Do you want me to have a go?" Zack motioned a steering wheel gesture in the air in front of him, looking at Graham.

"Nah, I have got it sorted now, I was just trying to mentally re-affirm myself that my holiday pay will cover this lavish five star cruise."

They all chuckled. Graham was very good at making subtly strange facial expressions when he joked. 'The Champion', although it was a pleasure yacht, had seen better days. It was probably all painted one colour, but after repairs, wear, and time it was now a rainbow of undercoats, primers, and a faded light-blue. Being the cheapest rental yacht they could find, it was worth what they had paid for it, which was not much.

"I think that's half the fun! When going camping on a distant island you have to ride there in style!" Zack added.

"I'm looking forward to it. We have all our gear packed below deck now." Mindy said as she looked out to sea.

"Yip, adventure here we come!" Beth, her best friend said.

Beth leaned over and gave Graham a quick kiss on the cheek. Graham and Beth had been together for nearly a year now. Over time their public displays of affection had become a lot less awkward for Mindy and Zack.

After some casual chatter, Zack stood up from where he was sitting and strained his eyes to look into the distance.

"What is THAT?"

He pointed to a dark cloud in the sky to the left side of the boat. The others were oblivious, enjoying the slow sail out. Graham looked around the blue sky only noticing the occasional white fluffy cloud. The girls were too busy sunbathing to be bothered.

"What are you on about?" Graham asked.

"Over there, look!" Zack said pointing to the edge of the horizon at the dark grey gloomy looking cloud.

"I don't remember that being there five minutes ago," Graham said as he stood up trying to get a better look. The girls sat up and tried to see what all the fuss was about.

The bleak oppressive cloud was distant on the horizon yet it looked to be very large. But as they all looked on they noticed it was spreading quickly across the sky, slowly at first, then faster and faster.

"Um… can a cloud do that?" Zack asked.

He looked at the others on the boat but received no reply. They all had their eyes glued to the blackness growing over the sky. Zack's thoughts started to drift to what a hassle it would be to turn around now due to the weather. Zack wasn't sure if it was quickly growing in size or moving towards them, or both.

"I don't like the look of this..." Mindy said trying to hide her nervousness but not succeeding. "...Maybe we should turn around?" she suggested.

The cloud had now spread over one quarter of the horizon. It grew in height as it spread out and everything beneath it looked dull and bleak. Stretching out, the cloud was now over 'Captain's Island' which sat on the horizon in front of them. They could hardly see the island in the darkness that was consuming all beneath the cloud wall. There didn't look to be any rain, and there was an eerie silence about it. The odd seagull that had been flying overhead had disappeared. Graham hurried back to the wheel and started to turn the yacht around.

"Yeah, I don't like the look of this guys and girls. Let's start to head back to shore and we will see how it goes."

The others nodded, still looking at the cloud as the yacht slowly turned. Zack felt uneasy, he felt like this looming wall of oppression was coming after him. The enormous blanket of darkness was still a long way from the boat. However, a rumbling sound of thunder started to grow louder and louder. The sound was not like normal thunder, being a brief burst of sound. This persisted constantly, growing in volume and intensity. Mindy and Beth put their hands over their ears. Now the thunder was so loud that they had to shout to each other to be heard over the dreadful din.

"Girls! Hey! Beth! Mindy! Go into the cabin and make sure everything is all secure, the seas might get a bit choppy," Graham tried to holler over the grumbling of the approaching darkness.

"What?" Beth yelled back at Graham, pointing to her ears to indicate that she didn't hear him. Zack heard muffled yelling from behind him, looking at Graham, he nodded then shooed the girls into the cabin. A deafening crack in the thunder made everyone wince with pain, their ears now ringing.

Zack turned around, momentarily frozen, staring into the oncoming doom. His heart started to race, he could hear the beating of his heart throbbing in his ears. The cloud above flooded over them in a roar of wind that knocked both of them to the deck. Lying in the entrance to the cabin, Zack lay on his back and tilted his head back as he saw the sky in all directions was now covered in thick dense cloud. The rush of wind subsided slightly. He stood up, watching Graham mutter some indistinguishable profanity as he too got back to his feet. Graham returned to the wheel and stopped it from spinning.

"What's going on?" Zack yelled, trying to be heard over the rolling thunder.

Looking back towards the shore he saw the cloud snuff out the last rays of light in the distance. Looking up, he could not distinguish where the sun was in the sky. A dreary light covered everything as if it were just after dusk. Everything looked muted and dulled.

Without warning the thunder stopped. The silence that replaced it seemed unnatural and was more worrying to them all than the previous noise. All Zack could hear was the slight ringing in his ears. Beth poked her head out from the cabin door slowly removing her hands from her ears. Mindy emerged from behind her shortly after. They all looked at each other in stunned silence for a moment.

"Well, who wants some lunch?" Zack said with a cheeky grin. The girls managed to choke out a nervous smile. Graham retained his concerned look. They all looked pale and scared. They resembled a group of rabbits caught in the headlights of an oncoming truck. Graham tried to regain his composure and posed like he was unfazed by the whole thing. Beth shook her head when she saw him. Zack could not get rid of the lump he felt in his throat.

The sky was torn apart like it was merely a painted backdrop. First a small dark hole, then it grew larger and larger. Like the world was a party balloon with a hole in it, air started to rush out into the darkness. Everyone looked up. Zack was terrified. He thought the very fabric of reality was leaking out into this void. The darkness grew in four directions quickly to form a massive cross shape in the sky. It was so black inside that it reminded Zack of lessons in high-school, learning that even light couldn't escape a black hole. But they certainly never mentioned a cross-shaped version.

There was a loud howling as air rushed to escape towards the huge cross dominating the sky. With a blinding flash the cross was filled with a brilliant light that burst outwards covering everything. The light was pure white and dazzling. A cross shape was burnt on the retinas of every living human. Somehow this occurred whether they had a clear line of sight to the sky or not.

As the light burst outwards, it was paired with a deafening sound which could've been mistaken for the tolling of a giant bell. It was deep and pure, it resonated with everyone at their very core. It was as if it spoke some long forgotten ancient language that everyone understood. It seemed to say:

"This is the end. Repent and be saved."

Zack dropped to the floor and curled up in a ball like a scared fetus. He felt like he'd die at any moment. He could hear the cries and moans of the others onboard flailing in the darkness. His breathing was panicked. The cross shape imprinted on his eyes reminded him of the cross on the top of the local Church.

He took his hands away from his face, blinking rapidly. He looked around, but the cross persisted in the center of his vision. It was like looking at the sun and still seeing its shape after you look away. He could see nothing but blackness everywhere else. He felt like his eyes were open and touched them with his fingers to check. He waved his hand in front of his face and could not see it.

"I'm blind!!!" he yelled.

Beth shrieked and began to cry. Zack could hear Mindy sobbing behind him somewhere. He strained his still ringing ears and heard Graham to his left fumble around the cockpit, muttering something. He blinked and rubbed his eyes and still he could see nothing but the cross. A trail of blood from each eye stained his face like cheap mascara running after a sad movie.

Zack couldn't understand any of it. How did the lightning happen after the thunder? Wasn't it supposed to be the other way around? Why was it a cross shape? And how did that cloud cover the sky so fast? What did 'Repent and be saved' mean? Zack tried to make sense of it all in vain.

The four of them now sat in silence, too dazed and shocked for conversation. Each of them were only able to see a cross in front of them. Darkness enveloped everything else.

Zack continued blinking for what seemed like an eternity. As abruptly as it left him, his eyesight instantly returned. The world seemed terribly bright. Yet as his eyes became accustomed, he realized that it wasn't as bright as it should be for the middle of the afternoon. He looked around to see the others rubbing their eyes and squinting. He waved at Graham, and Graham waved back. Zack looked out to sea and saw in all direction a thin fog had set in. He couldn't see the shore no matter which way he turned.

Ducking into the cabin, Zack re-emerged with the binoculars. Standing on the highest point on the deck, he slowly scanned the horizon. Starting with the horizon in front of the yacht he tried to peer through the gloomy fog in hope of seeing land.

"Surely we couldn't have drifted too far?" Zack muttered.

"What do you mean Zack? Oh, and what the hell is going on?!" Graham blurted out as he stomped around the deck at the back of the yacht.

"Yeah, that's not helping Graham. I take it you lot saw the cross thing too?" Beth stared at Graham in a disapproving look he knew too well.

"I did," Mindy piped up from where she was sitting, surprisingly calm.

"Yeah, it must have been a reaction to the lightning stuff that went on," Graham said confidently, stepping over the two girls, reaching for the binoculars.

"Yeah, I don't think so!" Beth said.

Zack turned to face them.

"Let's just get one thing sorted at a time guys. I have absolutely no idea about what just went on, but I think we firstly need to sort out where we are and, more importantly, how to get back home."

"Agreed," Graham said nodding as he took the binoculars Zack handed him.

Nobody spoke, though all their minds were racing, trying to understand what had just occurred. It was easier to pretend none of it happened for a moment and focus on trying to get back to land.

Finally, Zack again pointed out in to the distance.

"Hey! I think I can see land!"

Zack realized he was smiling and let out a small sigh of relief.

"Where?" Mindy asked surprised, "I've been looking all around and haven't seen anything!"

Zack stood next to her and pointed to the opposite direction of where she was looking. As he looked again to what he thought was land in the distance, his heart started to pound in his chest. For a second he froze. Snapping himself out of it, he grabbed Mindy and pushed her towards the cabin. Mindy looked furiously at Zack for his less than gentle actions, but then an expression of terror washed over her face and her mouth dropped. The two of them dashed back towards the cabin as Graham and

Beth looked towards them from the cockpit. They both saw what Zack had firstly thought was land.

"Get below deck!" Zack screamed.

It took them a moment for their brains to process what they were looking at. There was a raised section in the distance, higher than the surrounding water, but it wasn't the right colour for land or rocks. Then it hit them. There was a giant wall of water surging towards them. The tidal wave was of such epic proportion that it spread to cover the majority of the horizon in a few short seconds. It was hard for Zack to judge the height of the wave, but he assumed it was large enough to be lethal to all on board.

Graham and Beth made it into the cabin with Mindy and Zack close behind them. With adrenalin pumping through his veins, Zack frantically fumbled to shut the cabin door. He finally slammed the door shut and snipped the lock. Zack fell back down the stairs onto his back. He swung his head around and was pleased to see the others climbing into the bunks grabbing pillows and blankets in a panic. The girls were crying. Graham was squealing. Zack's mind raced as he tried to decide whether he had time to quickly go back outside and take the sails down.

Zack was launched mid thought into the roof of the cabin as the wall of water slammed into the tiny boat. Their yacht was like a rubber ducky in a bath when a child jumps in. Zack was thrown into the cabin wall, landing hard on to the floor. The boat started to roll at a dizzying pace, and Zack lost consciousness as his head bit into the bulkhead.

So it turned out the weather man was wrong.

Zack woke up with a jolt. He could taste blood in his mouth as he began to look around. He became aware that he was still inside the cabin now with someone looming over him. He was not in his bed at home awaking from what he hoped was a bad dream. He could hear water dripping slowly behind him, and his hair was wet. Mindy looked down to meet Zack's gaze as she noticed him waking.

"Are you okay Mindy?" Zack said with a wince. He felt a sharp pain in his chest as if he had multiple bruised ribs, which he had.

"You are always the gentleman Zacky. Yes, I'm okay. I managed to wrap myself in blankets as the wave hit. I have my share of knocks and bruises, but otherwise good," Mindy said slowly as she peered into Zack's eyes, trying to ascertain if he was fully conscious. She put her finger in front of Zack's face and moved it side to side.

"Yip, I'm Ok too," Zack said as he slowly sat up, ignoring Mindy's eye test.

"How's Graham and Beth?"

"Similar state to me I guess. Graham's arm looks pretty sore but he insists it's alright, and Beth's back is going to keep her moving slowly for the next few days. I'm just amazed that are all still alive!" Mindy said as with a smile she stood. Zack loved her smile.

Zack pulled himself up slowly. Using the wall for support he gingerly followed Mindy out the cabin door and into the cockpit. As he stuck his head outside he hoped to see blue sky. His face fell as his eyes met the sky, blanketed in a dark canvas of cloud and gloom.

"Good to see you are up dude," Graham said cheerfully, despite the circumstances. Zack wondered how he could remain sounding so authentically positive.

"Glad to see you all are in one piece too," he replied.

Zack looked around the top of the yacht, noticing the lack of mast. Most of the hull was splintered and broken. Large openings gaped where the mast and steering wheel should have been. Zack was confused yet delighted that they hadn't sunk. Their vessel now looked as bad as they all felt.

"So I guess we won't get our bond payment back on the rental aye?" Zack said with a strained smile.

Each of them had blood and bruises spattered over them.

"Do you want the good news or the bad news?" Graham asked with a grin.

"How can there be any good news?" Zack spat back.

"Well, we have no means of communication as the radio is dead..." Zack looked around for his phone. "Yes, I checked the mobile phones too," Graham added.

Defiantly, Zack grabbed his phone from his pocket only to see a 'no signal' message on the screen. He rolled it over in his hands, glad that it wasn't lost or broken in the chaos.

"…And I'm sure we all feel pretty broken, much like our fine vessel," Graham continued as he slapped the deck next to him. The yacht spat out a splinter as he did so.

"But we do now luckily, actually have land in sight. I think that mother of all waves washed us back to shore a full day or so's worth of sailing."

He motioned over his right shoulder. Sure enough, there was the shoreline with white water breaking upon the rocky coast.

Steep cliffs and roaring waves extended out to the right as far as the eye could see. As Zack gazed over the left side of the coast he saw the rocks become smaller with pockets of sand in between. The battered 'Old Coast Hotel' with its historic lighthouse was a little further inland and just within view. Zack could see that debris had floated on to the beach. He wondered whether he'd see parts of their boat. He was surprised by the lack of lights from the city of Brakenside that would usually be seen on the horizon.

"Good stuff, but how are we going to get back to shore?" Zack asked, looking to the back of the yacht where the reserve two-horsepower outboard motor should have been. Only a broken bracket remained.

"…Does the diesel engine still work?"

"Not at all, Zacky, and I'm surprised you didn't hear me swearing at it earlier. You must have really been out cold aye?" Graham tapped the side of his head.

Zack mirrored his gesture and quickly drew his hand away as his head rebuked him for prodding his own wound. He looked down on his hands; they were both splattered in blood. He started to shake, he had seen this gruesome sight once before. Though last time it was not his blood. He shook his head to rid his mind of the thoughts he dare not deal with.

Beth smiled triumphantly as she emerged from the cabin holding two cheap looking plastic oars.

"I found these under one of the bunks…" she said, handing one to both Graham and Zack.

"…I figured since I found them, you two can do the rowing."

She sat down with a smug look on her face.

Graham smiled as he moved to the left side of the boat to start rowing. Zack looked at Mindy who was rolling her eyes, and made his way over the broken hull to start the long painful row back to shore. After a few minutes it was clear that the two of them rowing would not be enough. Beth and Mindy pried broken planks from the upper deck and helped row.

After hours of tiring and tedious rowing, the battered yacht reached the shore. The four of them were out of breath and their arms were burning.

"Hey... let's... just... ground it... here on the... beach aye?" Zack said between gasps of air.

Graham looked over to him and nodded. He didn't want to try and talk, realizing he was more unfit than he thought. There was a scraping sound as the keel of the boat hit the sand on the bottom of the cove. Relieved, Zack paused his paddling. The four tried to row for another couple of minutes but made little headway trying to ground the yacht.

"We should really tie this up so it doesn't get washed out to sea," Beth said when she caught her breath.

"Sure thing," Graham replied as he stopped rowing and lay down to catch his breath. Zack collapsed too and closed his eyes, being happy in the moment. It felt good to forget all the crazy events that had just occurred and breathe in the fresh sea air.

Unbeknownst to everyone, behind the densely clouded sky, the sun set for the last time.

CHAPTER 3

OLD HOTEL

Zack was roused from his brief rest by a splash in the water behind him. Beth had jumped into the water at the back of the boat. Zack hurriedly got to his feet to see what was going on. He saw Mindy throwing a rope down to her.

"I didn't really want to wait for you two, so I thought I'd tie up the boat," Beth called.

She restrained the look of shock as the cold water made her doubt her enthusiasm on getting back to shore.

Zack smiled at Graham and saw his confused look fade from his face. He then watched Beth as she swam her way with rope in hand closer to shore, finding that she could now touch the bottom she waded the rest of the way to the beach. She found a suitably large rock and looped the anchor rope around it, tying it with a complex knot. Mindy tied off her end of the anchor rope around the front of the yacht with a random assortment of basic knots. Frustrated with the result she kicked the coils of rope as she got up and made her way back to the cabin. Zack turned with a questioning look on his face.

"It will hold," she said quickly.

"I'm sure it will," he replied letting her move past him.

"Ok people, let's see if we can get a phone line or something from that old place. We can return for our stuff later." Graham pointed towards the old hotel upon the cliff just out of view. He jumped into the water and made his way to shore.

Zack and Mindy followed close behind. Zack shivered and winced as the cold sea water pinched at his every cut and bruise. He was last out the water and found the others wringing their clothes on the small beach. The sand was course, with a large amount of tiny rocks scattered about. He could feel them under his bare feet with the occasional sharp prick underfoot reminding him to tread gently. He looked at the others who didn't seem to be noticing and then stomped out of the water.

Zack started to feel heavy as his soaked clothes stuck to him. He began wringing out his T-shirt as he stepped over the debris and broken pieces of boat that lay littered about them. The four trudged up the muddy trail that wound back and forth up the steep cliff face ahead. Large rocks jutted out into the path at various points, making it narrower than Zack would have preferred. Looking up he could just see the roof of the old hotel. They were all panting when they reached the peak. One at a time they sat on the grass at the top of the cliff to catch their breath.

"This is far too much exercise for a holiday," Zack said between breaths. Looking over at the lighthouse and hotel he smiled. Soon everything would return to normality, he thought.

Zack was wrong.

The lighthouse hadn't been in use since the major mineral mine, a few hours drive away, ran dry many years ago. The tall lighthouse was made of brick and had weeds making their way up almost to the top. Most of the glass windows were dirty and cracked. The white paint on the walkway around the light was peeling and the wood was starting to show through on the edges.

Attached to the lighthouse was a large brick house that had been converted into a hotel five years ago. The owner had attempted to make it a romantic get-away resort. Admittedly the sea-views were good, but the incessant cold sea winds and hours of driving time back to the city made it unpopular. It closed a year later. The two story building was forgotten by most people who lived in the closest town of Brakenside.

Zack's hope of finding help inside the hotel started to wane as his eyes absorbed the fallen state of the place. Some of the windows were boarded up and the surrounding gardens were horribly overgrown. It looked like there had been an earthquake recently as there were large cracks in the walls on the left hand side of the building. Parts of the roof had caved in and he could see into one of the second story rooms.

He could see grass growing in the gutters and a bird's nest in the top corners of the entry way. The roof had been painted blue, but was now spattered in bird droppings. He thought it would have been covered in graffiti but rationalised that it was too far out to be worth the trip.

His eyes looked over to the garage to see a grey ute parked with fresh mud in its tires and what looked like oil all over the ground beneath it.

"Hey, I didn't think anyone still came out here?" he said nodding his head towards the garage. The others looked over.

"That's probably the owner's car, Barney or something I think his name is. I heard he lives out here sometimes, bit of a weirdo," Graham replied as he started walking towards the front door.

The four of them wandered over to the hotel. Zack felt a bit uncomfortable turning up at a stranger's house, but he didn't say anything. He decided he would let Graham do the talking, as it sounded like he knew the owner. The paint chipped wooden door greeted them with silence. Graham knocked loudly on the door and stood back. The four of them stood in the entryway looking around for a moment. Graham knocked again. They waited.

"He must not be home. You think if he was he'd be trying to do something about all this damage," Beth said as she started to walk around the left side of the house.

Graham nodded at Beth and started walking around the right side of the house. Zack and Mindy stood in the entryway and looked at each other.

"I'll wait here with you Mindy in case he is just really slow at getting to the door," Zack puffed out his chest slightly as he spoke. Mindy raised her eyebrows at him and muttered "Okay."

Mindy sat on the grass in front of the hotel. She sat cross-legged, picking up the grass and ripping it into small bits. Zack turned to see Graham come around the left side of the building. He turned to the other side expecting to see Beth come around the corner, but she didn't.

"Where did Beth go?" Zack asked as he heard the front door unlock from the inside. The large wooden door slowly creaked open and Beth stepped out with a large grin on her face.

"Miss me?"

"What are you two doing? You can't just break into somebody's house!" Zack spat as Graham followed Beth inside. Graham turned and said in a calming voice

"Relax! The window was open, we didn't break anything, I'm sure the old dude wouldn't mind us using the phone. Besides, the place is half-busted up anyway."

"I don't like it," Zack said half to himself.

"Maybe he has some food?" Mindy stood up and sped past Zack through the door looking for the kitchen. Zack turned around like he knew there was somebody watching them.

Zack's eyes scanned the small bushes on the border of the cliff and the trees off to the side behind the garage. Seeing no movement he tried to calm himself. He felt frustrated that he was unnerved by nothing. Then his eyes caught a glimmer of light reflecting off the ute parked in the garage. He started to walk over to get a better look.

Zack realized it was nothing more than a reflection in the side window. As he came closer he could see there was mud all over the side of the vehicle too, not just on the ground beneath it. Confused he got closer and saw it wasn't mud at all, but it was a dull red color.

"Could it be blood?" he wondered.

He jogged across the small grass clearing and reaching the garage slowed to a walking pace. There looked to be bloodied hand prints smeared all over the window and door handle. His heart started to pump quicker.

Zack looked down at the ground beneath him and saw blood splattered in a disturbingly large area. He lifted his right foot quickly, realizing that he had been standing in it.

He peered through the blood-smeared window but leaned too close and got some on his nose. Zack hurriedly rubbed it off onto his sleeve. He could see the keys were in the ignition and the doors were locked.

Zack's mind recalled the few times he had locked his own keys in his car. He looked around and couldn't see the source of all the blood. Looking onto the walls of the garage he could see more smeared handprints. He walked around the side of the garage and saw another smear of blood in the grass. He walked over to it and saw more drops leading towards a small bloodstained bush on the edge of the cliff. He jogged over and leaned over the bush. The thought of a long fall onto the rocky wave beaten shore below made him lean back quickly. Looking again he saw only a rocky slope with waves lashing at the base. No injured hotel owner, no body.

"Hey!"

Zack quickly turned as he heard a voice shouting at him from behind.

"What *are* you doing?" Mindy looked at Zack puzzled as she made her way over to him. He noticed she was chewing and then saw the apple with a big bite out of it in her hand.

"Where did you get that from? You can't take the dead guy's food!"

She slowed her walk as she heard him.

"What *dead* guy?"

Zack jogged over and met her at the garage. He pointed towards the blood as Mindy looked over. She stopped chewing.

"What's all this?" She took a step back and checked that she hadn't been standing in the blood on the ground. Zack remembered that he did earlier and scuffed his shoes in the grass.

"There is a trail leading over to the cliff face too. Look."

He motioned for her to follow him but she started to walk back inside.

"No thanks," she replied.

They made their way back to the house. Zack rattled his brain for something to say when Graham yelled out something indistinguishable from inside. They walked through the front door and saw the others in the kitchen making sandwiches.

"Don't eat all the dead guy's food. There is a big mess of blood on that ute and it leads to the cliff. You are eating all his stuff!"

"Whoa. Slow down man!" Graham said chewing with a pleased expression on his face, obviously happy with his sandwich.

Zack told Graham and Beth what he had seen outside. Beth started to chew more slowly and put down her sandwich as Zack described the trail of blood. Mindy saw the look on Graham's face that showed he was regretting putting extra tomato sauce on his now half-eaten sandwich.

"Okay, so you are saying you couldn't find his body, right? There has to be a logical explanation, it doesn't mean he is dead," Beth said defiant of Zack's conclusion. She ate the rest of her sandwich.

"Yeah, maybe he went to try and get into his truck, 'cause he cut himself gardening that bush by the cliff and then decided he would not worry about it so left on a bike or something…" Graham's voice became quieter as he spoke, so it was apparent that he didn't believe his own story.

Zack just looked at him, shaking his head slightly.

"So what are we going to do? This is turning out to be a really awful holiday." Mindy spoke up as she started to assemble herself something to eat from the ingredients left on the table.

She pushed the tomato sauce to the furthest side of the table.

"Well the landline phone doesn't work, so we can't call anybody, I re-checked my mobile phone and that still has no signal." Graham muttered as he finished off the food in his hand.

Zack suddenly remembered his mobile phone was still in his pocket. He pulled it out and put it on the table. A small puddle of sea water began to seep out from it. Zack's face fell. Mindy patted Zack on the back.

Graham continued.

"So either the guy didn't pay his phone bill or that atmospheric event from before stuffed up the landline network too. Either way we may as well stay the night here."

"Can't we just drive back to town now?" Zack spoke as he thought about how long it would take to get back to Brakenside.

"Probably three hours driving a dirty ute, in the gloom with two people sitting in the tray on the back. And by the looks of the sky it's going to rain. No thanks," Beth said.

"We may as well have a warm night's sleep inside and tackle the trip tomorrow, especially with what we all went through today," Graham said.

Zack stretched a bit as sleep was mentioned and his tired body suddenly seemed heavier. A warm bed and a sleep-in tomorrow morning sounded pretty good to him.

"Good point." he admitted.

The others, feeling tired and worn, nodded.

Zack started to make himself some dinner. He couldn't think of any more excuses as his stomach became more and more insistent. Beth and Mindy went upstairs and laid claim to the master bedroom.

"You boys can sleep in the guest room," Beth said as she started up the stairs opposite the kitchen with what was left of her sandwich in her hand.

"Yeah, I'm dead tired, I think an early night is a good idea." Graham put away what was left of the bread and spreads and made his way into the guest room. He gave Beth a goodnight kiss at the stairs.

"What about our stuff in the yacht?" Zack asked.

"It will be fine there until tomorrow morning Zack. I doubt there will be two storms in one day," Mindy said as she disappeared up the stairs behind Beth.

Zack walked into the guest room and was relieved to see two single beds on either side of the room. Zack liked his own space. There was a large window covered by floral curtains in front of him. He heard Graham running water in the little bathroom to his left. Graham's jumper lay on the bed to the right. Zack dropped onto the other bed on his back. It was surprisingly comfortable and his eyes closed without thought as he started to relax. He took a deep breath and was glad he wasn't on the back of a ute driving back into town. He began to think about what had happened that day, but pushed it from his mind.

"I'm not ready to think about that yet," he mouthed quietly. "I have done enough hard work for one day".

After Graham had finished in the bathroom, Zack went in and washed his face. The cool water splashing on his face was refreshing. Looking in the mirror, he wiped some of the blood that had stained his face from the cut on his head. He made extra sure he had got the entire blood smudge off his nose.

"Time for bed my man! I've shut the front door and we don't need to do anything else today but sleep," Graham said as he collapsed into his bed.

He was now showing how much the day had taken out of him. Zack wriggled down into the blankets and drifted off to sleep.

Zack awoke with a jolt. Blurred images of blood, violence, rage and pain filled Zack's mind. He shook his head with a shudder, sitting up in his bed. He didn't usually get nightmares, though he didn't normally sleep in some dead guy's house either. Zack's suspicions were correct, though he couldn't convince the others Barney was dead. The owner of the hotel had been tortured and had thrown himself off the cliff breaking his neck at the bottom. The waves had moved the body down the shore out of view.

A slow scratching noise on the window made Zack turn his head. He saw only the dimly lit room, with Graham sleeping in the other bed. Graham was curled up and facing the wall, lightly snoring. Zack stared at the window, his mind trying to make sense of the sound. He wondered if it was the girls outside trying to scare them or maybe a cat.

Again he heard the scratching sound. Sounding like nails down a blackboard, it sent a shiver down his spine. He flicked off the blanket and sat on the edge of the bed. As he stared at the window he heard a scream that made him panic.

The cry sounded like the mix between a wounded animal howling and someone was trying to pronounce a foreign word.

Graham woke up with a jolt.

"Shut up Zack! I'm trying to sleep here," Graham spat angrily as he rolled over. As he watched Zack slowly shake his head in denial they both heard it again.

This time it was followed by some hissing and scraping noises by the window. This couldn't be the girls fooling around now, Zack thought. That sound couldn't be human.

Before either of them could speak again, the window shattered inwards. It sent glass flying into the room in all directions. The curtains were ripped off the wall and covered a dog size object now wriggling in the center of the room. Zack sat there frozen for a moment his mind absorbing all the details. He saw Graham recoil back up against the wall on his bed. Graham was just about to say something when there was a ripping sound coming from the pile of curtains on the floor.

Zack's eyes darted back to the mess in the middle of the room. There was shards of broken glass caught up in the curtains. He now saw something protruding from the curtains. It looked like a long boney finger, which pierced the curtain, and was now slowly ripping it as it went. Several other spikes stabbed through the curtain and started shredding it in all directions. Zack's mind raced. Whatever it was, it was quickly breaking free of its bonds.

"Could it be a cat? No, a dog? No, since when did they have six claw-like talons. A giant spider!?" Zack's mind tried to make sense of it all in vain. The tattered curtain dropped to the floor around it and Graham and Zack both gasped in horror.

The creature they saw looked like a demon from the depths of Hell. It was covered in what looked like armor made from bones or small rocks. Glazed in mud, it was twitching unnaturally as if jabbed by an unseen blade. Its head looked like that of a wolf with an elongated snout. It had three eyes deeply set into its head. The middle one looked like a wet crystal and was a brighter red than the other two eyes. It glowed faintly.

It had a thin forked tongue that flicked in and out around the sharp teeth. Large ear-like horns split in to three on either side of the rear of its head. A large crest of spikes arched backwards between them. It hunched forward slightly, tapping on the ground with its long arms to steady itself as it stepped out of the ruined curtain. The creature smelt like burning flesh and was hissing. There was no mistaking this creature was evil in material form.

When Zack looked at its chest, it did not rise and fall like his own when he breathed. The creature violently jerked its head and locked three eyes on Zack. He could feel the adrenaline flowing through his body and an awkward lump growing in his throat. Without thinking, Zack quickly jumped off the bed and sprinted into the bathroom and locked the door behind him.

Hiding in the bathroom, his heart was now thumping in his chest, his stomach turned over and over. The seconds seemed to inch by.

"This can't be happening…" his mind kept telling him "..this must be a dream!?"

A crashing noise in the room made him jump, his heart pumped quicker. Zack just realized he had left Graham out there alone with that thing. His mind raced as to what could be happening to his best friend. Zack pushed it from his mind and tried to quiet his breathing but with no success. Fear gripped Zack by the throat and he retreated to a foetal position on the floor.

Zack jumped again as he heard a scratch on the bathroom door. His eyes darted towards the source of the sound. A slow scraping by several claws on the door drowned out all other sounds. He hugged himself tighter. A noise behind him made him jump. He had bumped the shelf behind him and caused a shampoo bottle to drop. There was a moment of silence.

Zack's eyes were now fixed on the door once more. Nothing. He let out a slow stuttered release of breath. He heard the creature move away from the door. The door shook with a loud crash as the demon threw itself against it. The door shook, but apart from splinters of wood and paint falling off, it remained closed. The clawing and scratching was now in a frenzied rage.

Zack stood up against the back bathroom wall and desperately looked for a way out. There was none. A shrill screech echoed through the bathroom as the creature broke a small hole in the bathroom door. Small claws flashed in and out of the door ripping away more and more broken wood. The creature stopped and its claws disappeared. Zack heard the girls from upstairs open the door to the boys' room.

"What the hell do you think you boys are doing at this hour?" Beth yelled angrily as she opened the door.

Mindy and Beth's eyes both were set on Graham in a stern stare. Graham stunned, just sat on his bed holding his bleeding arm, his eyes looking towards the bathroom. The girls both followed his gaze as the demon came into view. Zack's ears were filled with the sound of his friends screaming at the top of their lungs. He heard crashing and movement and he could not bear it any longer. In desperation he whispered:

"God, help me."

He felt something he was not expecting. It was courage. He quickly convinced himself he was not going to remain hiding in a bathroom like a schoolgirl on prom night.

"Yo-ou piece of junk," he stuttered, barely audible, gathering his determination.

"So much for the battle cry," he thought. Adrenaline surged in his veins and his muscles burst into life as he stepped away from the wall. He scanned the room for some sort of weapon. Small hotel-sized bottles of toiletries and some toilet paper looked back at him reluctantly.

"Nope," he said.

With his stomach crawling up his throat he ran at the damaged door and shoulder barged in to it. The top hinge made a loud crack and broke away from the wall. The door crashed over onto the floor with Zack on top of it.

Zack's shoulders and face stung with pain, splinters lodged into his side and he winced. He realized that maybe just opening the door would have been a better option. The creature was not crushed under the door as he'd hoped.

Instead the beast was facing his friends. Zack's dramatic entrance caused it to spin around. It was so close to him now; he could see it in all its horrific detail. It had a row of spikes from the top of its head trailing down to the tip of its tail. Barbed horns jutted out from its wide shoulders. Two larger spikes sprung out from its back. They were draped with a torn membrane, which made it look like the creature had bat-like wings at some point, though they looked useless now.

Two thin arms split into two separate forearms, each with its own set of three-clawed hands. The claws were glazed in a red stain, which Zack correctly assumed was blood. Its thin torso had what looked like rib bones protruding in the front of its chest. Its hind legs arched backwards with its knees behind its body. Between each limb there were sinews that connected it to the body. Its body had what looked like veins and muscles on the outside of its body in various places. Dark-coloured liquid seeped out of gaps between bone and muscle. Zack noticed that its arms and legs were not identical in length on each side. Though it could move quickly and with obvious strength, it looked like it had been decaying for years.

Zack could see his blood-stained friends were clutching various wounds, each with tears in their eyes and fear on their faces. Zack quickly stood up as the creature approached and readied himself. He stepped towards it and kicked it in the head as hard as he could. The demon flew backwards a short distance, but immediately got to its feet. The creature cocked its head looking back. It was unhurt and almost seemed to laugh. Zack's foot was throbbing.

Zack's eyes darted about the room, looking for something to hit the demon with. He stumbled back a few steps and picked up the upper half of the bathroom door. Holding it in two hands he swung it with all his might on to the beast. There was a satisfying cracking noise as the door smashed the demon onto to the floor.

"Ye-eah, that's right punk, how do you like that?" Zack's voice rose in volume as he angrily yelled at the wriggling creature under the door. Zack still didn't sound as confident as he'd like.

Zack jumped into the air and brought his weight down with a double-footed stomp. The sound of splintering wood was pierced by a high-pitched shriek. He jumped again, this time slipping on to his right knee as the door piece broke in half again. He quickly moved back as the demon wriggled free from splintered wood. It emerged with no sign of damage or injury.

"This thing can't be hurt?" he wondered in panic.

The creature shook itself free of the door pieces and raised its head as Zack bent down and picked up a chunk of door. He held it like a baseball bat and waited for the creature to attack. Its three eyes locked onto Zack, and it launched into the air towards him. The creature's lunge was quick, but not fast enough. The length of door slammed into the creature and launched across to the other side of the room. It was like hitting a cat with a cricket bat.

Again the creature got up quickly, unhurt. Zack was starting to run out of energy. He ran across the room and kicked the creature with as much force as he could muster, lifting it off the ground into the wall. Zack's foot was now pulsating. The demon landed, regained its footing, and launched itself at Zack. Mid-air, it swung its four arms with claws extended.

The claws tracked deep gashes through Zack's right forearm as he tried to fend the demon off. The agony rose up in Zack till he could contain it no more. He let out a wail and fell backwards against the bed holding his arm. Tears now blurred his vision.

Zack felt overwhelmed. He had spent all his energy and not even managed to hurt the beast, and with one hit he had been dropped like an amateur boxer.

The demon let out a victorious sounding hiss and started to creep towards the girls who were still slumped in the doorway. Zack looked over towards Graham; he was still on his bed with a glassy expression on his face. Beth managed to start screaming again as the beast edged nearer. Mindy continued to wail. Zack felt a chilling cold wind from behind him. He turned around only to see the broken window. He noticed the bedside cabinet.

"Yes, that will do nicely," he thought.

Fighting against the fear and pain, he struggled to his feet. His resolve renewed, he decided he would fight this evil till his last breath.

"Get out of here everyone! I will keep the beast busy," Zack hollered across the room. He finally sounded confident.

The others looked like they were trying to crawl away, but much too slowly for Zack's liking.

The demon turned and trotted towards him once more. A snarled face and a low growling sound showed the beast's hatred for Zack's heroics. He waited till the beast was a little closer, turned, and picked up the entire bedside cabinet from behind him. Held in both hands, he raised it above his head, struggling beneath its weight. Zack let out a loud battle cry as he threw the cabinet down on top of the approaching beast.

With a loud crash the wooden cabinet broke into pieces over the creature. The contents of the drawers fell out as it shattered. A black book with a gold cross on the front cover dropped out and landed on the demon's tail. It was the Holy Bible.

It was put there years earlier and had never been taken out of the drawer until now. The room was filled with a high-pitched shriek. It sounded different to the other noises the demon had made before. It was a cry of pain. Graham, Beth and Mindy all turned to stare at it.

Zack, still out of breath, looked on intrigued as he tried to steady himself. The creature's tail was burning. The fleshy sinews and granite like scales started to melt away. The beast twitched and flicked its tail like a rat with its tail in a mousetrap. Zack dived forward over the beast, grabbing the Bible in his right hand.

The demon spun around and snapped its teeth close to Zack's face. The demon had a large mouth lined with barbed teeth, its lower jaw split into three, connected only by a thin membrane. There were three large fangs on the lower jaw paired with three on the top. The bottom jaw had teeth extending down from the roots of the three large teeth.

Zack grinned back at the beast as he held the Bible firmly in his hand. He smashed it into the demon's head with the last of his energy. The demon's head exploded in a violent burst like a pus filled balloon hit with a sledgehammer.

No head remained. Inky brown blood-like liquid gushed out from its neck. The creature's body flailed and thrashed as if burnt by an invisible flame. It liquefied as they all looked on. In less than a minute only a bubbling puddle of demonic goop remained.

Zack let out an exasperated sigh of relief. Exhausted, he lay on the floor. He closed his eyes momentarily.

"Please wake up!" he ordered himself.

"This isn't a dream, sorry Zack." Graham's voice was now calm again.

"A nightmare is more like it!" Mindy said between sobs.

Beth just cried. Zack wasn't sure if it was because of pain or the relief that it was over.

Zack stood and sat on the bed. Graham sat next to Beth and put an arm around her. The place was ruined. There were pieces of broken furniture, glass, and blood everywhere. Mindy had a deep gash on her left leg and Beth had a similar wound on her right arm.

As the adrenaline started to expire in Zack's system the pain resurfaced. He looked down to assess his own wounds. His right arm was bleeding profusely. He had minor cuts from the glass on the floor on his feet and many of his previous injuries were starting to bleed once more.

"I knew we should've packed insect repellent," Zack spoke quietly with a cheeky grin.

A tiny glimmer of light in the mucky sludge that was once a demon caught Zack's eye. He pulled the blanket from the bed behind him and used it to dig out a small stone. He rubbed it clean and saw that it was what remained of the demon's middle eye. It was now a glassy, dull red crystal. It looked dead and empty. He put it in his pocket before the others noticed.

Mindy found a basic first aid kit under the kitchen sink and started to bandage the weary four. They all talked about what had just occurred. Nobody was really sure what to make of it all. Beth suggested it was an alien; Graham thought it could have been a genetically modified dog-spider. Mindy mostly just kept quiet. Zack was just happy to listen for a while as Graham and Beth debated why their idea was more plausible.

"I think it was a demon," Mindy said interrupting.

"Do you mean like a demon-demon? Like heaven-and-hell type of thing demon?" Beth questioned.

Mindy nodded.

"There is no such thing as all that stuff…" Graham said.

"…That's just to keep you in-line when you are a little kid. There is no God, devil, angels or demons. That is all just fairytales and nonsense."

"Then why did the Bible hurt it?" Mindy replied.

Graham was quiet.

Zack felt cold. "Could this actually be real?" he thought to himself.

The four of them had been debating for over an hour when a flash of light burst through the windows and lit up their faces. They all stopped talking and looked to where the light source came from. As they started to approach the windows a distant yet loud explosion pierced their ears. Zack peered through the now-shattered window to see a large mushroom cloud of dust rising on the horizon. His heart sank as the realization hit him: his home town was burning.

The sky flashed once more as another large explosion echoed in the distance. The jolt caused a fragment of glass to fall loose from the window frame making Zack jump. He could hear the girls starting to sob behind him.

"Who would attack Brakenside?" Graham spat. His voice was muffled by subsequent explosions.

Several large fires were visible now. The smoke bellowing into the sky an unending scream of the dying inhabitants of Brakenside.

Mindy could take no more and retreated away from the window and sat on the bed. Beth followed her and they held each other. Zack and Graham both flinched as yet another large explosion burst outwards into the sky. The four of them stayed in the shattered room for several hours. They were all exhausted, but unable to sleep.

Eventually the frequency of the explosions began to diminish. Until at last there was silence once more. It was not as comforting as Zack had hoped. The bright daylight did not appear as everyone was hoping. The sky remained dim. No matter the direction Zack looked about the sky he could not see a source of light where the sun should have been. Day and night did not seem any different.

"We have to go and see if our family and friends are okay," Beth spoke what they were all fearing.

"We will all get killed. You've seen what's happened out there," Mindy spoke softly.

"We can't just stay here, and there hasn't been a sound for a while now." Zack turned to look out the window hoping another explosion wouldn't prove him wrong.

"We will run out of food here anyway," Graham motioned towards the kitchen.

Beth liked how practical he was.

Mindy thought for a moment.

"I'm hungry," she replied.

Zack smiled as he looked over at her. He didn't dare think too long about what had been going on, but felt glad he was with Mindy. He watched the others look around the room sharing strained smiles. Mindy got up and walked past them into the kitchen. Graham walked with Beth and followed Mindy. Zack reminded himself what good friends he had; his stomach reminded him how hungry he was.

After eating whatever they could find in the pantry, Graham stacked the remaining food on the table. The pile was a lot smaller than Zack hoped. The majority of the food was canned peaches. Zack cringed. He hated peaches. After another discussion they decided it best to head back to Brakenside in search for their friends and family.

None of them could have ever imagined what this task would lead to.

Chapter 4

Worms

Kephas turned the page in his Bible and read on…

Zephaniah 1

¹⁶ a day of trumpet and battle cry
against the fortified cities
and against the corner towers.
¹⁷ "I will bring such distress on all people
that they will grope about like those who are blind,
because they have sinned against the Lord.
Their blood will be poured out like dust
and their entrails like dung.
¹⁸ Neither their silver nor their gold
will be able to save them
on the day of the Lord's wrath."

And with that sobering thought Kephas closed his Bible and looked out the window at the rapidly darkening sky. Kephas knew this day would come. He had spent many years preparing for it when he was younger. Yet as he aged, he felt more sure it wouldn't arrive in his lifetime. So his preparations lapsed into infrequency.

Deafening thunder filled the air. Kephas was blown back into his chair as his windows exploded inwards. Flying glass burrowed into his face and chest. He fell over backwards in his chair and his head hit the floor.

Kephas remained unconscious for uncounted hours before he awoke. He was in pain and trembling. His right eye had swollen shut and he was covered in blood. Shards of glass were still lodged in deep bleeding wounds across his body. He took a deep breath, wincing as he did so and tried without success to stand up.

As he tried the second time, his good friend Deon West came in the door. Deon had been the bishop's gardener for eight years and the two of them got along very well. Deon wore dark green overalls that had mud splattered on them. His normally tidy black hair was messy and dirty.

"Bishop! Are you alright?" he rushed to help the old man, shocked at his injuries and more so that he was alive.

"Deon my good man, thank you…" Kephas struggled to say. Deon looked him in the eyes and nodded.

"You are going to be okay Bishop," he said looking around the room quickly looking for something to help stop the bleeding.

"Of course I am my boy!" The Bishop nearly managed a chuckle.

Deon smiled, remembering their previous conversations they had over the years. Thirty years his junior, Deon would refer to the Bishop with a 'Yes Dad, No Dad' when he was feeling mischievous.

"Don't move. I will be right back," Deon said as he remembered where he could find bandages.

Deon raced back out the door to retrieve what was left of the small rest home's first aid supplies.

When he returned he found the Bishop sitting in his chair pulling glass from his chest and flicking it across the room.

"Wooah, slow down ol' man. Let me patch you up," Deon approached with some bandages and gauze.

"It's just some pesky scratches," Kephas said, shooing him off.

"I wish it I could agree with you, but I'm thinking I can see the damage a bit clearer than you. At least let me patch up that eye?"

The Bishop nodded as Deon tended to his wounds as best he could.

"I'm sorry to be the bearer of bad news Bishop, and I'm not sure quite how to put it, but, well, um…" Deon lost his words.

"Deon, it's alright. How can I advise you today?"

"No, it's not what you think Bishop; I haven't touched a drop of alcohol this last week. It's, well..."

"Spit it out then."

"Everyone, Bishop... everyone is Dead!"

Kephas hung his head and listened.

"Not just the other elderly folk, the nurses, the staff. Everyone? It's just I can't find anyone else alive except you. I have been looking for hours/days. I'm not sure, up and down the street, everyone, missing or dead!" Deon started to fumble his dressings. He looked up at him, his eyes red from crying.

Kephas held him by both shoulders and replied confidently, looking him in the eyes.

"They have gone to be with the Lord. They are at peace now."

Deon nodded and tied the last bandage around Kephas's head.

The Bishop stood up.

"Come with me Deon, there is something you must help me do."

"Surely Bishop you need to rest and recover. Sit back down. I haven't even explained to you what else has been going on."

"I know this is hard on you my friend, and I will try to answer your questions on the way. I have been expecting this day Deon, and all the horror that is to come. We have made preparations. Quickly now, we need to get to the Cathedral. I'm hoping we are not too late."

They walked into the other room and Kephas opened his wardrobe. He pushed all his clothes aside to pull out an old suit bag from the very back.

"Deon, please can you collect any food or supplies that you can find close by and meet me at the front door?"

He nodded and did as he was asked. Once Deon had left the room, the Bishop opened the bag to reveal a dark grey trench-coat with a hood. It seemed strange to him to put on something he had not worn in years.

A faint smell of incense escaped the bag, with it memories flooded back to him as he put the garment on. The coat was durable yet ornate. It had strengthened layers of fabric and double stitching. There was a small white cross stitched into the front right shoulder. He familiarized himself with the multiple hidden pockets, checking their contents as he went.

Kephas replaced his slippers for his favorite black tramping boots. They met at the front door; Deon looked surprised to see the Bishop in his unusual attire. The Bishop returned a confident smile. Deon presented a small bag of supplies.

"Will this do?"

"Yes, thank you Deon."

Kephas and Deon made their way outside. A dying world reeking of rotting flesh and smoke assaulted their nostrils as they went down the path towards the street. Kephas gazed around with his good eye, swallowing hard at what he saw. The normally quiet suburb was a war-zone. The sky hung lifelessly above them. It was draped in smoke and endless gray haze, making everything look worse. Many of the surrounding houses had been smashed to rubble. Burning cars filled the streets. The normally luscious rest-home garden was dying. Kephas wondered how long he had been unconscious for.

"Too long," he thought to himself.

The neighboring houses were burnt shells and splintered wrecks. A line of tears ran down Kephas' bloodied cheek. He could hear nearby fires crackling rather than the usual din of lawnmowers and traffic noise.

The two of them slowly made their way down what was left of the street. Deep fissures in the ground and large bomb-craters made travel slow. Deon was silent as he walked next to the Bishop. He thought they needed to be hiding, though he couldn't think how to phrase this to his old friend. Deon got the feeling that Kephas had a plan in mind.

A barely audible strange screeching howl came from somewhere behind them and they quickened their pace. Deon looked at the Bishop in panic. Kephas recited scripture to Deon by memory.

Proverbs 18

[10] The name of the LORD is a fortified tower;
the righteous run to it and are safe.

"Remember this well, Deon?"

Deon nodded. Yet he continually looked for the source of the unusual sound.

A short while later they made it to the front steps of the Cathedral. It was built from light-colored large-sized bricks. Its classic gothic design had weathered the years well. It had accumulated several families of birds living on its roof. It was nearly one hundred years old, making it one of the oldest buildings in town. Brakenside continued to grow over the years despite the initially gloomy predictions. It had a thriving port, lots of shopping centers and suburbs sprawling in all directions.

The tall cathedral doors were wide open and two of them walked inside. Deon relaxed a little as the walked in. Kephas looked around expecting to see other survivors. He saw no-one.

"Follow me please," the Bishop added as he walked down the back pews to the rear right hand side of the church.

They stopped at a statue of Jesus. It was old, yet cared for. It was made from some type of stone, with paint covering it. There were a few chips in places that had not yet been mended. Deon had a puzzled look on his face as the Bishop knelt down in front of it.

"Sorry Bishop, Not sure if we have time for this right now, we should really find help."

The Bishop made the sign of the cross and then stood up again.

"I'm sorry too, Deon, We don't currently have the time this deserves to explain."

The Bishop turned and held down on the right ear lobe of the statue and pressed the big toe of the right foot. There was a faint clicking noise. A small hidden drawer in the plinth of the statue popped out slightly. Kephas opened it and removed a small key.

Deon's mouth was hanging open. The Bishop returned a knowing smile.

"This old dog still has a few tricks."

They made their way up to the large marble altar in the front center of the church. As before the Bishop knelt in front of it and made the sign of the cross. He placed the small key from the statue in to a small gap in the cross placard on the front face of the altar. He turned it and there was a satisfying click. The front panels of the altar popped open slightly. A waft of cool air escaped from the secret storage cabinet. It smelt like very old perfume and dust. Kephas opened the doors wider and removed a small black leather bag.

He very carefully took it out and placed them on the ground beside him.

"The church's secret liquor cabinet?" Deon asked, now not sure if taking the elderly bishop away from the rest home was such a good idea.

"Much more important than that Deon, you know…" The Bishop was cut off by the sound of pews being knocked over behind them. Deon flinched.

They both turned to see a small group of women and children standing up from behind the pews where they had been hiding. Deon started to relax as he walked over.

"Give me the bag now!" one of the ladies shouted as she strode over. She had long black hair, blood stains scattered all over her and a crazed look on her face. She wore ripped trendy jeans and a black top.

"Calm down, its okay, we'll…" Deon began.

"Shut your face and give me the stuff!" she demanded.

Deon noticed the large kitchen knife she had in her hand, which she promptly raised towards his throat.

"You're crazy," Deon yelled back as he tried to take a few steps backwards.

"Now! Give it to me."

"You're not seriously going to rob someone in the middle of a church, are you?" he pleaded. Deon was now starting to believe she would.

"Murder too, if you don't hurry it up!"

"As you wish," the Bishop added. He closed the bag again quickly after sneaking what he could as the others were arguing.

Deon took the bag from Kephas and lobbed it onto the ground in front of the angry woman. Kephas cringed as the bag hit the floor with a thud.

"Amanda, please!" one of the other ladies still standing with the children cried out.

"Quiet, Denise! We need this more than them. I'm taking care of it."

Deon backed away and sat on the floor with the Bishop. Amanda waved the knife towards the pair as a last threat as she trotted over towards her group, rifling through the bag as she went.

"What is this junk?"

She turned back towards them throwing the contents of the bag onto the ground. Some scrolls, parchments and a few small books fell out. Kephas stood up and walked over to her. She held the knife towards him.

"Where are your supplies? You can't have risked coming here for just some useless words. We need guns, ammo, food, water. All that stuff. Give me yours!"

"Or what?" the Bishop said calmly. "You'll stab me?"

The woman was enraged at the old man's comment, and in her current state that's all that was needed to send her over the edge. She took a step forward and lunged the knife into his stomach as hard as she could. The Bishop hunched over.

The woman and children shrieked. Deon cried out and ran over with his fists clenched. The Bishop stood perfectly still as he held up his left hand to stop his friend's advance. He then stepped back slowly revealing that his right hand was around Amanda's wrist, stopping the knife just short of piercing his stomach. Deon couldn't believe the old man could move so quickly. It took everyone by surprise.

"No harm done," he said, smiling at her.

Her face was pale.

"She probably had just slipped." He stepped to her side, taking the knife from her and covertly passing it to Deon.

"I'm so sorry, I don't know..." Amanda's now barely audible voice trailed off. Her eyes welled up with tears as she began to cry. Denise came over and held her.

"She... she.. It's been so hard," Denise pleaded with Kephas.

"All is forgiven my dear. We will look after you all."

They introduced themselves and were only talking for a few minutes when the Cathedral was perforated with light and shrapnel as a shockwave knocked everyone over. A home-made bomb had been detonated on the far wall of the Cathedral, blowing open a gaping hole in the injured bricks. Kephas pushed himself up off the floor eyeing a nail that had lodged itself next to his face.

Kephas quickly surveyed the scene and miraculously no-one suffered serious injury. He pulled Deon up on to his feet.

"Everyone out through the side door!" he commanded.

The structure began to creak and groan. A few small fires crackled and hissed. A loud crack made everyone jump as one of the roof-support beams broke above the hole in the wall.

"Move!" Kephas yelled.

They all scuttled out the door with Kephas the last one out. He managed to nab a few scrolls from the floor on his way. Kephas wore a hardened expression on his normally gentle face.

"Follow me quickly everyone!" he seemed to exude battle-tested confidence.

He herded the group of bewildered survivors down the church path into the car park.

"Deon, check them for injuries."

Deon nodded.

"I will leave them with you for just a moment." Kephas started to jog back to the Cathedral, despite Deon's desperate look.

He had only taken a few steps when the proud building where he had spent so many of his years crumbled to the ground. The group were enough distance away only to be slapped with a cloud of dust. Kephas let a bitter sigh escape between his teeth. He did a quick inventory of what he managed to grab from the cache moments before.

"This will have to do," he muttered.

Cries from the group grabbed his attention.

"Bishop! We've got blood everywhere," Deon said with panic trying to slow the bleeding on one of the children.

It seemed Kephas' previous assessment was not accurate. As the adrenaline started to wane others came forward holding bleeding limbs.

"Denise, was it? Help Deon sort the injured. Bring the serious ones to me, tend to the others as best you can."

She nodded her panicked face.

Kephas knelt on the grass on the edge of the car park and made the sign of the cross. He quietly prayed for a moment then checked his pockets. He pulled out a small scroll. It was yellowing and had a red wax seal on it. He ran his fingers over its length and broke the seal with both thumbs. Kephas peeled the scroll open and began to read the ancient text. It was plain and to the point, as one would expect of delivery instructions on the front of a courier parcel. The font was all in capital letters, and written in Latin. He read over the words, silently mouthing them as he went.

Deon and Denise carried over the first injured child and lay her gently on the grass on her side. She had lost consciousness due to loss of blood. Several nails were still embedded in her back. One had buried itself near the base of her neck.

"Ready the next ones," Kephas said surveying the girl's injuries.

Deon and Denise just stood there, wondering what Kephas was going to do next. Deon was puzzled how she managed to make it outside with the others. Her breathing was shallow and pained. Her matted black hair stuck to her face. She wore a white top and black pants, both were well worn.

Kephas held the small scroll in his left hand and made the sign of the cross over her as he prayed the holy words. He closed his eyes as he finished the prayer and let his hand rest on her shoulder.

"Amen," he concluded.

Deon echoed the same in a quiet voice.

Kephas then proceeded to pull out all the nails as fast as his hands would allow. Denise gasped and dropped to her knees.

"What are you doing?"

"Observe," Kephas replied calmly.

Each nail fell to the ground and Kephas wiped the wounds with his hand. His hands were covered in her blood. The girl spat blood into the grass and drank in a deep breath. Kephas stood up to move towards the next injured person. All heads followed him.

"Denise, look!" The young girl held out her arm. The deep wound on her arm had completely healed. There was not even a scar. She gleefully inspected each nail hole only to find no injury. Only blood smears remained. She stood up and went to find Kephas.

"Thank you sir!" the girl hollered.

"Thank the Lord God," he replied with a smile.

Deon and Denise starred at one another, mouths open in disbelief.

Kephas healed all in their group in the same way. As this was going on a few people walking past joined in and were also healed. Lastly the Bishop healed his own injuries.

Kephas addressed everyone.

"We must go to Saint Thomas Church and see Father Andrews. I will try to help all of you understand, as best as I can, but first we must get somewhere safer. Follow me and you may yet live."

He immediately turned and began to make his way across the broken street. Everyone followed.

Deon caught up with him at the front of the group.

"That was the most amazing thing I've ever seen in my life," he said.

Kephas nodded with a smile.

"Deon, it will be dangerous, and many will die on the road ahead. Take this."

He handed him a small wooden cross on a short rope. As he did so he quoted scripture:

2 Corinthians 10

> [3] For though we live in the world, we do not wage war as the world does. [4] The weapons we fight with are not the weapons of the world. On the contrary, they have divine power to demolish strongholds.

"Never lose this, keep it close to you," Kephas added.

Deon nodded, rolling the basic yet sturdy item over in his hand. It looked very old and well worn.

"Please can you go to the rear of our little band. Shout for me if you see something evil."

Deon looked puzzled.

"You will know when you see it." Kephas turned and strode on.

Deon went to the back of the group and kept both eyes peeled for something he'd know what, when he saw it, whatever that was. They walked on a few blocks further when Kephas' voice rung out.

"Everyone! This way. Do not look back." He pointed towards a small alleyway between two buildings.

"Hurry!"

Kephas stayed at the corner and shooed everyone down the alley.

One of the men stopped to talk to Kephas. But looking past him, his face grew pale and he sprinted past the others, yelping like a small dog. More people turned then followed with frightened cries.

The others rushed past until Kephas and Deon remained.

A shrill scream cut the air as they both turned to see several small demons scramble across the debris in the street towards them.

Kephas pulled out the rosary beads that had been around his neck and wrapped them around his fist. He began chanting what sounded to Deon like Latin. He jumped forward, catching a leaping demon mid-air with a wild right hook. It flew across the road in a bubbling mess.

Another demon lunged towards Deon snarling and hissing. Deon was frozen in panic, his mind not comprehending what he was seeing. Kephas quickly turned and smashed the demon with a spinning back-fist. The creature crashed into the curb.

Kephas ran to meet the remaining demons. As he did so he tripped on some rubble on the ground. Losing his balance he toppled forwards. With the skill of a martial-arts expert he dropped into a forward roll like he planned it. He exited the roll with a flurry of punches, squishing a demon into the door of an abandoned car.

The whole time the Bishop kept chanting. The words he proclaimed sounded to be filled with holy wrath. They matched the rhythm of his movements. The last remaining two demons launched their attack simultaneously from both sides. Kephas tried to dodge but received a deep gash in his back. All Deon could do was watch, gripping the cross in his hand tightly.

Kephas steadied himself for the next assault, clenching the rosary beads in his bloodied right hand. This time he caught one mid-jump by the tail and swung it into the ground. The demon let out a defiant cry, which was cut short by Kephas' fist, cracking its head like an egg. The last demon jumped again, slashing its claws in a frenzy. Kephas grabbed it by the throat in a left-handed choke hold. The demon stabbed its sharp limbs into his forearm. A swift right punch removed the demon's head. He threw the remains into the gutter.

Panting, Kephas turned towards Deon.

"Demons... they cannot stand against anything Holy or Blessed."

Deon looked at his cross.

"Yes, now let's get those good people to safety."

Deon gently turned Kephas by his shoulder to tend to his back. His coat was ripped but there was no blood. He saw underneath a second layer of dark gray leather was undamaged. Kephas pulled up his ripped sleeve to reveal the same.

"What in the world?" Deon stammered.

"I have been training for this day Deon for a great many years. And in truth I was unsure if it would be within my time on this green earth. But let us discuss this later." Kephas turned down the alley after the group.

Deon and Kephas met them around the end of the next building.

"We thought it best to wait for you Priest," Denise said.

Kephas nodded. "Onwards young ones. We must get to Father Andrews. He will know what to do."

They ran along the battered streets, collecting more people as they went. They stopped only briefly to heal those who were badly wounded. The suburbs were broken with torn pavements from the earthquake and craters from what looked like an air raid.

Rounding a house on the corner of the block the group came to a halt. Another gang of demons patrolled the street.

"Deon with me, you others stay back," Kephas called.

"Kephas! What do I do?"

"Hit them with the cross!"

"God help me," Deon said quietly.

"He will," Kephas replied smiling.

Deon secured his cross onto his right hand with the attached rope. They ran into the middle of the road and were greeted with snapping jaws and slashing claws. Deon could hear Kephas' war-chant once more. The Bishop stood in front of him pounding demons left and right. A demon jumped over the top of a car and charged towards Deon. Kephas was too busy with his own fight to assist this time.

Deon found himself running forward to meet the evil creature. It jumped at him and clawed his arms. Pain shot through Deon's body. But he did not flinch or stagger. He swung punches back in reply, finally grazing it on the leg. It fell to the ground squealing. Deon grabbed it and delivered the finishing blow.

Somehow energised by this small victory he joined Kephas, who now stood with numerous broken demon bodies on the ground around him. They fought until all the demons had been killed.

"You fought well Deon. Thank you."

"Thank *you* Bishop," Deon said with hands on his knees, catching his breath.

Kephas made the sign of the cross and healed Deon's wounds.

Deon's mind began to boil over with questions as he saw the steeled look on the Bishop's face.

A loud, booming sound rippled up the street. Smoke started to billow up from the next block over.

"No!" Kephas yelled as he sprinted off towards the smoke. The survivors ran after him.

Deon saw the tall steeple of St Thomas Church as he ran around the corner of the street. It was shrouded in a thick black smoke. The cross at the top sat slightly on an angle. He made it past the last building and smiled.

The old brick church still stood, to everyone's relief. It was smaller than the Brakenside Cathedral but similar in design. It remained mostly intact despite an earlier attack by a group known as 'The Sons of the Snake'. A homemade explosive was tossed over the tall metal fence. The fence was comprised of rows of tall thin pipes that were capped with a small cross.

The bomber threw a lead pipe jammed with explosive powder and shrapnel clear over the fence with ease, however it got lodged in the branches of a small tree in the church courtyard. This significantly decreased the resulting damage to the structure.

Yet all the windows on that side of the church had blown out. Some shrapnel had lodged into the walls and roof. A generous splashing of scorch marks were everywhere, and the tree was vaporized. But the Church still stood. Unfortunately, a splintered chunk of wood from the tree flew across the grass and lodged itself deep into Father Andrews' neck. A number of people received minor cuts and gashes.

Deon saw Kephas run through the gate and amongst the people gathered around Father Andrews' body. Father Douglas Andrews had been the parish priest for ten years, and one of Kephas' best friends. He had his fortieth birthday party in the church hall a few weeks earlier. Kephas and Douglas had often travelled together to do missionary work. Deon would later learn that this entailed so much more than anyone expected.

"Go in peace now to be with the Lord, my dear friend," Kephas said as he closed Douglas' vacant eyes.

"I'm sorry Bishop, I know he was close to you," Brother Christopher said as he emerged from the crowd.

Brother Christopher had wild brown hair, glasses, a pale complexion and a wiry figure. He looked to be wearing his gardening clothes.

Kephas nodded.

"Tell me Brother, did he ever tell you about what we did on our missionary excursions?"

"Yes. Father Andrews made a presentation to the whole church whenever he returned; the photos he had taken while in Papua New Guinea made a lasting impression," he replied.

"Anything about how he got that scar on his arm?"

"No. He did say after the last trip he would discuss the details with me when the time was right. I think he correctly sensed that I had felt apprehensive about myself going abroad on my own missionary work. Why?"

"Ah." Kephas realized that things had just got a lot more difficult.

Everyone was looking to him to know what to do next. Kephas took a deep breath and closed his eyes. He stood and raised his face skywards. He slowly exhaled, and upon opening his eyes he spoke.

"First things first then. I have people following me here. We will need to get them into the church. Please gather everyone you can."

"Yes, Bishop."

"I will address everyone in the church shortly, but first find enough men that we can watch the church from all sides."

"Watch for what?"

"Those that come looking for aid, and those that do not."

Brother Christopher nodded, despite a worried look on his face.

A short while later everyone had gathered in the church. Kephas and Deon were walking around the fence line. Kephas had pulled a small ornate incense burner out of one of his pockets. It was spherical, metal and had cross-shaped holes cut in to it on all sides. He held it with a metal chain. Kephas slowly prayed as he went dispersing the musky smelling concoction all around the boundaries of the church property.

Kephas took it with him inside the church and did the same around the walls of the church. Inside people had begun to get quite rowdy, arguing with each other about what had been happening. Kephas continued regardless. Slowly people stopped talking and watched him. Kephas gave off a presence that he knew what was going on. He was strangely calm and pragmatic.

Once he had finished he handed the incense burner to Deon and made his way up to the pulpit. He made the sign of the cross as he did so.

All eyes were on him.

"My good people…" he began.

"…My name is Kephas and I have been the Bishop of this wider area for the past eight years. More importantly I am a member of the Ordinem Sal et Lux, the Order of Salt and Light. This Order was established hundreds of years ago to protect human kind in these End Times."

Some people in the crowd scoffed, others gasped.

"Let us summarize the basics quickly. Number one: yes, God, Heaven, Hell and the Devil are very real. Number two: yes, those creatures which some of you have seen are demons from Hell. Number three: yes, we will do all we can to save you all. Number four: no, you are not safe and many of you will die."

At this a man in the crowd stood up and shouted: "Who are you to dictate this to us old man?! I am not fooled by your propaganda! I have no use for you and your talk. I shall make my own way."

He started to make his way past the others, as he headed towards the door. Many others started to follow him. He had not made it far when Kephas replied.

"Thirteen. My gardener and I killed thirteen of those evil creatures on the way here. At least give me that many minutes to try and help you understand, and then you can make an informed decision."

The people stopped and looked at him once more. Another few men stood up and yelled angrily.

"Ridiculous! Those creatures cannot be killed! You can only slow them down or escape. I was the only one who made it out of my building."

"What can you do old man?!" another yelled.

Kephas reached into his pocket and pulled out a fist full of dulled red gems and held them for all to see.

Deon had not noticed Kephas collecting them earlier. He tried to remember how many he had killed himself. He couldn't think of any past two.

The crowd quietened down. Almost everyone in the room had seen those red gems, the third eye in the head of the small demons. Those that who were lucky enough not to witness first hand recognised the expressions on the others faces.

Kephas continued.

"We must prepare, everyone can help. We need to fortify and stock these grounds so we can continue living. May God bless you all!"

Explosions in the background seemed to punctuate his sentences, yet he did not flinch. Everyone listened to him all the more. Kephas answered questions for twenty minutes before saying:

"Allow me time to better fortify this place, then we'll continue this discussion, without any unnecessary loss of life."

It seemed to satisfy the crowd long enough for Brother Christopher to stand up and answer questions as best he could.

Afterwards, Brother Christopher met Kephas and Deon at the church gate. Kephas was applying some scented balm from a small ornate metal container to the fence posts. He was praying as he did so. Deon walked in front shaking the fence, checking it was structurally sound, and clearing fallen branches and debris away.

"Bishop, how can I help?"

Kephas turned, stood up and looked Brother Christopher intently in the eyes.

"Do you love Jesus Christ, the Lord God Almighty in Heaven and dedicate your soul to his service?"

Startled, Brother Christopher replied, "Yes, I do."

He repeated the question towards Deon, who answered the same way.

"Kneel and receive the blessing."

Deon dropped what he was doing and knelt next to Brother Christopher.

"Repeat these words after me, my solider brothers: My Lord and Saviour Jesus Christ, fill my soul with your light…"

The men repeated the words as Kephas went.

"Cleanse me and guide me. I pledge all that I am to your service Lord God. I will be Salt and Light in this world, I will be your holy sword and shield. Amen."

The Bishop made the sign of the cross and put his hands on their shoulders.

"Stand, my brethren, the war is just beginning."

As they stood Kephas continued.

"Write these words on your heart, and if your memory is like mine write them on paper too." He finished with a smile.

"What would you have us do?" Brother Christopher asked.

"We must ready the people, protect them, and save as many as we can. Please enlist two people under you and instruct each to do the same, so that if you die in battle all your knowledge is not lost. But first I will try and teach you all I can."

Over the next few days they trained under Kephas and the community stocked and strengthened the facilities. The people collected food, bottles of water, medical supplies, blankets, clothing and gardening tools from the church buildings. Broken sections of fence were reinforced and the top points directed outwards with the edges sharpened.

Kephas had spent the majority of his time directing others and healing those that had arrived. When he had time, he retreated to the late Father Andrews' office. There he poured over the relics he managed to extract from the now ruined Cathedral. There were numerous scrolls, basic diagrams and a few small metal boxes. Deon had seen Kephas open a few of them to confirm their contents.

An old map was also amongst the artefacts. It was a leather backed parchment which had been rolled up for many years. Multiple layers of ink were across its surface. The original older ink had been redrawn over time to maintain legibility. Kephas rolled it up and placed it in his inside coat pocket when he realized Deon was peering over the desk at it.

"First we must train our troops Deon," he said smiling.

Deon waited for some details with a blank expression. Deon thought that Kephas sometimes forgot that he was really the only person with any clues about the current situation.

"Please go out and gather as many people as you can. Who are willing to go outside the safety of our fence line to search for survivors, food and supplies?"

Deon nodded and left the small church office.

"And bring all the gardening tools too. I'll meet you all in the courtyard shortly," Kephas called to him.

"Why?" Deon asked obviously puzzled.

"We will need them to make some weapons," Kephas replied.

A short while later Kephas walked out to meet the volunteers with Deon and Brother Christopher. He recognized Amanda among them. Kephas walked over to her and smiled.

"I am happy to see you with us Amanda."

"I will earn my keep," she said, looking at her shoes.

Next in line was Adam, Kephas' mechanic for the past few years. Adam was tall, broad and rugged. He wore blue overalls that had many oil stains on them. He had a long black beard and a shiny bald head.

"Nice to see you, Aaron."

"It's Adam, Bishop"

"Oh yes, I'm sorry."

Kephas could never remember his name, despite his many polite reminders.

"Well at least he's getting closer..." Adam said quietly to Deon. "...I'm not James this time."

Deon returned a knowing smile.

Kephas continued to the last two volunteers.

"Hello there, what are your names gentlemen?"

David replied with his name first. He wore tatty blue jeans and a brown hooded sweatshirt. He had neat, short blonde hair and a moustache the size of his ego, which was huge.

"David Jones is the name, Sir. I'm sure you'll never forget my name."

Kephas would.

Kephas smiled back at him.

William introduced himself next. He had long brown hair tied up in a ponytail. He wore a business jacket over black cargo pants.

"Call me Will."

Kephas nodded and turned to address them all.

Many other people had begun to gather to see what was going on. Kephas picked up a spade from the pile of tools and inspected the blade. He held it above his head as he spoke.

"As you are all aware, we have had people come to our little community from the local neighborhoods. We have been stocking supplies, and we have established ourselves as best we could. Now I ask you to join with me in venturing out with me to bring back more people and supplies. This shovel will be your weapon against the demons out there. I will bless you and our weapons. I ask all who remain here to pray for us. I am confident that we can fill this place with people."

He passed the spade to Adam and motioned the others to collect one each. Will picked up another spade and David selected a pickaxe. Deon held a rake and Brother Christopher chose a pruning saw. Amanda held a pair of hedge clippers awkwardly. Kephas walked over to her and requested to look at them.

"May I?"

He undid the bolt holding the hedge clippers together and handed her back one half. He pulled something from his pocket that looked like a small candle with no wick. He ran it up and down the blade a few times.

"This is blessed wax; it will enable your blade to cut the demons. It will wear off after some use, but God willing it will be enough for this outing. We will look for some better options as we go. You can still hit the demons without blessed or holy items, but you will do naught but waste your own strength."

Kephas handed Amanda the other half and the small wax stick. She started to coat the second blade.

"Thank you."

Kephas gestured them to follow Amanda with applying the blessed wax. Kephas picked up a broom. He propped one end against the curb and kicked the brush end off, leaving a sharp looking point on the end. He wrapped his rosary beads around the pointy end. Deon watched carefully and did the same. Kephas gave them all some basic instruction on how to wield their crude weapons.

Kephas said a prayer and they set out through the gates. As soon as they left they heard the demons cackling and hissing from somewhere out of sight. Clang! The metal gate shut behind them making the scavenger crew jump.

"Stay together," Kephas commanded as he stomped across the muddied grass verge.

They rounded the edge of the street and saw a single demon on the footpath. It eyed them and snapped its jaws.

David ran ahead.

"This one is mine!" he declared.

The others ran to keep up with him.

David ran at the demon swinging his pickaxe. The creature snarled and jumped towards him, slicing his arm as he went past. David let out a cry and swung his weapon around again, this time connecting with the demon. It split into pieces as it was burnt and boiled by the holy wax coating on the blade.

Victorious, David turned to face the group. Kephas sighed and nodded. Will, who was lucky enough not to have seen a demon this close before, gripped his spade tighter. Adam clapped.

Panting, David jogged over to them.

"Did you see me cream that little bugger?"

"Yes, good work, but please remember we need you to save your energy to bring back people and supplies," Kephas replied as he healed his injuries.

"I have loads to spare!" David said, holding his hand up for a high-five. Brother Christopher awkwardly patted his hand.

Kephas directed the others to keep a look out and they called for survivors.

"Hello!? Is anyone here? We can help!"

They walked to a small convenience store. A metallic click spun everyone's heads around. Behind the counter a bedraggled man pointed a shotgun at them.

"Get out! Or I'll blast you back out the door." The owner of the store wore a black tattered beanie, with a fine spattering of blood over it and his face. His eyes were peeled so wide Deon thought he must have lost his glasses.

"Out!" he yelled.

Kephas held his hands up and started to walk backwards out the door.

"We mean you no harm. I could heal your wounds."

The chewing gum dispenser next to them exploded in a mess of buckshot and plastic. The owner pumped his shotgun, readying another shot.

"OUT!!!" his voice strained.

"We're going," Kephas replied.

The group backed out and continued around the corner of the building.

"We must go back for him," Brother Christopher insisted.

"In time yes. He is not ready to listen to anyone right now," Kephas replied.

Brother Christopher was silent for a moment, then nodded.

"Hey! Can you really heal these wounds?" a voice from behind the nearby bushes called out.

"Yes, really," Kephas called back.

Two teenagers stepped out from behind the bush. Both were holding kitchen knives. One of them was clutching his arm, the other held her shoulder. Their clothes were dirty and looked like prior to recent events they had been living on the streets. Kephas passed his weapon to Deon and walked over to them. They readied their knives; David stepped forward with his pickaxe.

"Peace be with you all. There are no enemies here," Kephas declared.

Kephas continued, despite the readiness of everyone to stab each other. He walked over to them with his hands up, showing them his palms. He approached the young man and put his hands on his arm. Stinging pain made him flinch and in turn others flinched. Kephas closed eyes and prayed. Deon tried to remember the holy words. Kephas opened his eyes and wiped the blood from the young man's arm. The gash that was there moments ago was now gone. Stunned, he dropped his knife to examine it closely.

Everyone relaxed a little, even David. Kephas continued to the young girl and healed the wound on her shoulder.

"Come with us, we will take you to safety, where we'll have time to discuss all this with you."

They thanked Kephas and joined their group.

Deon smiled.

"I'm Deon, and this is Bishop Kephas, Brother Christopher, Adam, Amanda, David and Will."

Each person waved in turn.

"Jamie and Sandra," Sandra said.

Kephas waxed their knives for them and told them that they could now cut the demons.

The group continued recruiting people all afternoon. They were now about twenty all together when Kephas called it time to return to the church.

Deon and David killed a few more demons on the return journey with few injuries. The group heard screaming coming from the church. Kephas ran ahead, signalling the others to join him. Several demons were snapping at the church fence to the terror of those inside. They jumped, scuttled and hissed around the fence, but would not touch it. By now everyone had seen or been wounded by one of the evil creatures.

"Attack!" David yelled, charging towards the closest demon. The demon turned in time to have its face split into a gooey mess by David's pickaxe. Deon and the others joined him in the fray.

Amanda was impressively adept at timing her strikes. Two demons circled her and pounced at her. She managed to cleave the limbs off one and cut the other in half at the same time. She proceeded to drive the blade into the head of the demon wriggling around on the ground whom had its limbs removed.

Brother Christopher approached cautiously and caught a demon in his left hand. They exchanged a series of rapid stabs, resulting in many punctured bleeding wounds on his left forearm and a dead demon with many slices and holes on the ground.

Adam and Will were getting used to fighting with their spades. They managed to bat attacking demons with the flat side of the spade and return swing with the waxed edge to finish them off. Deon used the length of his cross staff to good effect, stabbing and swiping from a safer distance.

Kephas stayed a little closer to the group of people they were leading back to the church. He circled them and made short work of any demon that came close.

"Run to the gates!" Kephas commanded.

The scared group of people ran towards the church with the crew cutting down demons on all sides.

Reluctantly, the man on the inside of the gate opened it in time for them to come flooding in.

Kephas patrolled the fence line, killing the remaining demons. Finally the scavenger crew made their way inside and the gate clanged shut behind them. Kephas came in last.

"Healing," he called.

He worked with Brother Christopher showing him how to perform the healing prayer. After intently observing several gashes heal, Brother Christopher successfully healed a small wound on an elderly man's arm. After wiping the blood away he collapsed onto the ground, utterly exhausted.

"To channel such power can leave you feeling drained," Kephas explained as he sat with his head in his hands on the grass, worn out.

After some time inducting the rescued people Kephas retreated to the church office. He sat down and let a big sigh escape his lungs. He began to close his eyes when the door swung open with Deon behind it. He knocked on the door as it opened.

"Not interrupting anything am I?" he asked.

"Come in, sit down my friend."

"I thought I'd ask you about that map," Deon said, sitting down on the office chair.

"Ah yes, you're right. We probably need to prepare for this early."

Kephas pulled out the ancient map and unrolled it onto the desk, brushing the desk clutter aside as he did so. Some ink had seeped over the small details. The top left of the map looked more or less like Brakenside, with the rivers and the hills in the respective places. Kephas' finger traced from the city past the coast, through the large hills, along a river and left his finger resting on the picture of a cemetery.

"This is where we must go."

…

Beth returned from her search of more supplies.

"Look what I found team," she said, as she placed a torch, a radio, two water bottles and a jacket on to the kitchen table.

"Good work," Zack replied.

Zack was still clutching the Bible since last night. He felt like it was all he needed. He flicked though its pages. He was daunted by large amount of words, and there were no pictures. His eye stopped on the some verse, which he read aloud to his friends.

James 1

²Consider it pure joy, my brothers and sisters, whenever
you face trials of many kinds, ³because you know that the
testing of your faith produces perseverance.

Graham stopped counting the food on the table and just looked at Zack vacantly.

"This book has been really useful so far. I'm going to hang on to I," Zack replied.

Graham began:

"Okay, we need to get our stuff sorted. I just want to get home as soon as possible. I'm over this holiday. I think we should get our stuff back from the yacht and chuck it in that ute."

He pointed as he spoke.

"Then we can drive back to town and go from there. Is everyone happy with that?"

Zack and Beth nodded.

They all noticed Mindy was not there. Zack shouted out her name and began to look for her.

"I'm coming," Mindy replied as she made her way back inside.

"Look I'm really sorry everyone, I'm not quite sure how to say this but, the yacht is gone."

"It'll be there, don't stress," Graham said as he ran past her to get a look from the top of the cliff.

Looking over the bushes he could see the little cove where they left the yacht. The rope was still attached to the rock on the shoreline. But there was no boat on the other end. He looked up and down the coast but Graham could not see it. He trudged back into the house poorly hiding his disappointment.

"Its nobody's fault. Soon we'll all be able to look back on this and laugh, or something," Zack said as he saw Mindy retreat away from Graham's look.

"We must be due for some good luck soon," Beth added.

Once the four had extracted everything useful from the hotel they carried what little they had to the ute. Graham had found a spade in the garage, which he used to smash the passenger window. He unlocked the doors and the girls hopped in where it was clean. The boys climbed into the tray with some of their gear. Graham continued to flail the spade about.

"Watch it!" Zack said as he ducked a near miss.

Graham returned an apologetic smile as they drove down the long, windy gravel driveway. The ute came to a stop at the bottom. Mindy leaned out from the passenger's side window.

"Are you two Ok on the back?" she asked.

"Yup. All set," Zack replied. "We will be home in no time."

Zack was wrong. They would never make it back to their homes.

The ute pulled out on to the misty road. Beth put the headlights on and drove at a slow speed. With the boys on the back she took extra care. Mindy played with the stereo, but yielded nothing but various flavors of static.

Wild-looking grass fields surrounded them. The infrequent lines of tall trees and wire fences were the only interruption. Occasionally Zack heard Graham give directions. Zack's mind started to wander. He was looking forward to forgetting all of this holiday and getting back home.

They continued on down the pothole-scattered road until they approached a car stopped in the middle of the road. Beth hit the brakes harder than she needed to and they jolted to a stop. Everyone felt uneasy; no-one wanted anything else unexpected.

"It doesn't look like anyone's in it," Beth stated.

Graham jumped down off the back of the vehicle with his spade in hand. Zack followed him.

"I don't think they'll need help digging anything, Graham," Beth said, leaning out the window with a smile.

Graham poked his tongue out at her. As the two of them got closer they confirmed what Beth suspected. The pale blue car just sat there awkwardly, like an ugly kid at a school dance. Zack leaned in the driver's window and saw the keys still in the ignition.

"What's going on?" he heard Mindy yell from the ute.

"Nobody around, I don't know," Graham replied.

Zack hopped in and tried to start the car. Nothing happened.

"It's dead; shall we just push it off the road?"

Graham nodded and helped Zack do so. They returned to the others waiting in the ute.

"I don't see why anyone would leave a perfectly good car in the middle of the road," Zack said.

"Perfect, other than the fact it doesn't go, you mean?" said Graham.

"Well, yeah."

The four of them drove past the empty car and continued on their way back to town. They passed a few other empty cars on the side of the road, which they didn't stop to investigate. They turned on to the main road and appreciated the better road conditions. Zack and Graham turned to watch the road ahead.

Zack peered into the distance, hoping to see a glimpse of the city between the hills and trees. He saw a dim glow of brake lights up ahead. There were cars queued up at a small bridge. The bridge was narrow and arched over a small river, high enough to obscure the view of the road ahead. They joined the other cars and waited.

After a few minutes of no movement the driver of the car in front got out and walked up the queue. Other drivers soon did the same. One driver returned to his car obviously angry and honked his horn, kicked his car, and started walking back towards town. Zack jumped down and ran over to him.

"What's going on up there?"

The middle aged man turned around. He wore dirty brown overalls and smelt like a cow shed.

"The road is completely blocked kid, it looks like an accident up there, but no-one has turned up for hours. No ambulance, no police nothing, I'm sick of it. I'm going to walk."

He stormed away before Zack could ask anything else.

"Thanks," Zack called and returned to the others.

"So, what's up?" Beth said, voicing what the others were thinking.

Zack repeated what he heard and hopped back on the ute.

After some time passed, Graham's patience ran out.

"If these people are all leaving their vehicles…" he began, pointing to another driver ahead leaving their car, "We may as well walk too. We won't be getting through."

Graham was cut off by a loud explosion that boomed from somewhere on the far side of the bridge. Everyone turned to look. More drivers got out of their cars to try and see. The group ran up to the bridge between the empty cars. Zack leaned past a white van blocking his view. He saw a short distance up the road two cars had a head on collision.

There was glass and debris everywhere. No-one was inside the damaged vehicles. On the side of the road there was a body with several items of clothing draped over it. There was a first aid kit and other supplies scattered around. The surrounding grass had been flattened.

Some people were running down the road towards where the explosion was heard from. Zack could see both lanes were filled with empty cars heading out of town.

"No wonder there was a crash," Graham said, pointing to the cars, most of which had there headlights and bumpers damaged.

Zack wondered what would cause both lanes of traffic to be filled by people fleeing town and what that explosion could have been.

Mist veiled the road colored by the dim glow of vehicle lights. It reminded Zack of many an early morning spent in traffic.

"Somebody died." Zack pulled Grahams arm to show him the body.

"What are you two talking about?" Mindy said appearing on the other side of the van. Zack pointed and watched the two girls' faces fall as they saw it. Shouting and commotion could be faintly heard from down the road.

"Come on dude, let's go help," Graham said as he weaved his way up the road between the cars.

A loud scream pierced the still air. Zack's heart thumped loudly in his chest. Everyone stopped for a moment. A figure burst through the mist ahead, sprinting towards them. It was one of the drivers with a crazed look on her face. She ran past them crying. More shouts and screams filled the air. A few people ran past them back towards the bridge, some of them were bleeding.

"Get back to the ute," Graham commanded.

A terrifying scream chilled Zack's blood. This scream was not human. His previous injuries seemed to sting with increased vigor. His mind raced. Where did he leave that Bible?

He looked down at his empty hands and found himself running back towards the ute with the others. He tried to hurry Mindy along who was in front of him, not running as fast as he'd like.

Upon making it back, they saw someone had left a car close behind their vehicle. The girls hopped in. Graham went around to try and move the blocking vehicle. He peered through the window of the locked door.

"No keys," he muttered.

More screams cut through the air. Zack reached into the back tray of the ute and grabbed his Bible. He walked a little way down the road. A wounded man with blood all over him ran past him. Zack's head turned back to the road. That's when he saw it. At first he thought it was another person stepping through the mist. After an intentional blink his mind accepted the horror before him.

It was a demon, but much larger than what Zack had previously seen. It stood on two thick hind legs, roughly shoulder height of an average human. Its head and features resembled the smaller demons, just bigger and stockier. Its arms were longer and muscle-bound. Its legs were shorter than a human's and its knee joints were backwards. It trudged forwards, with large claw laden feet spread widely.

"Run!" Graham's voice rung out.

Zack clutched the Bible in his hand tighter. He slowly started walking backwards. He turned to run and tripped on someone's abandoned handbag on the ground.

A deep guttural grunt burst from the demon focused on Zack. It stomped forward with more speed than you'd expect of a heavily built creature. Zack scrambled to his feet as Graham ran past him swinging his spade and yelling.

The garden tool smashed in to the side of the beast's head, nearly knocking it over. The demon turned and grabbed the spade with its long clawed arms, wrenching it from Graham's grip. Graham stumbled and started to back away. Zack got up off the ground and ran towards Graham. The demon chased after them both as they ran back towards the ute.

Zack could hear the girls screaming inside the vehicle. Beth slammed the ute backwards into the vehicle behind them, crushing the bumpers and smashing the lights. It struggled and skidded, gradually pushing the other vehicle back.

Pain shot through Zack's spine. A smaller demon had just jumped on to his back, stabbing its claws in to him as it did so. Zack swung his right hand, gripping the Bible into the demon, causing it to squeal and release its grip. Another strike sent it hurtling to the ground.

The large grunting demon grabbed hold of the front of the ute. Its strong arms and long clawed hands punctured the bonnet of the vehicle. Mindy started screaming even louder. Beth shifted into gear and the vehicle lurched forwards, pushing the large demon back. She planted her foot onto the accelerator and pinned the demon between the ute and the vehicle in front of them. The beast let out another wild grunting cry.

Another small demon jumped out of the queue of vehicles ahead of them and ran at them screaming. Beth kept revving the engine, but was not able to crush the large sturdy demon. It punched more holes into the bonnet in a rage.

"We gotta go!" Graham yelled, pulling Mindy out of the passenger's side.

Zack held his bleeding back with his left hand. Beth jumped out her door. The four of them ran up the street in the direction they had originally come from. Zack was trailing them and nearly bowled Mindy over when she quickly stopped. Ahead of them in the road were three smaller demons. There was blood splattered over the ground around them.

Another loud grunt from behind them, followed by the sound of tearing metal told Zack the larger demon would soon be free. Zack's eyes were drawn to a wooden gate on the side of the road.

"This way!" he yelled, tapping Graham's shoulder as he ran past him. The others followed him with the small demons hot on their heels. Beth climbed her way over the fence and helped Mindy. Graham and Zack stood on the roadside of the fence and looked at each other.

"You go," Zack said, holding up the Bible in his hand. "I'll hold them off."

"Follow us quick, man!" Graham replied as he hopped over the fence and ran into the grassy field with the others.

Zack took a step forward, his body trembling with adrenalin. A small demon jumped at him, swiping its sharp claws. Zack retorted with a swing of his Bible, clipping the evil spawn, which scuttled backwards.

Another booming grunt signalled the larger demon making its way out from between the damaged vehicles. Zack could hear the crunch of glass under its feet as it approached. The mist obscured the demon from view, but it sounded like it would find them soon.

Zack turned and scrambled over the old gate. A small demon leapt at him as he did so and he fell on to the grass on other side. The demon jumped down towards his face but was bashed by Zack's Bible. A strong grip wrapped around Zack's arm and pulled him up.

"I couldn't leave ya," Graham said smiling.

Memories of their time at school flashed into Zack's mind. They had been friends for years and were always there for each other.

"Let's go," Zack replied.

They sprinted into the misty field. It didn't take long before the wooden gate behind them was lost in the fog. Zack looked behind them, relieved that the demons didn't seem to be following.

"Where are the girls?" Zack asked.

"I told them to follow the fence line, but I thought we would've come across them by now," Graham said with a concerned look on his face.

They continued running until they made it to the end of the fence. A hill rose on their right with a few trees scattered over it. On the far side of the fence was a small stream, winding its way further into the country-side. The two young men stopped to catch their breath.

"Beth! Mindy! Hey!" Graham said, half whispering, half yelling.

The sound of snapping twigs made them both jump as the girls came out from behind a bush a short distance away.

"Thank goodness!" Zack spilled.

Before anyone could speak further a loud grunting sound echoed out through the fog behind them.

"Run!" Graham spat as he climbed over the fence. The others hurriedly did the same as they ran along the grass verge next to the stream.

After they ran out of breath they stopped and rested. After a few minutes Graham stood up.

"We have to keep going."

Everyone's expressions complained, but they knew he was right. Panting, the four got up and continued walking. The creek was several strides wide with the deepest point in the middle being knee deep. The water was running clean and clear, with small rocks and plants surrounding it. Zack thought he saw a small, fresh water fish out of the corner of his eye. His dry mouth told his brain that he was thirsty.

"Can we drink this?" Mindy stole the words from Zacks mouth.

They stopped and assessed. Graham stepped gently into the water and scooped some water up in his hands and smelled it.

Beth laughed. "Does it smell like water?"

Graham shrugged and sipped a little. He threw the rest of water back into the creek and shook his hands.

"Tastes okay. Actually tastes really good." He bent down and drank his fill.

The others followed suit.

Zack drank and let out a satisfied sigh. For a moment he forgot their situation and enjoyed the company of his friends. Beth playfully splashed Graham. Graham splashed her back. Zack turned and looked at Mindy. Zack was met with a 'splash me and I'll kill you look' on her face. Graham swooped Beth up in his arms and the two of them kissed.

"Oh get a room," said Mindy as she splashed them.

Graham met Beth in the local pizza shop where she worked. After hanging out there for pizza whenever she seemed to be working, after a few weeks he asked her out. Zack was envious of his courage.

Not long after that Zack saw Mindy for the first time. She was working at a fruit and vegetables shop on the checkouts. Beth needed to drop off her car keys to her and Zack had offered to drop the couple off in town on his way to work. The three of them went into the shop, and Zack saw Mindy.

"Oh wow, I hope that's the chick." Zack remembered thinking as the three of them walked over. Zack found her overwhelmingly attractive. She had some intangible attributes that Zack couldn't figure out. He just wanted to keep looking at her. Even in her gaudy green vegetables uniform Zack thought she was amazing. When it came time to say hello, Zack stumbled over the big lump in his throat trying to say his name.

"Oh... er, yeah hi, I'm Zack," was the best he could manage.

Mindy smiled and said her name without problem. Zack wanted to imprint that smile in his memory forever. After a few brief minutes they left the shop and Zack dropped Graham and Beth off and continued on to work.

Zack worked for a security company and his shift on that night was at a chemical warehouse. The chemical company stored some drugs that could be used to make some illicit recreational substances. However the building was securely fenced, employed lots of lighting, and had frequent stock movements. This meant almost a guaranteed boring night for

Zack. He didn't mind, as he was happy to think about Mindy for the whole shift.

After finishing high school Zack didn't have a clear idea of what he wanted to do with his life. He thought protecting people sounded like a good thing and applied at Gold Star Security Services. He liked the way that he would normally get quite a variety of placements. He had been to supermarkets, shopping malls and many warehouses. He hoped he would be able to get to do the bank runs. Normally that was given to more experienced employees.

In the months that followed Zack became less awkward around Mindy and the four of them spent lots of time together. They had been to music festivals, beaches and spent lots of time just hanging around. At one point Beth joked about the four of them going on a double date. That sounded great to Zack, but the expression on Mindy's face made Zack think she wasn't thinking the same. Zack continued to try to be a gentleman regardless, hoping to eventually win Mindy over. Yet he was never bold enough to make any recognizable advances.

Beth turned and splashed Mindy and Zack. Mindy returned splashes and soon after the four of them were soaking wet and laughing happily.

Zack started to walk out of the water then realised he didn't know where he was going.

"Where to guys?" he asked.

Mindy replied, "I'm starving, where can we find food around here?"

"Good point," said Beth. "We left all our stuff back in the ute."

"There's bound to be a house around here somewhere right?" Graham added.

"Yeah, let's do that and then we can work our plan from there," Zack said.

The four tramped through more grassy fields keeping the small stream on their left. It seemed like hours passed. Zack's stomach was getting more and more insistent. A few groups of trees and the occasional fence was all they encountered. The four peered into the mist but to no avail.

"Has anyone got anything to eat? I'm famished," Mindy pleaded.

They stopped walking and sat down to rest. Zack checked his pockets. He pulled out a small remainder of a stick of chewing gum. He held it up in delight, only now remembering that he put it there. The others checked their pockets too but had nothing edible. Zack felt all eyes on his gum and passed out a piece to Beth and Mindy. He split the last piece and gave half to Graham.

"Thanks mate," Graham said and lobbed the gum into his mouth.

"I guess this is dinner then?" Beth said as she chewed her piece with a funny look on her face.

Zack put his gum in his mouth and then understood.

"Strawberry with a hint of seawater, it's fine dining in some parts of the world," he said with a smile.

"What time is it?" Mindy asked.

"Seven thirty," Graham said, still chewing.

"That's weird; it's not even getting dark," she replied.

Zack looked up in the sky looking for the sun or the moon. He couldn't find either. Only cloudy skies and mist in every direction. They all begrudgingly swallowed their gum and after another drink in the stream they started walking again. Hours passed and there were still no houses in sight.

"Yes, yes!" Mindy pointed at a vague shape in the mist.

"It's got to be a house!" she said with delight.

Excitedly, they all jogged to where she pointed. A large tin shed made its way out of the fog to greet them. They slowed to a walk. As they got closer their hearts sunk further. The old neglected shed was barely standing, covered with weeds and fallen leaves. The tin roof had many holes and missing supports. The wooden walls were wobbly and rotting. The small shed had once been used to store hay. But the owner quickly found it too small and built a bigger one on the other side of the nearby hill, unbeknownst to the four.

Graham grabbed the wall and shook the shed, trying to confirm it would not fall down on them if they were under it. The shed creaked and groaned but moved less than Graham expected.

"This will do," he said, walking in and clearing the ground with his foot.

"Charming," said Beth.

"I'm exhausted," Mindy said yawning.

The four lay down and tried to sleep. Zack and Graham lay facing the door, wary that the last time they slept a demon attacked them.

"I'll take first watch Graham. Get some rest" Zack offered.

"Thanks, I'll try," he said rolling over. Zack kept his eyes on the door. He yawned.

Zack held up the Bible in his hands and flicked through the pages. It would have been too dark to read at this time of day in normal times. But strangely now, there was enough ambient light to read. Zack thought about that for a few minutes but couldn't make sense of it. Indeed no-one could. God had stopped the sun's light reaching earth directly. Now there was no day and night cycle, just persistent dim conditions.

Zack read a passage to himself:

Philippians 4

[11] I am not saying this because I am in need, for I have learned to be content whatever the circumstances. [12] I know what it is to be in need, and I know what it is to have plenty. I have learned the secret of being content in any and every situation, whether well fed or hungry, whether living in plenty or in want.
[13] I can do all this through him who gives me strength.

Zack dwelled on what he read.

It seemed like many hours passed. Zack flicked his eyes to the door occasionally and soon his eyes were too heavy to keep open. He leaned over and gently prodded Graham, who opened his eyes and nodded. Zack nodded too and rolled over to try and sleep.

It was very cold. Graham and Beth snuggled together to keep warm. Zack was shivering; he looked over at Mindy who was shivering too. He thought it over and over in his head but wasn't sure what to say. Everything Zack thought of seemed silly or awkward. Finally his cold body overpowered the swarm of butterflies in his stomach.

"Hey," he whispered.

Mindy just looked at him and nodded.

Zack started to move over towards her. His mind raced.

"Hey? Hey what? Should I say something else? Does she even know what I mean? What side should I lay on? Should I ask her again?"

He eventually made his way next to her and gently lay his arm over her.

She slowly moved closer to him. Zack's heart was pounding in his chest. He breathed slowly and tried without success to not move at all. He could hear her every breath. Her hair smelt like wonderful with a dash of salt water. He could feel himself slowly warming. Mindy snuggled closer.

After a few minutes Mindy fell asleep. Zack could hear the subtle change in her breathing and he knew she was sleeping. Zack relaxed a little. Zack was in Heaven. He had a huge smile on his face. He thought about the two of them growing old together, with matching rocking chairs. He didn't want the moment to end.

"Thank you God," he thought to himself.

All the recent horrors left his mind. Zack closed his eyes.

A twig snapping nearby woke Zack up. He quickly turned his head and looked around. It was just Graham's foot. He lay there holding Mindy, smiling.

Hours later, Beth got up, followed by Graham. They both went outside. Mindy wriggled slowly and Zack lifted his arm.

Mindy woke and sat up.

"Morning," she said with a sleepy face.

"Good morning," he replied.

They got up and met the others outside.

"It doesn't seem to get darker or bright anymore. It's six fifteen," Graham declared.

"Dunno, solar flare, eclipse or something?" shrugged Zack.

"Surely we can find a house this morning, right? Beth asked, wiping her eyes.

"I sure hope so, one with food," Mindy replied.

The four walked back to the creek and after a drink they set off. They walked for hours.

The mist slowly became less thick and finally Mindy pointed out a house in the distance.

"There! That's got to be a house!"

The tired and hungry four picked up their pace. After some time the group approached the large home. It was a colonial bungalow, with white wooden walls and a light green roof. There were vegetables growing in the back garden and an old tire swing in a tall oak tree at the side of the house. On the far side of the house they saw a driveway leading to the road.

They walked up and Graham knocked on the door. Zack looked at the carrots in the garden and contemplated grabbing one to eat. They heard the sound of a lock sliding, and then the wooden door swung open. In the doorway stood a large man. He wore old jeans and a faded brown T-shirt. He had a short gray beard and wispy gray hair. His face was weathered by many hours in the fields. He had bright young eyes set amongst an aging face.

"Even more of you?" he announced.

"Uh, what?" Graham said.

"I'm just surprised you came to the back door," the man said.

"I'm sorry to intrude Sir, there has been some crazy stuff going on."

"You are right about that," he said, interrupting.

Graham continued:

"Yeah, we've been stuck out in the countryside for a few days now. Your house is the first one we've seen. Could you please by chance spare us some food?"

The man laughed.

"What? Seriously? How far have you traveled? Surely not from the other side of the Wilson's farm?"

Graham shrugged.

"I beg pardon, where are my manners? My name is Ronald, you are all welcome to come in and eat if there is any food left. It's just you lot are about the fifth group of people in the last day or so. I guess it's just because we are so close to the road."

Zack peered around the side of the house as they were speaking, seeing the main road at the end of Ronald's driveway. He wondered to himself how they didn't find the road sooner. The four followed Ronald inside. The house was old but tidy and filled with people. A dozen people filled the lounge and kitchen; each looked to have been through a similar experience as Zack and his friends. There was a family huddled on the couch trying to sleep. Another group sat on the floor tending to wounds on a lady's back. An older lady was stirring a big pot on the stove and directing others on where blankets were.

"Hi young-uns, I'm Martha. Find a seat, soup is nearly ready," she said as she opened the pantry looking for something. Martha wore a light blue floral dress and a white apron. She had curly brown hair tied up in a short ponytail.

The four gave their enthusiastic thanks and filed into the lounge. Ronald was called from elsewhere in the house and disappeared.

Zacks stomach yearned for Martha's soup. It smelt like she had mastered the perfect mix of herbs and spices, and they teased his nose. He could just about taste it. He was pleased to be inside, and sat down on a stool. The others sat down nearby.

A large man approached Zack from across the room.

"You've seen them too?" his eyes stared at Zack desperately.

"Yeah," Zack replied, knowing just what he meant.

The man's face fell and he sat back down, rolling a hat in his hands over and over. He looked like a crazy person to Zack. Something about his eyes seemed strange. Martha went around and bandaged up the four's wounds as best she could, in between stirring the soup.

Martha announced that the soup was ready. She poured it into what looked like every bowl, cup and mug in her house and handed them out. Zack followed the others to the kitchen. He thanked her as he received his soup in a pink pony drink bottle. It was still steaming hot. He raised it to his mouth and hot chunky soup flowed in.

The pumpkin was expertly cooked, and it seemed to melt in his mouth. Zack detected croutons and some other vegetables. He wondered if there was bacon. His stomach pangs lulled. The household quieted down as everyone drank their soup. A few minutes later many of the refugees thanked Martha and Ronald.

"Ok, everyone, I'll just say this again for the benefit of you new people. As you've seen, we have been happy to help all of you, but I can't let you eat us out of house and home. You can all stay the night, but first thing tomorrow you must move on," Ronald announced for all to hear.

There were a few groans and whines from the people.

"There is a service station just up the road and town is not far beyond that. I'm sure you'll all get to where you need to go."

"But what about those, those, things? They'll kill us?!" a frightened young boy yelled out.

"We should all go to the church, we'll be safe there," a man stood up as he spoke.

He had a bald head, gray business shirt and pants. He was holding rosary beads in his hand. Zack found out later his name was Matthew.

A heated discussion ensued. Zack kept wondering if he should speak but kept quiet.

"Look, there isn't enough food here for everyone, what happens when it all runs out? We'll have to move on then anyway, come with me," Matthew said.

The man who talked to Zack earlier with desperate eyes stood up.

"No-one can make me go out there again!" he was shaking as he spoke. Zack's heart started thumping again. The feeling in the room got very tense.

"This is my house! You are guests! Act like it!" Ronald yelled.

Crazy-eyes grabbed a heavy looking ornament from the table and held it high. Ronald grabbed a knife from the kitchen.

"Is that how you want to play it, sonny?" Ronald yelled back furiously.

Matthew jumped in between the two men.

"Calm down!" he said sternly.

Before anyone else could move, the kitchen windows smashed inwards, covering everyone in a shower of glass. Two small demons tumbled over the kitchen bench and onto the floor. Screaming filled the air. Everyone tried to flee. The demons hissed and cackled. Crazy-eyes dropped his weapon and fell backwards over the couch. Ronald turned his knife on the demons, slashing wildly. Matthew ran forward, manoeuvring people out of the way of Ronald's wild attacks.

A small demon jumped onto the table and leaped at Ronald. Despite all his previous missed strikes he stabbed the demon square in its chest.

The demon was knocked backwards on to the floor. The other demon hopped into the lounge towards Beth and Mindy.

Zack jumped to his feet. Adrenalin flooded through his body. Mindy screamed. The demon leapt towards a young girl sitting next to her. Mindy punched the demon mid-flight, knocking it back. Zack grabbed the Bible and brought it down to crush the demon. It scuttled underneath the coffee table before the blow landed. Graham and another man flipped the coffee table over, smashing the glass top. Crazy-eyes threw the heavy wooden ornament at the demon and succeeded in knocking it over.

The demon ran across the top of the couch, swinging its claws as it did so, slicing several people. It jumped at Crazy-eyes and dug its claws into his arms. He wailed and thrashed, trying to shake it free. Zack jumped across and swatted the beast with his Bible. Crazy-eyes threw its carcass to the floor and started to stomp on it.

Zack turned to see Ronald and others with fresh wounds cowering in the corners of the room. Matthew had somehow managed to wrap his rosary beads around the demon's neck and was choking it. The creature squealed as the rosary beads burnt their way through its neck until its head fell off onto the blood-splattered floor. Crazy-eyes was still stomping the remains of the other demon.

"Its done, it's over," Matthew declared.

He sat down on the floor. Matthew had a calming affect on the house. Zack felt like he could trust Matthew, and despite all that was going on he felt things would turn out alright.

"Is everyone Okay?" Graham asked as he checked people.

"I couldn't kill it!? I stabbed and stabbed it? I've done a fair amount of hunting in my day, and I'm sure it's not of this world," Ronald said, nursing his bleeding arm.

"It was a demon," Matthew said adamantly.

Zack felt like he'd have to accept this was actually happening.

After that, everyone decided the church would be the best place to go, including Ronald and Martha.

"Grab everything and anything. We leave as soon as we can," Ronald said emptying a cupboard into his bag.

"These are cursed times," Martha muttered to herself.

They spent an hour collecting everything from the house that could be of practical use, including food, tools and clothes.

"When these crazy times end, I expect each and every one of you to buy me a few dozen beers," Ronald said, half in jest as he watched people empty his house.

Graham found a baseball bat and a large coat, Zack carried a small bag of tinned food, Beth had a roll of bedding over her back and a few water bottles, Mindy carried a small bag filled with all sorts.

Matthew was first out the door, now carrying a backpack over one shoulder.

"For those of you who don't know me, my name is Matthew. Follow me."

He set off walking down the driveway.

"Why aren't we driving?" demanded Crazy-eyes.

"The roads are busted and clogged with cars, it'll be faster to walk," was Matthew's reply.

Many of the people at the house had already abandoned their own cars, with only a few managing to drive to Ronald's house.

The group of about twenty people walked up the empty road. Smoke was rising in the distance towards the city. There was broken branches and scattered debris over the road, like after a big storm. Zack looked up ahead and saw another car accident. Both cars were empty, but must have collided recently. He looked up at the smoke plumes rising. He felt like things would get worse before they got better.

Zack was correct.

After a few hours of walking the group came across a large fissure in the ground, which split the road and nearby ground. Matthew approached carefully and peered down. The sides were steep and crumbling. Zack came up alongside and looked into the chasm. He could see it was about as deep as a house is tall and about as wide as the road at its widest point. Zack turned his head and looked to see how far it went. It continued as far as he could see to his left, getting wider and deeper as it went. He looked right and saw it continue somewhat narrower.

"Shall we climb down or go around?" Matthew turned to ask Ronald who came up behind him.

Just as he was about to reply a large chunk of rocks and earth fell from the opposite side. A car parked on the edge gradually slipped in and toppled over onto its roof.

The people near the edge quickly stood back.

"We must go around," Ronald decided.

The others agreed.

The group pushed their way through some small bushes on the side of the road and walked through a well overgrown field. Tall weeds swayed in a gentle breeze. Small shrubs dotted the plain, with the occasional tall trees offering its shade to smaller plants nearby.

As the group trudged on, the ground began to slowly degrade into a bog. Water collected in recessions in the ground. Mud seeped up through the grass. The group followed the large fissure up until Matthew announced:

"We should be able to make it across here."

Matthew stepped his way down into the shallow gouge in the dirt and clambered his way up the other side. Ronald's refugees made their way slowly through the muck and up onto the field on the other side.

Screams rang out from the rear of the group. Zack had just climbed his way out of the fissure. He turned to see three demons claw their way out of the mud further up in the deep gap in the ground.

"Run for your lives!" Crazy-eyes yelled as he bolted ahead.

Matthew, Ronald, Graham and Zack helped the others over the muddy ledge.

An elderly man was the lagging behind. He had terror in his eyes as he stomped through the muck.

"Come on!" Ronald yelled.

The demons screamed as they scrambled along the ground towards him, eager to collect their next victim. The old man dropped the bag he was carrying, ran up the bank and threw up his arm. Ronald and Matthew grabbed a hold of him and started to pull him up. However they were not quick enough.

The demons pounced onto him, stabbing in their long claws. The old man cried out in pain. Graham jumped down with his baseball bat, clobbering one demon. Zack jumped in too, swinging his Bible into the back of another demon. It shrieked and skidded off the old man's back, floundering around in the muck until there was nothing left. The third demon had climbed its way up the old man and sliced deep into his neck. The old man suddenly fell limp. Ronald slipped, Matthew lost his grip and the old man's body fell into the mud.

The demon that Graham batted away got up and leaped onto Graham, stabbing its claws and biting his shoulder. Graham cried out in pain and tried to knock the beast off with his bat. Zack ran over towards him. Graham grappled the demon with his other hand and threw it to the ground. There was a spray of blood from Grahams back. Graham's pain and rage fuelled his strength and he rained down onto the demon with his baseball bat. The demon was driven into the mud.

After a few moments Graham's pace slowed and finally pausing to take a breath, the demon pushed itself up out of the mud, unharmed. It chattered in such a way that it almost sounded like laughter. Zack swung his Bible down on it with both hands. It burst like an evil juicy watermelon.

Matthew had jumped down into the mud too. He was wrestling with the last demon and jammed his rosary beads into its snapping jaws. He then punched them shut. The demon thrashed and dissolved into the mud. Matthew reached his hand into the muck and pulled out his rosary beads.

"I concede man," Graham said panting. "They have to be demons. Only that holy stuff can stop them, I'm sure of that now."

Zack nodded, panting.

Graham dropped to a knee. His back and shoulder was bleeding profusely. A loud grunting sound echoed down the muddy trench. Zack's mind froze. He recognized that sound as one of the large demons. Graham had a panicked look on his face.

"What's that noise?" Ronald asked slowly stepping towards it.

Further up the trench the large demon Zack had seen earlier stomped into view. It opened its large jaws and hollered another loud grunt.

"RUN!" Zack spat, running towards Graham to help him out of the mud. Ronald and Matthew scrambled up and over the ledge with Graham and Zack close behind. Zack saw the rest of their group ahead a short distance away, standing beneath a tree.

An older lady watched them intently, looking for the old man. She started to cry when she saw the men running away from the ledge without him.

"Run! Everyone! Run for your very lives!" Matthew yelled.

The group turned and started running away as best they could. Some dropped their supplies, others tried to lug them with them.

Zack saw Mindy and Beth running ahead with the main group of people. Some people split and ran off by themselves. The fields ahead were covered in deep thick grass with small trees becoming more densely packed as the group ran into the forest. There was a small wire fence a short distance ahead. The group clambered over it as fast as they could. Zack looked behind him to see the grunting demon lumbering after them. He could see a few smaller demons coming up from behind it.

"More are coming!" he yelled across to Matthew.

Matthew repeated the call across the group.

"Let's lose them amongst the trees!" Matthew added.

Zack reached the fence to find more supplies and bags abandoned. The group could see the hulking demon across the field now and it ran with increased vigor. Zack tried to keep Beth and Mindy in sight as they ran between the trees ahead of him.

Graham collapsed on the ground behind Zack. Blood loss and exercise were taking their toll.

"Help me!" Graham said between heavy breaths.

Zack ran over to him and with Ronald's help lifted him to his feet. The three of them made their way into the forest as fast as they could, which was not very fast. The lush undergrowth slowed their advance further. Fallen leaves and branches covered the ground. Zack heard more screams from ahead of them.

The majority of the group was now out of sight in the trees ahead. Zack's heart pounded even faster. The men made their way around a bunch of trees to see the group ahead of them standing still. The sound of rushing water became louder as they approached. The cause of screaming was not demons ahead, but a fast-flowing river. The banks on either side were rocky and steep with the water level below the ground level around it.

Some of the group had started to make their way alongside, but the ground was difficult, with trees leaning towards the river and slippery rocks around them. Zack could hear the demons rapidly approaching from behind.

"We gotta fight," Matthew declared.

Zack pleaded with his eyes to find another means of escape. But they found none. On the other side of the river the forest looked even more dense. Graham held up his baseball bat defiantly.

"Let's do this! We can at least make time for the others to get away."

Crazy-eyes jumped into the river and was promptly washed downstream. Zack never saw him again. Beth, Mindy and the others started to make their way along the riverbank. A man that Zack didn't know picked up a fallen branch and stood ready to fight.

Zack looked ahead at the approaching demons. He felt tight knots churn in his stomach. He could feel a lump rising in his throat. He started to draw in deep breaths.

"God please help me," he whispered.

Matthew and Ronald charged forward meeting the demons head on. Zack and Graham followed behind. The smaller demons nimbly jumped through the trees and leaped forward screeching. Ronald was carrying a rock and swung it full strength into an oncoming demon. It flew into a tree and dropped on the ground.

Matthew had his rosary beads wrapped around his fist and lunged at another demon. He clipped it as it tried to evade. The injured demon fell victim to Matthew's follow up punches and became a stain on the side of a fallen log. The other smaller demon hopped around, slicing the arm and back of the man holding the branch. He swung and missed a few times before one swing connected and Zack finished the demon with a swat of his Bible.

The larger grunting demon trampled his way into the small, clearing breaking branches as it went. It dropped its large jaws baring its jagged teeth and let out a deep growl.

The men stood around it, hesitant to attack the beast. It looked like it had seen years of battle.

Matthew stepped forward and took a swing with his beaded fist. The grunting demon attacked. Random-guy smacked it on the back of the head with his branch. It turned towards him and knocked the branch out of his hands with its strong, clawed arms.

Matthew took the opportunity to jump on its back, wrapping the rosary beads around its neck. The beast howled in pain and its neck started to bubble and leak dark colored pus. As the beast had a layer of muck over it, it took time for the beads to meet the beast's flesh and start to burn.

The large demon swung its larger right arms around and stabbed Matthew straight through his chest with a spike on its arm. Matthew gasped out in pain and spat out blood. The demon twisted and struggled but could not get free from the holy beads around its neck. The men simultaneously assaulted the creature, smashing it with all their might. The branches, bats and rocks did no damage, but Zack's Bible tore a big chunk flesh out of its shoulder. The demon howled and pulled the spike out of Matthew's chest to fend off the incoming attacks.

Matthew spluttered and hacked, barely staying conscious, holding on around its neck with all his remaining strength. The demon stabbed Matthew in a dying flurry as its head came off in a bloody mess. The demon fell backwards onto Matthew and started to slowly dissolve in to a stinking pile of mud, blood and muck. Matthew coughed, and his last breath left his lungs.

"He can't be dead. Help him up!" Ronald shouted. "He seemed to be the one guy with a clue about this whole mess."

Ronald pushed the demon corpse remains off him and checked his vital signs.

"He is dead," he finally admitted.

Zack's heart plummeted. Ronald plied the rosary beads out of the mess and held on to them. Ronald stood up covered in dirt and blood. He realised that the demon had cut him earlier and held his arm. Graham dropped down on to a log.

"Bandages! Help someone!" Zack yelled going over to him.

The people making it slowly along the riverbank returned and the group tended to their wounded and took stock as best they could.

"I'm sure there were more of us. Where's that old lady and that guy in the biker jacket?" Ronald said.

"And that family with the teenagers," added Martha.

The group called out but no-one returned. Mindy did a good job of dressing Graham's wounds, and he wasn't looking as pale now.

"Are you okay Mindy?" Zack asked

She nodded "I'm okay."

"Where are we going? What's the plan?" Random-branch-wielding-guy asked.

"We can't stay here, let's try to get to that church Matthew was talking about," Ronald said.

"Where is it?" Graham asked.

"I think he was referring to that old white church on the corner of Railway Road."

After some discussion and filling of water bottles in the river the group set off. They followed Ronald slowly through the forest. Eventually the trees became more spread out, and the undergrowth gave way to long grass. Zack walked along while his mind struggled with all that had happened recently.

The group walked for hours before reaching a small road. Ronald looked both ways, turned left and set off down the road. There were trees on both sides, with fields stretching as far as the eye could see beyond that. Zack felt a squishing under his foot. He lifted his shoe. It was covered in blood. Zack gasped. On further inspection, he saw that it was a large, squashed red worm under his foot. It was a bloodworm. Zack remembered a year ago when they were all over the news. Some scientist was saying that bloodworms were common enough in some parts of the world, but only a fraction of the size.

Normally they were no wider than a pin and half the length of a typical worm. These new variety were the thickness of a thumb and the length of two hands. Zack hadn't paid much attention at the time, but since he had just stood on one he remembered all he could. The scientist on TV was warning that this worm would be a serious problem as it had somehow appeared globally at the same time. There were reports from multiple countries that they had seen an alarming decrease in the standard earthworms at the same time.

News footage showed this new large bloodworm eating a standard earthworm. This wasn't particularly interesting to Zack, but to others it was astonishing. The bloodworm had a sphincter of six small jaws lined with tiny sharp teeth that it used to eat worms and bugs alike. Zack scuffed his foot off in the grass and carried on walking.

The cuts in his arm demanded his attention. Zack inspected his bandages and winced as he prodded the wound.

"Checking you're still awake?" Graham asked.

"Yeah, wish I could wake up from this nightmare," he replied.

Up ahead Ronald stopped by a bend in the road.

"Over this way!" he yelled as he climbed over the fence on the side of the road and walked on. Zack couldn't think of why they would need to venture off the road. It seemed others thought the same.

"It's a shortcut..." Ronald assured them. "...We can cut across Lindsay's property to the railway line and then just follow that to the church."

Ronald was a local and he seemed very confident, so the group followed. The grassy plain seemed to go on and on. Zack had much more exercise lately than he was used to.

Finally amongst the wild grass they spotted the railway line. Ronald made a victorious 'I told you so' face as he walked on to the tracks.

"What about trains?" Martha called from behind him.

"After all those earthquakes earlier? No chance. And if we happen to see one, we can ask for a ride," Ronald replied assuredly.

Zack looked down the tracks; they went on into the distance winding their way gently around a small hill. Zack ached all over. He just wanted to be at home watching TV. A cry from amongst the group jolted Zack back to reality. His heart started to throb.

"Surely not more demons?" he thought.

He jogged ahead past the others to see what was going on.

The field ahead of them was covered in blood, and it was wriggling. Thousands of bloodworms covered the ground. The occasional cow carcass and small bush broke up the writhing mass.

"What in the hell?" his voice trailed off.

The bloodworms had grown in size and appetite. This horde had consumed an entire herd of cows.

CHAPTER 5

HARD LESSONS

Kephas closed his eyes. He drew in a deep breath. He could not remember how long he had been awake.

"Bishop?" Deon asked quietly.

"I'm not sleeping," Kephas said opening his eyes, smiling.

"Yes, this map. It shows the location of the closest armoury, which is at an old cemetery. It is a long distance from here considering that cars will not be of much use with the roads all broken up as they are."

"Armoury? That sounds good, but why store things so far away?" Deon asked.

"Yes, well, I did not expect that things would get this bad so quickly. The late Father Andrews and I had actually discussed it. Alas, with hindsight we would have changed so many things. Regardless, before we plan this trip we must unite as many people as we can in this city. As you saw many churches were bombed, but there may be many others that are intact. We'll have to send out people to establish connections. Together we may be able to get through this."

Deon nodded.

Kephas continued: "I'd like to think that if we can set up a safe zone at each church; we can save more people than trying to lead everyone across town back here."

"How do we begin?" Deon asked.

Kephas smiled. Deon knew that the situation was dangerous and that lots of hard work lay ahead, but he didn't let that stop him pitching in to help.

The door burst open. A middle-aged lady stepped in. She had short brown hair and a blue blouse and jeans.

"Help! At the fence, please come quick!"

"Yes Sandy, we're on the way," Kephas replied.

The three quickly left the office, ran down the small hallway and out the door towards the front fence line. There were a group of people gathered close to the fence. They were bending over looking at something on the ground. As the three approached one of them stood up.

"It's okay now," David said confidently as he tapped the dirty pickaxe in his hand.

"What happened exactly?" Kephas asked.

"One of those little snappers jammed its head through a gap in the fence. It was trying to squeeze its way in until I pegged it to the ground with this." He held his pickaxe up again, just to make sure that everyone could see.

"I've got this sorted Bishop, don't worry," David added.

"Thank you, er, um, my good man for your defence of these precious people."

David thinly veiled his disappointment when Kephas forgot his name. But his expression changed when he was thanked in front of so many people.

Kephas continued.

"However, I'm afraid that if those demons could press themselves up against the bars, the incense I used earlier must have completely dispersed. We will need a more permanent solution. Sandy, could you please find as many Bibles that you can muster and bring them here? Ask others to help you. We must work fast. Deon, please find everyone who has seen combat and ask them to patrol the fence line. We must be prepared for an attack at any moment."

"Yes Bishop," Deon said as he ran off with Sandy behind him.

"Oh and bring lots of tape," Kephas called after Sandy.

She nodded.

"I'll watch the front," David said as he left.

A few minutes later all sides were being watched and Sandy returned with Amanda and a big stack of Bibles and a few dispensers of tape.

"What now?" Amanda asked.

"Do as I do," Kephas replied.

Kephas picked up a Bible and a roll of tape and walked to the fence line. He looked at the Bible in his hands and took a deep breath. He then ripped the book into two parts, splitting it down the spine. Sandy gasped. Kephas repeated the process several times, and then taped the pages around the bars in the fence. Amanda and Sandy understood and followed suit.

"This should provide better protection from the evil ones," Kephas declared.

Others joined the ladies in their task. Slowly but surely the fencing was being sanctified. There was a feeling of vulnerability in the community. The safety that they had all felt wafted away in the slight breeze.

Deon was anxious; he walked the fence line holding his converted rake weapon tightly in his hands. His eyes darted around expecting to see a demon pop out at any moment. He saw deep cracks in the road, broken glass, abandoned cars, and empty war-zone like streets. But he saw no demons.

Kephas walked all around the boundaries holding his right hand up while he was praying. Eventually he circled back around to where he started.

"It is done," he proclaimed. "We should be safe now, you can tell all our people patrolling that they can rest, though I hope we can find one volunteer, to maintain a standard watch."

"Thank God," said Sandy earnestly. She went to pass on his message.

Deon was walking around the back of the church when Sandy came along.

"Take a break Deon, Kephas says the walls are okay now."

Deon let out a big breath. He felt sure that any minute they were going to be attacked.

"Thank you," Deon said as he lowered his weapon and walked back to the church office. He dropped onto the couch and closed his eyes.

Hours passed. Deon's legs were starting to go numb and he woke with a jolt. He sped down the hallway to Kephas' new office.

"Sorry! I dozed off, what can I do to help?" he said, opening the door.

Kephas was sitting at the desk pouring over the manuscripts from the hidden church cache.

"A well-earned rest. Feel free to take a few more hours if you want. There should be a bed somewhere around here," Kephas replied.

"I'm okay now, I felt like I had been up for so long, but it's still not dark yet?" Deon asked as he peered at the sky through the window.

"Yes, I noticed that too. It doesn't seem to get as bright as day normally would be or as dark as night would be. I think this will play to our advantage, fighting those demons in the dark would be even more difficult. But I don't assume to know how that has happened,"

Deon shrugged.

"What are you reading?"

"Some very old prayers, blessings, exorcisms, notes and a pile I'm not too sure on yet. That would be the big pile," Kephas smiled. He looked very tired.

"Have you had any rest bishop?" Deon said, concerned.

"Not yet, perhaps when I have sorted through the rest of these scrolls."

"Oh I insist, let me keep an eye on things for a bit. You'll be able focus better after some sleep."

Kephas started to open his mouth to protest, and then nodded slowly.

"Wake me immediately if the people need me."

Deon nodded then walked out of the office and shut the door behind him.

Kephas lay down on the office floor and closed his eyes; he fell asleep before he thought about a pillow. Several hours later Kephas woke and found Deon. He was talking to Sandy outside the church hall.

"Hi Bishop, we were just saying that the tap water is no longer functioning."

Sandy was very practical and easily kept her cool in stressful situations. She was a member of the board of trustees of a local school, a netball coach, helped out at the local soup kitchen, and a mother of three teenagers. She was always willing to volunteer where she could. She was happiest when busy, and since arriving at the church she had helped out in innumerable ways. She was holding a water bottle in her hand. It was half empty. She held it up when she saw Kephas notice it.

"There is a stream not too far from here. I thought we could get some water from there?" she suggested.

"I was saying that it'll be dangerous," Deon added.

"Yes, I see. Thank you for identifying this. Okay. Sandy please bring all the water containers you can find and volunteers to carry them. Deon, please find everyone who is willing for combat duty and bring them here too." They both nodded and went off.

A short while later a large group of people had assembled in the car park. Kephas addressed them.

"My good people, we are about to undertake another mission out into what's left of our broken world. Any of you who wish to remain here feel free to do so. I cannot guarantee your safety. However there are still many who we can save! Also we will need food, water, weapons and materials in order to keep this place going."

Kephas quickly counted those standing in front of him.

"Ok, those who went out fighting with me last time can take three new volunteers each. Amanda can you please take your group out and look for more survivors?"

"Yes! We'll get it done," she replied.

"Will, can you please take your group to look for food?"

"Sure," Will nodded.

"And can, you..."

Kephas looked at David, and didn't remember his name.

"...My good man, please look for weapons and materials?"

Kephas handed him a long list on a scrap of paper.

"You want me to get all of these?" David's eyes widened.

"Anything from there would help a great deal," Kephas replied.

"We'll sort it."

"Brother Christopher, I'd like your team to try and contact other churches and gatherings of people and help them setup their own safe zones."

He handed him two sticks of the Holy wax that he had applied to the weapons before the last venture outside the gates.

"Thank you, I will put these to good use," he said.

Kephas continued.

"Alan, can you please ensure this place is well patrolled? We want to intercept anything before it gets close."

"I will keep this place safe," Adam replied with a smile.

"Sandy, if you would hold the fort and managing incoming people and supplies please?"

"Yes, but does someone know where the stream is?" she asked.

A young boy raised his hand. He had short black hair, a bright green T-shirt and blue jeans. His name was Brendon.

Kephas invited him to speak up.

"Do you mean the creek than runs under the bridge that crosses Northcrest Way?"

"Yes that's it," Sandy replied.

"Okay good. We will need the rest of you to help carry water back. Deon and I will provide protection for the water team. Are there any questions?"

Will spoke up. "Do you have anymore of that holy wax for us?"

"Ah, yes thank you."

Kephas pulled out his last wax stick from his pocket.

"Deon, could you please?"

Kephas motioned towards the bag sitting on the ground.

Deon bent over and picked it up. It was filled with all sorts of bladed and blunt implements. It contained lots of kitchen knives, steak knives, a few garden tools and some metal rods.

"As I hope I mentioned earlier, this wax will wear off over time. I'm really hoping weapons team can come through for us. Otherwise future mission will be much more difficult."

David held his pickaxe high.

"We got this."

"Yes. Be aware we are running low on blessed wax."

"What do we do about the demons?" Amanda asked in a loud voice.

"Avoid them wherever possible. If not, kill them," Kephas replied.

Amanda nodded.

"I expect things will get worse before they get better. Return here if the situation gets too dangerous. Stay safe," Kephas added.

Kephas raised his hands over the group.

"May the light of God the creator of all things and the Lord Jesus Christ shine upon you and bless you. Amen."

"Amen."

The groups started to move out.

Kephas turned to Sandy.

"Please ask all who are staying behind to pray for us."

"We will, and good luck!" she replied.

Amanda and her group was first out the gate. She turned left and followed the broken road until she was out of sight. Will's team crossed the road and weaved their way between the buildings. David's team followed the road to the right and turned right again down the next street. Brother Christopher's team followed the water team down the road.

Deon was walking with Kephas at the front of the water collection group. He constantly searched for demons. They were in a suburban part of town with many houses and a few shops around. Debris lay on the ground everywhere. Some of the buildings had been wrecked by the earlier earthquake. Others were relatively undamaged. Low cloud covered the entire sky, yet it was not raining.

Deon scanned the buildings ahead. No movement was seen yet. They carried on down the street and turned another corner. Brendon pointed down the road to a bridge. Underneath was the water they were seeking.

A lady came running out of her house crying. Her dress was torn and splattered with blood.

"Help me!" she sobbed. She ran up to Deon and cowered behind him. She stuttered and pointed back towards the house she came from. Then she broke down into tears. Deon and another lady from the group consoled her and walked her along at the back of group. Soon more and more people fled from their houses and joined them. Kephas was trying to keep the group moving towards the bridge further down the road, but it was becoming more difficult.

"Deon!" he called over the commotion.

Deon left the lady he was helping with another member of the group and went to the front to meet Kephas.

"Can you run these people back to the church and rejoin us at the bridge?"

"Yes."

Kephas called for Brother Christopher.

"We need your group to carry on to the nearest church to see if it is intact. Otherwise we'll be swamped with people. And we'll have nowhere to house them."

"I agree. I'm hoping the church on Wilford Street is okay. It's just a few blocks from here."

With that he and his helpers departed.

Kephas addressed the newcomers.

"Attention please everyone! It is not safe to stay here in the street. Follow this man to safety. It is not too far."

Deon waved to get their attention and started to escort them back to the safety of the church. Deon realized that it was down to only him to protect these people. He turned and called out to those following him.

"We are going to pick up the pace!"

Deon started to jog. He seemed to instil just the right amount panic and the others started jogging too. They came around the corner of the street and on the roof of one of the houses was a small demon. Deon couldn't help but stare; he started to think about what he should do when a woman behind him started screaming.

"It's one of those things!" she wailed.

The demon quickly turned its head and locked its eyes on its new prey. Deon's thoughts of sneaking past were dismissed. His heart started pumping faster.

"Stay close!" he called.

He continued jogging up the street on the side furthest from the demon. It shrieked and leapt down off the roof towards them. Two more demons scrambled over a fence behind the house.

"Lord God, give me strength," Deon prayed quietly.

Deon gripped his weapon tightly and stepped forward to meet his enemy. The demon scuttled down the road towards the people at the back of the group. Deon sprinted to intercept. The demon was quicker and lunged into the screaming people, slashing its claws at everyone in range. A middle-aged man earned a long gash across his arms and shoulders for standing in front of a young boy.

Deon caught up and swung his weapon in a double-handed arc. The demon jumped over the first attack and leapt at Deon. Deon stepped forward and punched it square in the face with a fast left jab. The demon was knocked back against a parked car and then impaled by Deon's subsequent thrust of his sanctified sharp rake weapon. Screams from the front of the group pierced the air. Two more demons were scampering across the road.

"Run!" Deon screamed.

He pointed his rake ahead and the group started running for their lives. Deon ran towards the demons and threw his rake at the closest demon. The rake skimmed across the road and spun around, hitting the curb and clipping one of the demons. Deon ran forward and kicked away the second demon. He gained a gash on his leg from its fast claws in the process. He lunged towards his rake and quickly brought it down on the demon he clipped earlier with his lucky throw. His attack landed and the demon split and popped in graphic fashion.

The last demon ran towards Deon. He threw his weapon again, this time missing badly. The demon jumped at him, slicing his arms as he tried to defend himself. Deon now realized throwing away his only weapon was not such a good idea. He punched the demon repeatedly and threw it to the ground. It quickly got up and leaped at him again. This time Deon's defence was too slow. The demon landed a savage blow across his head and into his right eye.

Deon screamed out with pain and fell backwards onto the road. The concrete curb punched into his back and shoulders. He held his hand over his face, his body wracked in pain. He opened his good eye to see the demon approach. He had nothing to defend himself with. He looked across the road to see his weaponized rake behind the demon, well out of reach.

Deon kicked and thrashed with the demon as it rained stab after stab into his body. He grabbed the demon by the head with both hands and started to squeeze. It had little effect. Deon's mind raced. He knew he was going to die.

"Lord God, help me."

Deon had barely started to pray when the demon on top of him exploded all over him. He wiped the blood and muck off his shocked face. The man who he had helped earlier was standing above him holding out his hand. In his other hand was Deon's rake.

"Thanks!" Deon managed to utter.

"Let me help you up buddy, now we're even," the man said.

"Deon."

"Jacob," he handed Deon back his weapon.

"Let's go."

The two men ran down the road catching up to their group. Deon left a trail of blood dripping from his many wounds. But he kept on running. Somehow he blanked the pain from his mind. He was determined to get these people to safety or die trying. Deon scanned the way ahead with his one functioning eye. The group made its way past the end of the street and saw another group coming out of a connecting road. It was Brother Christopher's group. They too had lots of new-comers in tow. Many were splattered in blood. Deon saw Brother Christopher's face drop when he saw him. Two groups met in the middle of the road.

"Deon! Let me heal you," Brother Christopher insisted.

He held his hand on his bleeding face and his other hand on his shoulder. He prayed the holy words Kephas had taught him. Deon's body felt numb. He then felt a surge of energy wash over his whole body. It felt like a mixture of adrenalin, pins-and-needles and a profound peace. Deon shivered. He wiped the blood from his face and opened both his eyes. He could see again. Deon stopped leaking his blood all over the road.

"Wow," was all Deon could think to say. He touched his eye, and his face. He felt a new scar. It was as if it had been there for a long time, but moments before his face was a bloody mess.

"Sorry, I haven't managed to heal like Kephas yet. That scar is a doozey," Brother Christopher said with a smile.

"No problem, the ladies love scars right?" Deon replied.

Before Deon realized, Brother Christopher had healed the others injured in his group.

"We must get these people to the church," he said.

Deon nodded.

They ran down the road with renewed vigour. Deon watched for more demons with both eyes. Soon the group had made it back to the safety of the church. Adam and his team escorted them in. Brother Christopher was panting hard.

"I'm exhausted."

He lay out on the grass as soon as he was in the gate. Deon still felt energized from when he was healed.

"Thanks again, I'm off to help with the water collection."

Brother Christopher waved.

Sandy directed the new people towards the church hall. As Deon walked past her she tapped him on the shoulder.

"Deon, can I talk to you a moment?"

"Sure."

"We were low on supplies before you all left, now you've brought in even more people and no supplies. Please ask Kephas what he plans to do. I'm not saying we should turn people away, I just don't want to starve either."

"Understood, I'll pass that on."

Deon ran out the gate and down the roads until he met up with the others fetching water from the stream. He spotted Kephas standing in the middle of the bridge surrounded in demon remains. Kephas maintained a watch for more enemies. The roadside dropped away to a grassy verge that lead down to the creek. Small plants and trees encased the creek as it wound its way through the suburbs.

Deon could see the volunteers walking up and down the slope passing buckets, drink bottles, and other containers up to the side of the road.

"Deon! Good timing, we had a bit of trouble but are nearly finished now," Kephas called.

"Yeah, me too. Those people are safely back at the church."

"I knew you could do it. Oh and Brother Christopher seems to have helped out too?" Kephas pointed to Deon's scar over his eye.

"Yes! That healing business seems to be quite draining. How do you manage to keep going Bishop?"

"Practice, my boy."

"Ah right, oh. Sandy said we will be getting desperately low on supplies at this rate. What is the plan?"

"Trust in God..."

Kephas repeated Bible verse from memory:

Matthew 6

[25] "Therefore I tell you, do not worry about your life, what you
will eat or drink; or about your body, what you will wear.
Is not life more than food, and the body more than clothes?[26]
Look at the birds of the air; they do not sow or reap or store away
in barns, and yet your heavenly Father feeds them.
Are you not much more valuable than they?

Deon nodded.

One of the volunteers walked up on to the road with the last container filled with somewhat clear water.

"We're ready," he said.

"Good work, let's get back," Kephas replied.

Kephas picked up the two largest containers and set off at a pace that seemed surprisingly fast for the weight he was carrying.

"Are you Ok with those?" Deon asked.

"If you can catch me, we will swap," Kephas said with a smile.

Deon picked up some water and set off after him.

The water collection group made it back to the church with no incident. Sandy was waiting anxiously at the gate.

"Bishop, please, a moment?"

"Yes Sandy?"

Kephas put his water down and went over to Sandy. A moment later Deon and the others filed in, puffing. Deon sat on the grass and caught his breath. He looked around; there were people everywhere. Their numbers of only a day or so had doubled. Deon was reminded of days in his youth spent at large music festivals, with practically standing room only.

Sandy took Kephas aside.

"I had Adam and his friends dig a long drop toilet behind the church. The plumbing everywhere is no longer functioning."

"Great thinking," he replied.

"The other teams have also returned bringing more survivors with them. This is great news, but we simply don't have room for everyone. And we certainly don't have enough food."

"I see," Kephas took in what she said and thought for a moment.

"The school," he declared.

"Sorry?" she replied.

"There is a primary school across the road from here. We will secure it and will be able to house people there. Tell me, have the demons come inside the fence line while I was away?"

"No, we've not seen any."

"That's good news. Please summon volunteers and all the remaining Bibles you can find, we will sanctify the school fence immediately. We will need fighters to clear out the school, too."

"Yes Bishop, and what about the lack of food?"

"One thing at a time young sparrow."

Kephas walked out the gate again.

A short time later a large group of volunteers and ten fighters crossed the road to secure the school. Kephas opened the gate to St. Thomas School and walked down the concrete path towards the classrooms. There were numerous buildings on the property, all with blue tiled roofs and light cream walls. Deon walked behind Kephas looking for demons. He was surprised that there was relatively little damage from the earlier earthquake. A small number of windows were broken; a few deep cracks in some of the walls, but all the buildings were still standing.

Deon looked down at the paint on the concrete. It was covered in different games. Hopscotch, animals and the like. Deon smiled as he walked his way down a long, green snake with numbers painted on it. He heard a chuckle from behind and turned to see Amanda smiling. She joined in the game too.

Upon reaching the first block of classrooms Kephas turned to address them.

"Okay, let's spread out from here. Search everywhere, stay safe."

Deon saw David and a few others disappear behind some classrooms. Deon walked through the benches where the students sat to eat their lunch. There were cracks in the ground, some of them knee deep. He walked along further to the administration building. He went to open the door but it was locked. He began to wonder what he should do next when screaming filled the air. His heart skipped a beat.

Deon ran down towards the rear classrooms. He rounded the corner just in time to be covered in a spray of blood. One of the new fighters had his arm cut off by a large demon. This one was large for its type; it stood nearly as tall as a human. To Deon it looked like the small demons he had fought, but just much bigger and stronger. Its hulking arms swung again and impaled the man with one arm. His screaming abruptly stopped. The demon withdrew his long spikes from him, flinging the body to the ground.

Deon had not even learnt the man's name yet. He thought he'd have plenty of time for that. The dead man did not think anything. Deon wiped the blood from his face. The demon turned to face Deon and started to charge. Deon jumped to the side and swung his weapon.

"Help! Everyone! Over here!" he yelled, like his life depended on it, which it did.

The demon turned after missing its attack and let out a roar as it lunged at Deon. He fended off the first blow with his weapon but the second hit him in the chest and he fell backwards onto the ground. The demon charged again. This time Deon intercepted with a quick thrust to its right leg. As the blow connected a chunk of what looked like a mixture of dirt, rock and muscle was knocked off the creature. Not the crippling blow Deon was hoping for. The demon seemed to be encased in protective armour of some sort. Deon saw that the demon's right leg now looked slightly red where the armour had come off. Deon scrambled to his feet, narrowly avoiding losing a limb.

"Oh, boy!" David yelled as he came around the corner of the classroom to help.

The demon turned to face David. Deon promptly stabbed the beast in the back, dislodging another chunk of armour. David swung his pickaxe at it and removed yet more from one of its arms. The demon howled and charged at David, slicing his arm and chest and throwing him into the wall. Deon targeted the large demon's right leg again and managed to land a blow where the armour was already missing. The blessed cross on the end of his staff drove into its flesh, boiling and ripping it apart. The demons leg was severed. It screamed and howled, thrashing violently in all directions. Its right leg was spitting dark ooze onto the ground.

David took another swing with his pickaxe and missed. The demon smashed David up against the wall and drove its barbed elbow into his face. David let a wail of pain escape his lungs. Deon thrust at the creature knocking off more armour. The large demon slapped him to the ground. Deon's head smacked against the concrete curb and he began to bleed internally. He held his staff up in front of him, struggling to stay conscious.

The demon attacked and Deon's arms were cut deeply and he dropped his weapon. The demon loomed over him and raised its arms to deliver the killing blow. The demon's midriff exploded outwards, covering Deon in muck. Deon blinked and saw a sanctified blade protruding from the creature dangerously close to his face. Amanda had stabbed it from behind where Deon had hit it previously. More people rushed in and pummelled the demon until it was spread over the classroom wall like graffiti in a bad neighbourhood.

"Thanks," Deon said amongst the blood in his mouth.

"You're welcome," Amanda said as she tried to help him up.

Deon cried and fell back to the ground. His head pulsated with pangs of pain. He stumbled to a knee and looked at the guy who lost his arm, and his life. He choked down the lump in his throat.

Kephas arrived at the scene and checked on the dead man.

"Can you heal him Bishop?" Deon said pointing.

"I will try."

Kephas felt for a pulse and didn't find one. He put his hand on the man's chest and closed his eyes for a moment.

"He has passed away, I cannot heal him. I'm sorry."

One of the people standing there teared up and left.

"I don't get it? Why don't you heal him like those other injured people?" Amanda asked.

"His soul has left him, this body is just an empty shell."

"Jesus rose people from the dead in the Bible, can you do that?" Deon added.

"Yes, he did. But no, I can't. I am sorry. I did not expect Mortkin would be here."

"A what?" Amanda asked.

"That large demon was a Mortkin, the killing type. The small demons, the Scarkin, are the torturing type. Both are very dangerous and the very essence of evil."

Kephas closed the dead man's eyes. He then stood between David and Deon and healed them both, one hand on each of their shoulders.

"But don't be discouraged, the one that lives in each of us is greater than the one who is of this world. This young man has gone to be with the Lord God in Heaven now. Come, let us secure the school. There are many people depending on us."

Deon felt a peace wash over him once more. His head stopped bleeding. He drew in a deep breath.

"You're right, let's get this school safe," David said as he picked up his weapon and set off.

After a few hours searching and a few Scarkin killed, the group were confident that the school was secure. The sanctification team moved in and wrapped the fence with Bible pages. Kephas watched the last pages go up on to the school gate. He then proceeded to pray in Latin the blessed words of protection.

Deon let out a big sigh.

"Thank the Lord."

The team of fighters broke up to patrol the boundaries of the church and the school. Brother Christopher, Deon and Bishop Kephas returned to the church office to talk with Sandy. Approaching the church gate Deon saw even more people had squeezed into the church compound. They weaved their way through the crowd and found Sandy. Amanda started to lead people across the road to the school.

"As you gentlemen can see you secured that school just in time! More people have joined us while you were out."

"Did anyone bring food with them?" Deon said with a smile.

His stomach was reminding him he had not eaten in a long time.

"Sadly no, and that's just the thing. We need a way to feed all these people."

"How about the supermarket?" Brother Christopher asked.

"Agreed," said Kephas. "Assemble some volunteers. We set out at once."

A short while later Kephas, Deon, Amanda, and David left the church heading for the supermarket. Deon had hoped that he could rest inside the safety of the compound, but understood the need to move quickly. His stomach thought it was a good idea too. They walked amongst the empty broken streets. Few people remained in the suburbs around the church. Fewer still were alive.

After a while the group reached the supermarket car park. Only a small number of cars were parked there. Deon saw the front glass doors of the supermarket were smashed in. Rubbish and debris littered the car park. Deon had thought that many survivors would've been here trying to get food also, as it was the only supermarket in the suburb.

"Grab a trolley," David said to Deon as he walked past them.

"Good idea." Deon wiggled a trolley free from the others in the stack.

The loud crack of a rifle spilt the air. A single bullet narrowly whizzed past the group and shattered a window of a parked car.

"Get down!" Kephas commanded.

Deon's heart kicked into high gear as his mind scrambled to find somewhere to take cover. A few panicked seconds later the group hid behind the car with the broken window.

"Did anyone see where that came from?" David asked.

An unfamiliar voice rang out over the car park.

"Get out of here! This is our supermarket."

Amanda peeked over the bonnet of the car. She saw three men holding hunting rifles standing on the roof of the supermarket. Kephas stood and walked a step towards the supermarket with his hands in the air.

"We mean no harm, we just..." Kephas was cut short by the sound of another bullet punching into the car next to him.

"The next one goes in your face!" a bedraggled man yelled as he looked down the scope of his rifle.

"Okay, okay, we're going," Kephas replied.

He motioned to the others to get up. They cautiously stood and started to back away from the supermarket. The men on the roof kept their eyes on them as they moved. Kephas turned and they hurriedly walked away.

One of the men on the roof argued with the others.

"We can't just let them go; they'll be back with more people."

"It's fine, don't worry about it."

"I'm not taking any more chances."

David's shoulder burst in a spray of blood as a bullet tore through it. He screamed and tumbled over onto the concrete.

"Run!" Kephas yelled.

Another shot skidded off the concrete close by. Kephas went to David's aid and pulled him to his feet. Deon ran with Amanda desperately trying to make it around the building at the edge of the car park. A few seconds later they were out of line of sight of the supermarket snipers. Kephas and David appeared shortly afterwards. Kephas lay David down and assessed his wound.

David spluttered, trying to speak. Kephas closed his eyes. He spoke the holy words of healing over him and moments later David was standing.

"Thank you again Bishop, let's go," David said.

No-one needed convincing. They were all aware how lucky they were to be alive.

After they were safely a few blocks away they stopped and discussed their next move. Amanda spoke up: "Let's try the convenience store we were at a while ago. He may have changed his mind by now."

"Good idea," Kephas replied and they set off.

An hour later they came upon the convenience store with the shotgun-wielding owner. Kephas walked in with his hands in the air.

"We come in peace, is anyone here?"

The distinctive sound of a shotgun being loaded drew Kephas' attention to the back of the store. The owner had blood running all over his face and his arm was crudely bandaged. Much of the shop was in disarray and there was blood splattered over the counter.

"Don't move!" he spat.

"We've come to ask if have any food that you could spare us please?"

"You've come to steal! Just like all the others."

David walked into the owner's view just outside the door next to Deon and Amanda. The owner trained his shotgun on each of them and then kept it pointed at David. Like the others David held his hands up. The owner stared at all the blood on David and his ripped shirt.

"Whose blood is that? Your last victim?!" the owner demanded.

"It's mine." David opened the rip and smeared the blood away from where his wound was.

The owner's eyes widened when he saw his shoulder was intact.

"Lies!"

"This old man healed me."

"Don't lie to me."

"Look, if I was going to lie to you I'd have a more believable story than that pal."

The owner grimaced. He was obviously in pain. He was quiet for a few moments.

"Okay then. How?"

Kephas stepped forward. "Let me show you, you are obviously hurt. Let me heal you and we will go."

"You'll steal my food!"

"No, we can find food somewhere else. Just let me help you. Please."

Kephas approached cautiously.

"Okay then, but I've got my eyes on you."

Kephas walked around the end of the aisle of groceries and saw the store owner's body was covered in gashes and blood.

"I'm Kephas, what's your name?"

"Gregory."

"Okay Gregory, just relax."

Kephas closed his eyes and placed his hand on to Gregory's shoulder. He prayed the Latin words that Deon was slowly starting to memorize. A deep peace washed over Gregory and he dropped his shotgun, lunged forward and hugged Kephas.

Deon relaxed a little and lowered his hands.

"Thank you, thank you, thank you! I thought I was going die!"

"By looks of the blood you've lost, you soon would have. But don't thank me; it is through the Lord God that I was able heal you."

"What? Really?"

"Yes."

"Which God?"

"The one true God, the Almighty, the creator of heaven and earth, the.. "

"Alright, alright. The Jesus one?"

"Well, Yes..."

"Okay good. Look, I'll get the long version when we get outta here. You've got somewhere safe right? You lot look in much better shape than others I've seen."

"Yes, St Thomas Church and the primary school are now safe."

"Great! Let's go!"

"We.."

"Yes, yes, take all the food, take everything you want. Just keep those beasts away from me."

"Thank you, we will."

Gregory grabbed the keys to his van and the four of them filled it with as much as they could.

A while later they drove carefully out of the garage behind the store and onto the broken streets. They traveled at a walking pace around the deep cracks in the road, sometimes driving over the footpath and grass. Eventually they made it back to the church in one piece.

"This is very generous of you, thank you Gregory," Kephas said.

"You're welcome! I'm happy to help."

Sandy was eagerly awaiting their return.

"Thank the Lord you have returned!" she said greeting them.

"Yes indeed," Deon added.

"The supermarket trip looks like a success."

"This is all from Gregory's shop; the supermarket is a no go."

Deon's face told Sandy she'd be filled in later.

"Thanks Gregory, I'm Sandy, let me show you around."

They distributed the food and supplies and set up a return trip to get was left behind at the store. Deon was starving. After Sandy had carefully rationed the food, Deon came to collect his share. His dinner comprised of two peanut butter sandwiches, an apple and two lollipops. This wasn't quite what he had hoped for, but his stomach was delighted nonetheless. While they were away Sandy had set up a return trip to restock their water.

Over the next few days the church and school became progressively more organized, with several expeditions to bring in new people from the surrounding neighborhoods.

Kephas was talking to Brother Christopher in the churchyard when Deon and Jacob came up to them.

"Excuse me Bishop, but Jacob here has something he'd like to show you," Deon said.

"Yes, what is it?"

"I've been talking with Deon and well, I've made this." Jacob handed over a cloth covered object to Kephas.

Kephas unfolded it to see a makeshift axe. It had a wooden handle with wrapped rope around as a grip. The metal blade had an inscription carefully etched into it.

"Jesus Christ is the light of the world."

Kephas smiled as he rolled it over in his hands, and stepping away slightly from the others he swung it around with surprising skill.

"This is wonderful! However did you make this?"

"The school workshop Sir. It has a good selection of tools. I'd be able to make much more too with a few more items."

"This is such good timing. We've already had many weapons lose their usefulness as the blessed wax on them has worn off."

"Yes, Deon had shown me his weapon. I thought that if it was etched into the blade itself. It wouldn't wear off."

"If you allow me, I'll try this one out against the demons first, then please make as many as you can."

Jacob had a big smile on his face. His mechanic shop had gone out of business a few months back and he'd found it tough getting another job. He felt great satisfaction in being able to contribute.

"I have some scrolls that I have nearly finished translating that I think would add even more zing to these weapons," Kephas said happily.

Amanda came running from around the other side of the church in a panicked state.

"Has anyone seen Brendon? Young boy, black hair, blue jeans and green top. This high," she indicated with her hand.

Everyone shrugged or shook their heads.

"No, why?" Deon asked.

"He's missing. I think he may have gone to collect water with the others, but they are still not back and I'm freaking out."

"Let's go and find him them," Kephas said. "How many blessed weapons have we got left?

"I still have one; I think the others were taken by the water team," she replied.

"Okay, let's go."

Kephas, Deon, Amanda and Brother Christopher set out.

"Here Deon, you can give this axe a try."

"Thank you Bishop."

Brother Christopher held one of the small ancient crosses in his hand; Amanda had one half of her blessed hedge clipper blades. Kephas had who knows what up his sleeve. The four of them left the church at once and followed the same streets that the water collection team had taken. Deon held the new axe in his hands tightly. He never got used to the feeling of risking his life. Deon missed the easy days of tending to the gardens.

Deon surveyed the streets as the four jogged. There were deep cracks in the road. Some of the houses had all but collapsed, yet others seemed largely intact. Deon felt fortunate that he had not been crushed, as hundreds of other people must have been. Deon looked upwards. The gray sky felt oppressive and although they were outside the air was stale and stagnant. He peered around and couldn't see the sun in the sky. Deon had given up on tracking the time of day. He felt tired all the time.

"There," Brother Christopher pointed out and ran ahead.

A body lay on the edge of the street motionless. It was face down with the feet farthest from them as if it has been running towards the church.

"I recognize this man; he was on the water team," Brother Christopher said.

The man was covered in deep cuts all over his body. Blood had saturated his clothing. He had a panicked expression frozen on his dead face. Kephas looked up the street to see a trail of blood leading away from the dead man.

"He must have bled out. I'm sorry but we should hurry to see if anyone else is still alive."

As the four stood, Deon closed the man's eyes. He thought about how crazy things had become that there were dead bodies laying in the street.

Distant screaming and sounds of fighting quickened the pace of the group. They rounded the street and saw what was left of the water collection team. Two people stood back to back surrounded by a large group of Scarkin. More bodies littered the surrounding area. Spilt water containers flooded the street in bloody glaze.

"Help!" one of the two survivors shouted at the top of her lungs.

It was Denise. She looked near the point of collapse with multiple injuries staining her clothes. She held a blade defiantly in her hand. The encircling Scarkin hissed and lurched forward, snapping at any opportunity. Denise and another survivor swiped and swung their weapons desperately to keep them at bay.

Kephas shouted something in Latin as he threw a small spherical object towards them. It smashed into the ground amongst the Scarkin and exploded in a splash of clear liquid, then a burst of light-blue flame. The demons boiled and writhed as the holy oil burnt their flesh. Denise and the other survivor ran back towards the group, dodging attacks from the remaining demons.

The rescuing group charged forward past them and carved up the evil creatures. Deon swung his holy etched axe into a Scarkin, splitting it in half mid-air. The demon detonated into a mess of dark-colored muck. After a few moments of fighting the humans stood victorious catching their breath amid the demonic remains.

Kephas and Brother Christopher quickly set about checking the bodies. Kephas managed to save one lady who looked to be dead lying near the side of the bridge, still clutching a water container in her hand.

"There was too many of them," Denise said, looking at her fallen comrades, sobbing.

"You did all that you could," Amanda said. "Please tell me you've seen Brendon?"

"Um, yes he was here with us. I don't know where he is now though. Sorry, I lost track in the fighting."

Amanda called out Brendon's name and kept looking for him. Deon trudged down the slope to the river. He picked up a water bottle and was making his way back up when he heard a rustling in the bushes behind him. He dropped the container and held up his axe. A young boy with black hair emerged from the bushes. He looked like he had been crying.

"Brendon?"

The boy ran towards Deon and hugged him.

"I, I, just hid," he started to cry.

"It's okay now, you're safe. Come with me."

Deon lead him up back to the road and Amanda swallowed him up in a big hug.

"Oh my dear Brendon. You're alive, you're alright!"

The group spent some time paying respects to the dead and collecting water, then made their way back to the church.

Upon their return Deon sat down on a bench in the churchyard under a tree. He closed his eyes. He sucked in a big breath. As he exhaled he tried to make sense of all the feelings bouncing around inside him. He wasn't sure where to start.

"Deon!"

He opened his eyes.

Amanda was approaching him. "Kephas is asking to see you in his office. And thank you for your help out there today."

"Okay. No problem," he said with a smile.

Deon stood up and made his way to the church office and knocked on the door.

"Come in."

Deon entered to see Kephas, Brother Christopher, Adam, and Will looking over a map of Brakenside.

"Ah, good. Deon, please join us," Kephas began. "I'm sending you four out to link up with the other churches. I think we are established enough here now that we should see how people further out are doing."

Deon looked down at the map spread out on the table. It was a tourist map of the small city; it was colourful and had the sight-seeing attractions and restaurants marked out on it. There were icons of churches and meeting halls scattered about it.

Kephas continued: "We know that the Cathedral was destroyed..." He pointed to a church with a red 'X' drawn over it on the map. "...I have a feeling that you may find others in a similar state from all those explosions a few days ago. If what you find is secure tell the people to stay put. Otherwise direct them back towards us. I'll be sending out other patrols after you to keep an eye out."

"So we are to move on from each place immediately?" Brother Christopher asked.

"I trust your judgement. If lives can be saved, do what ever you deem needed. We will need to understand the state of the whole city when we can. I don't know if we are the worst or the least affected."

"Understood."

"We'll be supplying you with enough food and weaponry to make the trip. But try to avoid combat if you can. We've been given Mrs Jameson's car so you can take that as far as you can manage. But I expect you'll likely be on foot most of the time."

"You're not coming with us Bishop?" Will asked.

"I'm afraid not. As I hope you've seen, the prayers that I have managed to translate so far have been invaluable. I hope to get the remaining ones done before I set out again. Besides you've all proven yourself capable fighters."

"Good idea. Thanks."

"Jacob has been busy while we were out."

Kephas unfolded a blanket in the corner of the room and pulled out a spear and placed it on the table. It was followed by a large club and a converted spade. These were made of a combination of wood and metal, with holy words etched into the metal at the business end of each weapon.

"Oh yeah, this will do nicely!" Will picked up the club and rolled it around in his hands. There was rope bound around the grip and it had a strong looking wooden shaft with a heavy looking metal smashing-end.

"Thanks," Adam said as he picked up the spade with sharpened knife blades attached to it. It had a strong shaft and new handle.

Brother Christopher inspected the spear. Its blade was in the shape of a cross with sharpened edges. There was also a small spike on the other end. Both had holy words on them.

"Thank you."

"Deon, I trust your axe has been effective?"

"Yes Bishop, please thank Jacob for us."

"May the light of Jesus Christ shield you from all evil and may God bless you that you may return safely back to us."

"Amen," they all said.

The four men set out.

…

Zack looked out over the bloody field. It was about ankle deep in bloodworms. The railway lines disappeared out of sight underneath the wriggling mess. The group stood at the edge of the worms unsure whether or not to go any further.

"They are just worms. Come on," Ronald said. He stomped ahead into the worms, squashing them under foot as he slowly moved forward.

"Wait!" Martha yelled. "They killed the cows!" She pointed to a cow ribcage protruding out of the worms in the field ahead.

"Nonsense. It must have been dead already. Let's go," Ronald replied.

The rest of the group still hadn't moved. Zack's mind tried to make a decision and failed. Graham stepped forward and stomped a worm flat. He then stomped on a few more.

"It's not so bad," he declared.

"It is horrible and gross," Beth retorted.

Zack watched a few more people from their group stomp a few worms. They were trying to prove to themselves that it wouldn't be dangerous. They were wrong.

Zack turned around and tried to see if he could see the road. He couldn't. His tired legs reminded him of how long he had been walking. He didn't feel like walking back the way he came. But he didn't feel like walking through a field of bloodworms either.

Ronald made his way further ahead of the group with no problems. Mindy watched him for a few more steps, and then she too stomped on a few worms at the edge of the field of blood.

"We can do this guys, they are just bugs," Graham said.

"I don't like it," Beth replied. "I have a really bad feeling about all this."

"I think we all have a bad feeling about this, but let's just get this done. We're heading the right way. I don't want to get lost again."

"Okay," Beth said eventually.

More of their group had already started to follow Ronald. The four made their first steps. Zack felt multiple worms squish under his feet as he stomped his way forward. It was like walking into the kitchen after someone had dropped carnivorous spaghetti bolognaise on the floor.

After a short while the group had made it past the small hill that had previously blocked their view of the way ahead. Ronald's body language as he first saw the field beyond made it clear that it was also covered in bloodworms.

Zack's legs were complaining about all the extra effort required to stomp each step. He had seen that if he followed in footsteps of the others in the group, he could follow, saving some effort. The others noticed this too and soon the whole group was walking single file across the seemingly unending, writhing ground.

Ronald continued to lead the way and walked towards one of the cow carcasses. As he approached he could see only the bones were left. Some worms were still consuming the last grisly parts, but it was largely picked clean. Not long afterwards, Zack, following in the trodden path, walked past the same remains. Just as he did so the cow skull cracked open and a gooey mess of worms burst outwards. Zack gagged.

"Oh that's truly foul," Graham said, covering his mouth.

Zack redirected his eyes ahead, desperate to see the end of the worms. Several trees and shrubs lined the base of a small hill ahead of him to the right. A deep ditch wound its way across the way ahead to the left. Zack wondered if there was water there. His mind told him that even if there was, drinking anything that was surrounded in blood was probably not a good idea.

"I think it's this way," Ronald called.

He was kicking and stomping a small clearing in the worms around him.

Zack remembered that he hadn't walked over the railway lines in a while. He too stomped a few extra worms trying to find the tracks buried beneath all the worms. Ronald gave up looking for the tracks and pointed towards a large hill towards the horizon.

"It's gotta be this way. Come on, nearly there."

Zack was pleased to see that the hill he pointed out was green in colour.

"I'm exhausted," Mindy said quietly.

"Yes me too," Beth replied.

Graham and Zack nodded.

"I'm really over these stupid worms," Zack added.

The group walked on begrudgingly until someone shouted.

"Demon!"

Zack spun around searching with panicked eyes. Off towards the distant tree line a Scarkin was slinking through the worms. It didn't seem to be slowed as much as the humans were. Zack's heart started thumping in his chest. He retrieved the Bible from his bag with fumbling hands.

"Watch it!" Ronald yelled as he pointed to more Scarkin arising from among the bloodworms in front of them. The worms didn't seem to want to consume the demons.

Branch-wielding-guy and a few others moved as quickly as they could towards the front of the group to join Ronald. Zack and Graham followed close behind.

Zack's ears were filled with panicked whimpers from the group. Soon the demons were galloping over the top of the worms towards them. The humans readied themselves for their attack. Swings of a baseball bat, a branch, a Bible, and a Ronald's rosary beaded fist met the first demon attacks. A few frantic seconds later a demon had been killed, and several people were slipping over in the worms.

Graham and Zack worked together to bat-and-then-Bible oncoming demons. Zack swung his Bible at a demon as it jumped but slipped on the worm carpet beneath him. He fell backwards and worms made his landing soft but horrible. However he somehow managed to knock the back of his head on the hard ground beneath the worms. Zack became face to face with the disgusting little creatures. He saw one worm open its mouth to take a bite, at which Zack jumped up to his feet. He proceeded to stomp on that worm for good measure.

"Zack!" Graham yelled.

Zack spun around just in time to be knocked over by a Scarkin flying into him. He struggled with it, suffering several cuts to his arms and chest, then managed to swat it with his Bible.

Graham came over and helped him up.

"A few more," he said, nearly out of breath.

Zack was amazed at Graham's calmness. He was good at focusing on the task at hand. The pair skidded and slipped their way over to the others battling the demons. Branch-wielding-guy was on the ground thrashing against a Scarkin and a bunch of worms. Graham stepped forward and belted the Scarkin off him with his bat. Zack jumped at it as the demon landed and crushed it into the ground. The pair helped Branch-guy up, brushing off worms from him. He offered his thanks and pulled off a worm that had bitten into his arm. A spurt of blood made him screw up his face in pain.

"Little buggers," Branch-guy said, throwing the worm to the ground.

"Let's help Ronald," Zack said.

They made their way over stomping worms as they went. Zack saw Ronald had already killed a couple of demons with Matthew's rosary beads. After a few minutes the men had killed the last of them.

"Ok we're good," Graham declared.

Zack started to relax a bit. Screams and cries for help from behind them sent his mind into a panic once more.

"Martha!" Ronald yelled, pushing past the others.

Martha was yelling and struggling on the ground. Others in the group had also fallen over with worms washing over them. Beth and Mindy were both helping others up. Zack looked around. He was sure that their group was bigger than the people he could see. Some had just gone.

Ronald dug away the worms from his screaming wife. She was covered in blood. It was difficult to tell what was hers and what was squashed bloodworms. Ronald kept saying her name over and over. Zack made his way over to help. Soon they had killed enough worms that they could pull her up off the ground.

"Help me carry her," Ronald said to Zack.

Ronald grabbed Zack's wrist and motioned for him to do the same. Branch-guy continued to pull worms off her as they lifted her off the ground on to the seat made from their arms.

It was clear Martha had lost a lot of blood. Zack felt her breathe heavily against him as they started to carry her out of the field of blood. She was a slightly built woman, but stomping through bloodworms after all they had gone through, she seemed very heavy.

Zack turned to see Beth and Mindy both helping two ladies wade through the worms. Graham's previous wounds seemed to have reopened and he was walking slowly trying to stay focused.

"I'm James, thanks for your help before," Branch-wielding-guy said.

"Zack, and that's Graham. You're most welcome."

"This one must be a strong lady, looks like she suffered lots of bites," James added.

Ronald nodded.

"We'll get her out," Zack said adamantly.

"The church is on the other side of that hill." Ronald pointed ahead of them.

Each heavy step didn't seem to bring them any closer. Zack could feel her blood soaking into his clothing. Martha's breathing became progressively shallower. Zack's heart sunk. He didn't think she would last much longer. She now had her eyes closed and rested her head on Ronald. Ronald was talking quietly to her. They trudged their way through the worms and gradually made progress.

"I can see the edge of the worms!" James said with a smile on his face. Zack smiled too. He thought any new horror that awaited them surely had to be better than this.

"Finally." Graham jumped on a worm and kicked away another on the edge of the field.

Zack nodded to Ronald. He felt Ronald's strong grip on his wrist. He was nearly at his limit but pushed on.

More sighs of relief escaped the others as the group started to walk on solid ground, leaving the worms behind them. They slowly made it up the small hill. Zack felt the cuts in his arm from earlier start to bleed. He was grateful not to be walking on worms, but even the slight incline of the hill was seemingly harder work.

"There!" Ronald pointed out their destination peeking over the top of the hill.

The small colonial church had stood the test of time for many years. There were some deep ruptures in the ground nearby, but the building stood with no damage from the earthquake. The white paint that covered the church looked like it had seen better days, with some of it starting to flake off. A small steel cross protruded up from the roof into the sky. Zack kept his eyes on it as he walked slowly over the peak of the grassy hill.

"Nearly there," Beth said from behind him.

At the bottom of the hill they carefully carried Martha over a small wire fence and then crossed the narrow country road to the church. Zack was breathing hard now, conscious of every step before he could put Martha down. He looked over at Ronald; his face was like stone, acutely aware of the severity of her injuries. James hopped up the steps to the church and knocked on the door.

"Hello? Please, we need help! Hello? Anyone?"

He knocked again and after a few seconds of no reply, tried the door. It was unlocked. James opened it slowly, clutching his trusty branch in his right hand.

"We don't mean any harm. We're coming in."

He peeked inside.

"Wait here just a second," he said to Ronald then went inside.

Zack stood quietly in pain for a few moments. The door swung open again and James stepped out.

"It looks safe, bring her in. However there is no-one here."

Everyone was hoping for some help to be waiting for them inside. Ronald and Zack carried Martha in and lay her on a wooden pew. She groaned quietly as they did so. Zack was relieved to hear her make some noise. Ronald checked on her wounds. Zack helped Graham in and they sat down on another pew.

"I'm spent," Zack said quietly.

"Yeah."

Beth walked in helping a lady in with her. The lady was middle aged and had many worm bites and cuts over her body. Beneath the muck and blood she wore back pants, a brown top and had a mixture of dyed short hair. In the introductions that followed Zack would learn her name to be Cynthia.

Mindy came in next, also with an injured lady. It wasn't clear who was helping who. This lady was similarly clad in blood, mud and injuries. She wore blue jeans and a red top. She had long blonde messy hair. Her name was Rebecca.

Only nine people from their original larger group made it to the church. They tended to their injuries as best they could. Mindy had a towel in her bag, which was used to wipe the blood off people to try and find wounds among the bloodworms remains. Everyone was tired and hurting.

Martha had been lying perfectly still for some time.

"No! No you don't!" Ronald started yelling. He shook Martha and tried to rouse her. Rebecca came and sat next to him.

"I'm so sorry."

"She'll make it through. She's got to, she's...." his voice trailed off.

Zack blinked back tears. Hours passed and confirmed everyone's thoughts: Martha was dead. Ronald sat next to her sobbing, holding her hand. Beth rummaged through a bag and pulled out a can of fruit salad. Zack's stomach jumped to attention. He didn't know how long it had been since he'd eaten. Zack wondered how they'd open the tin, and before he thought of a solution, Beth took the lid off. It was one of those pull-ring type tins. Zack smiled with relief.

Beth pulled out a few more tins and handed them around. Everyone ate a little, except Ronald. The fruit felt so good in Zack's mouth. He could finally lose the taste of blood and dirt. The peaches were sweet and juicy and he savoured every bite. He was tempted to open all the food they had and eat all he could. Though he knew they would need to make it last.

Graham lay down in a pew, slowly but surely covering it with his blood. He started to become more and more pale. Zack sat next to him.

"Are you okay, man?" Zack asked.

"I'm cold."

Zack was surprised that Graham didn't have a witty retort. He thought he must be feeling really bad.

"I'll see what I can do."

Zack got up and looked around the church. There were no warm blankets anywhere. He pulled a curtain down from one of the windows and laid it over his friend.

"You'll be okay, just rest."

Beth sat next to Graham and stroked his dirty hair.

Time passed and Graham moved less and less. He closed his eyes and slept. Everyone was worried. Zack couldn't help but look at the slowly growing puddle of blood beneath the pew.

"We gotta get him to a doctor," Zack announced.

"How will we do that?" Beth snapped.

Zack shrugged. "I'm sorry, it's just I don't know what to do."

"I know what you mean," Beth replied.

Zack walked out the front door of the church and looked around. This really was a rural church. Grassy fields and trees was all he could see. In the distance he saw a house burning. He went back inside.

"Perhaps I should go and find some medicine and come back?" Zack heard how desperate his idea sounded.

Beth had tears running down her cheek. Mindy was trying to keep herself busy rummaging through her bag. The thought that his best friend was dying swelled in Zack's mind.

Zack dropped to his knees in one of the pews. He looked up at a large crucifix hung on the wall. He had heard about Jesus in school but didn't remember most of the details. He looked at the painted statue hung on the cross. He was bleeding too. Zack thought about how it all wasn't fair.

"Why does it have to be like this God? Why is there so much suffering? Even Jesus suffered on the cross. Why?"

Zack hung his head and closed his eyes.

"Please God, help us. I know that I have done terrible things and I don't deserve your help. Just, please, please help Graham, God. Amen."

Zack finished praying and looked around, hoping beyond hope that a doctor would somehow turn up. After several minutes he sat back up on the pew. Zack let out a long wavering breath.

A loud knock on the door drew everyone's attention. Zack jumped up and ran to the door. The door swung open as he approached. A man stepped in.

"Hello, I'm..."

"Please help our friend, he's dying!"

Zack grabbed him by the arm and lead him to Graham. The man looked over his injuries and felt for a pulse. He began to pray the holy words of healing:

"In nomine Patris et Filii et Spiritus Sancti..."

Zack looked on in awe as Graham opened his eyes and started to slowly move. The man closed his eyes and sat down for a moment to catch his breath.

"Thank you sir! I... I... feel like my wounds are gone?"

Graham sat up and lifted up his shirt trying to check the wounds on his back. Zack leaned forward to see scars all over his back, like his injuries had somehow had months to heal.

"Thank the Lord God, not I," the man replied.

Zack wiped some blood from Graham's back, and prodded his scars. "Amazing!"

All the others crowded around, inspecting Graham's scars in disbelief.

"Please stranger, heal my wife," Ronald said as he rushed over.

The man walked over and checked for a pulse. Martha's body felt cold to his touch.

"I am so sorry, she has already passed on to be with God."

"But, but please, there must be some miracle that you can do here?"

"Sincerely Sir, I wish I could, but her spirit has left this body."

Ronald slowly nodded and sat down.

"I'm Beth, this is Mindy, Zack, Ronald, James, Rebecca, Cynthia, Martha and Graham. Excuse me, but exactly who are you?" Beth pointed to each of them in turn.

"My name is Brother Christopher, and I have so much to tell you all," he replied.

CHAPTER 6

HOMESICK

Brother Christopher talked with the group for hours, answering as many questions as he could. He spent a lot of time talking with Ronald to try and help him deal with Martha's death. Brother Christopher explained that the spiritual forces that had always been in the world had now manifested physically.

Zack showed Brother Christopher the Bible he was carrying and asked where he should start. Brother Christopher flicked through, folding down the corners of several pages. He then returned it to Zack, pointing to a specific verse.

Matthew 6

⁹ "This, then, is how you should pray:
"'Our Father in heaven,
hallowed be your name,
¹⁰ your kingdom come,
your will be done,
on earth as it is in heaven.
¹¹ Give us today our daily bread.
¹² And forgive us our debts,
as we also have forgiven our debtors.
¹³ And lead us not into temptation,
but deliver us from the evil one.

As he talked, Brother Christopher healed the rest of their injuries. Abruptly he stood up and checked his bag.

"It is time. I must go. There are many more people like yourselves who I need to help."

"Please stay with us, we need you!" Beth implored.

"I wish I could. Ah, here it is." Brother Christopher pulled an old stick of wax from his bag. It reminded Zack of one of those shaving soaps that his grandfather had. It looked to be even older.

"Please pass me your bat."

Graham gave it to him with a confused look on his face.

"As you'll remember me telling you the demons can only be killed by Holy means. This blessed wax will make this baseball bat a deadly weapon. But be warned, it will wear off over time. James gave him his branch and Brother Christopher coated that too.

"Are you sure that will work?" Graham asked with a sceptical look on his face.

"Certain." He held up his spear that was dirty with muck and blood.

"How did you get out here from the other side of town so fast?" Zack asked.

"I assure you it wasn't as easy as you've made it sound. But I was able to use a car for a good part of the journey before the deep gaps in the ground stopped me. I left the keys in it, a blue station wagon on Cumberland Street. You're welcome to it if it's still there."

"Got it. Thanks," Zack replied.

"I'm going to the Westward Community Center next, then all the churches I can find on this side of the river before I return. You are welcome to come with me or go straight to St. Thomas'. But I better get going soon."

After a brief discussion they decided to make their own way to St. Thomas'. Zack was feeling quite confident now they had some real weapons against the demons. Zack's headache had even gone away for a while.

"May the Lord God bless you all with protection and guidance. May the peace of Jesus Christ rest on you all," Brother Christopher prayed with his right hand held high.

He put his bag on his back and walked out the doors.

"I'm staying here," Ronald announced.

"What? No, come with us!" James said.

"I need to bury Martha, my place is here," he replied.

Everyone could see he had made up his mind.

"Thank you for all your help Ronald, you are a good man," Graham said.

Ronald shook his hand followed by Zack and James. Beth and Mindy gave him a big hug.

"Good luck to you all."

The group packed up what little they had and walked out the doors.

"Let's stick to the roads this time," Graham said.

The others agreed. They walked down the country road towards town. After a few hours they made it onto the main highway into Brakenside. Zack looked around. Overhead the low cloud spread all over the sky. The rolling, grassy fields had slowly started to give way to smaller sections with houses on them.

Up ahead Zack could see Brakenside in the distance. Plumes of smoke rose from the battered city. He could hear a car alarm blaring in the distance. He smelt a sickly smoke, like there was plastic burning somewhere nearby. Abandoned cars were scattered about. Fissures in the road and ground made travel difficult.

Zack felt glad to be back near civilisation, but in the back of his mind he was scared of what the people would do. He remembered articles in the news before all this happened; people didn't seem to need an excuse to be violent and cruel. This apocalypse seemed like a huge opportunity for horror.

"Shall we swing past our place?" Graham asked.

"What, why?" Beth replied.

"It's kinda on the way there, and we could restock our supplies. Maybe even sleep with a roof over our heads."

Thoughts of Zack's home flooded to mind. He worried about his family and friends and if they were still alive.

"I want to go to my house too," said Rebecca.

Soon everyone was making a case why their house was the most sensible place to go to next.

"I don't think it will be easier, just because we're in town. Shall we just see how we get on?" Mindy stated.

They continued to talk as they walked, but agreed their trip would largely be dependant on what they encountered. The group turned on to the road where Brother Christopher had left the car. Unfortunately they ended up walking the full length of the road and did not find it.

"Someone else must have taken it," Zack said.

"Thanks Captain Obvious," Graham replied with a cheeky grin.

"Oi!" Zack gave him a light punch in the arm. He was glad to have their casual banter back again.

Soon the group had made it to the edge of suburbia. Zack didn't feel at ease, like he thought he would. He was suddenly aware of all the places close by that a demon could be lurking. They were walking down the middle of the road when Graham stopped.

"Listen!"

Zack strained his ears. He scanned the front yards of the houses around them. There was no-one around. Then he heard it. The sound of a car. It seemed to be coming closer, yet still a block or so away from them. The engine sound was then drowned out by the sound of breaking glass and crunching metal. Then all was quiet.

"Good grief," Beth said.

The group stood still, listening and watching. Then a loud scream rung out.

"We must help them!" Zack announced.

"We don't even know what is going on," Cynthia said.

"We must try," Graham replied.

They started to run in the general direction and then the screaming was suddenly cut short. Zack couldn't help thinking that whoever it was, they were dead. Zack was right.

The group cautiously made their way up the road. In the distance a booming noise started another plume of smoke rising into the murky sky. Zack longed to hear the familiar annoying sound of a lawn mower. He didn't get his wish. Ahead of them in the distance Zack saw someone run across street.

"There, I think I saw someone," Zack pointed as he spoke.

The group continued down the street.

"Hey, are you okay in there?" Zack yelled.

"Shut up!" Graham insisted. "We don't want to attract attention."

They did attract attention.

On the opposite side of the street a Scarkin jumped up onto the roof of one of the houses.

"Demon!" James yelled.

Graham looked at Zack in a very 'I-told-you-so' kind of way.

Zack rolled his eyes.

Another three small demons emerged from behind nearby houses. They snapped their strange jaws, cackling to themselves. The group drew closer together in the middle of the road. The demons scuttled over fences and bushes and made their advance. Zack remembered what Brother Christopher showed him:

Ephesians 6

[10] Finally, be strong in the Lord and in his mighty power.
[11] Put on the full armor of God, so that you can take your stand against the devil's schemes. [12] For our struggle is not against
flesh and blood, but against the rulers, against the authorities,
against the powers of this dark world and against the
spiritual forces of evil in the heavenly realms.

Zack felt a confidence he didn't think was possible staring into such evil.

"Let's do this," Graham said.

Zack and James nodded.

The three ran forward into the demons, swinging branches, bats and Bibles. Graham connected with his first strike and burst a Scarkin into muck, spraying its remains across the road.

"Woohoo sucker!" Graham exclaimed. He was delighted that his blessed bat was now effective.

James was finding similar success with the blessed wax on his trusty branch as he pummelled a Scarkin into the concrete.

Zack swung his Bible, but was finding it difficult to hit his mark. Soon, the three men encircled the last demon and crushed it with a barrage of strikes.

"Good work guys! That guy was right," Graham said with a smile.

Zack's arm alerted him to a new injury. A shallow, but long cut on his arm.

He clenched his teeth. "I've got an idea."

The others watched curiously. Zack walked to the side of the road and broke a branch off a small dying tree. He then proceeded to secure his Bible to one end by using his belt. He swung it around a bit to test it out then jumped up and down to check his pants would not fall down. Happy with his results, he returned to the group with his new Bible-club.

"Oh good idea," Mindy said.

"Thanks," he replied.

Before anyone could speak further a man rushed out the house Zack had initially thought someone was hiding in.

"Oh thank you, thank you!" he exclaimed.

He was in his late fifties, wearing a business shirt and pants covered in blood and dirt. He had long wavy gray hair and a pained look on his face.

After a few minutes of talking they learnt his name was Winston. He decided to join them on their way to St Thomas'.

Zack looked at Graham with an 'I-told-you-so' expression on *his* face.

"Yeah yeah, I know," Graham said smiling.

Zack liked the feeling that he had helped someone. He recalled a conversation with his mother when he was finishing high school. Zack was not sure what he was going to do, but decided he didn't want to do any more study. Zack recalled her saying:

"You really like helping people, find a job that does that."

At the time Zack found that perfectly unhelpful. But now Zack thought his mother was onto something. Zack liked the idea of protecting people. This was not at all what he had in mind for a job, but was happy enough to smile.

"What are you smiling at Zack?" Mindy asked.

"Oh, just happy that we helped someone. Let's get going."

With Winston in tow they made their way further down the street. Zack was on the lookout for more people he could save. He could hear others in the group talking about what had been happening lately. Winston asked many of the same questions they had asked of Brother Christopher. He had mentioned Bishop Kephas would know more. Zack was keen to meet him. He had questions of his own that he needed answered, though he couldn't ask them in front of his friends. Zack looked down at his feet. Deep feelings of guilt washed over him; bad memories flooded into his mind.

"There!" James yelled.

Zack snapped back to attention. He looked in the direction James was heading towards. Zack felt whenever he had a few minutes to forget the current situation a new danger would appear.

"What is it?" Graham asked

"That's my street up there. Let's drop by my house." A grin spread across James' face.

"Is that all? I thought we were under attack."

Everyone's heart rates slowed back normal.

"Oh, sorry, I'm just keen to get back."

"I get it, but do we have time for a stop?" Beth asked.

"My house has a bunch of food in the pantry, and I'm sure we can find other useful things."

That seemed to make sense to the group so they diverted to James' house.

"There it is, the one with the red roof," James said.

Zack looked down the road and saw a simple weatherboard house with a red metal roof. The front yard was bare, with grass and a single tree. The surrounding houses looked similar but with better gardens. James ran ahead and ran up the small path to his house. He was shouting out someone's name that Zack couldn't quite make out. The rest of the group followed James inside.

Zack looked around the simple house. It was orderly, but it looked like the place had never been vacuumed.

"Found him." James came out from one the bedrooms holding a small dog.

"This is Bradley everyone!" he said with a smile.

The small shaggy dog looked happy to see everyone. Everyone seemed happy to see him too.

"Sorry, but a toilet stop would be great," commented Cynthia.

"Sure. First left down the hallway. Make yourself at home everyone," James replied.

Zack walked into the lounge and sat down on a worn green couch. It was so comfortable that he nearly fell asleep. Mindy and Beth checked out the kitchen for supplies.

"Oh yum! Do you mind James?" Zack heard Mindy say from behind him.

"Be my guest, take anything you like," James said, still patting his dog.

Zack willed himself up from the couch to see what the others were doing. Graham sat closing his eyes in one of the armchairs. Rebecca was making a sandwich and Beth and Mindy were eating nectarines. Zack opened a few cupboards and found a pack of muesli bars. He started to munch on one as he looked around.

"Sweet TV James," Zack complemented.

"Oh, thanks, yeah it's the new sixty inch model with 'three-point-one pure sound'. Pity I can't show you, I imagine the power is still off everywhere."

Zack tried a light switch on the wall and confirmed James' thought. James put Bradley down and he excitedly ran around between everyone's legs. The group spent a short time at James' house eating and packing anything they thought could be useful.

"I guess we better head off," Graham said.

James stuffed a few more random things into his pockets.

"Yeah, let's go."

As they walked outside James ran up to his neighbor's house and knocked on the door.

"Mrs Gunderson? Are you home? It's James from next door."

He waited for a reply.

A distinctive click was heard from inside. The door slowly opened. A pistol made its way out of the door attached to a little old lady. She was wrapped in a cream coloured dressing gown, and had short gray hair.

"Whoa, it's just me," James said in alarm.

"Who are all these people?" she said as she flailed the pistol around in her hand.

Everyone put their hands up.

"We mean no harm," Beth said assuredly.

"Have you heard from the Government?" she asked James.

"What? No, but you should come with us, we are going somewhere safe. Now lower that gun!"

She finally pointed her pistol away and everyone relaxed slightly. Zack couldn't help track the pistol with his eyes as she talked; she waved it around with each word. Zack wondered if she had any idea if it was even loaded.

"I'm waiting here; they'll be coming to get people soon."

"Who is?"

"The Government people of course, I've been listening to the radio, they have that emergency message playing."

"Have you been outside? No-one is coming."

"They can't just leave us like this, I've heard some nasty things going on. Of course they will come."

James debated with her for a few minutes getting nowhere.

"Okay look, when the Government comes, they will want to get people out fast right? Let's go somewhere safe where everyone else is waiting."

"Oh, like an evacuation point?"

"Sure, like that."

"Okay, let me get my bags." She shut the door in his face and disappeared for a moment.

She appeared again towing two large luggage bags behind her as if she packed for an overseas holiday.

"Be a good lad?"

She gave them both to James then pulled out another handbag from inside and locked her front door. She still carried the pistol in one hand pointing it at anything and everything.

"How about we put that gun in your bag just for now, Mrs Gunderson?"

She paused for a moment.

"Okay, it was a bit heavy," she said as she stowed it in her handbag.

Zack saw James roll his eyes.

"We're going now," she announced as she walked down the path.

Zack couldn't help look at Graham and grin as she even stopped to check her letterbox and her rose garden on the way out.

Rebecca offered to help carry Mrs Gunderson's large handbag, but she was not successful. They introduced themselves as they walked along down the street. Zack ended up walking next to Mrs Gunderson.

"Have you seen any, um, creatures?" he asked her.

"What creatures?"

"Yes, um, they are about this big." Zack held out his hands. "Claws, evil looking things."

"Russians."

"What?"

"Of course, they have been cooking up all sorts since the end of the war. My late husband knew it was just a matter of time before they attacked."

Zack didn't know what to say.

She continued: "The army will sort them out Sonny, don't worry."

Zack smiled politely.

"I hope so."

The group walked down the street. They had nearly reached the end when Graham spoke.

"So shall we go to our place next?"

Zack had thought going to their flat would be a great idea. He thought of all the things there that would come in handy. A fresh change of clothes would be so nice. He couldn't shake the grimy feeling he had. He missed his daily shower.

"It's not to far from here, right? I think it'd be worth dropping by," he said trying to hide his strong feelings on the matter.

"I don't want to be late for extraction," said Mrs Gunderson sternly as she walked on ahead.

Graham wore a confused look on his face. The group walked into the intersection at the end of the street and stopped. It was time to decide where to go next. Beth spoke up.

"My place has plenty of food in the cupboards that would be invaluable."

Rebecca said something similar. Cynthia said she needed to check on her pets. Another discussion arose. Zack saw a blur of movement that interrupted his thoughts. He looked down the road to see a horde of Scarkin washing over the road.

"Run!" he screamed as he quickly turned and knocked into Mrs Gunderson.

"You watch where..." her voice trailed off as she saw the approaching demons.

She quickly turned and started running. Zack was impressed at the speed at which she moved for her age. In a matter of seconds the whole group had seen the danger and was running down the road on the opposite side of the intersection to the demons.

"We won't be able to outrun them!" James yelled.

"What do you suggest?" Graham yelled back.

An idea sprung into Zack's head. He swerved off the road and ran up the path of a town house. He ran up to the door and kicked it open. The lock busted and splinters of wood went flying. Zack felt like an action hero. He hoped Mindy had seen it. But he then slipped on the front door mat and tumbled over.

"Get in here!" he yelled back at the group from the floor.

Graham, Beth and Mindy were already running up the path. Mindy smiled at Zack. He couldn't tell if she thought it was funny that he slipped or was impressed by his idea. Rebecca, Winston and Cynthia ran up the path and went inside. James hurried Mrs

Gunderson inside and Zack closed the door behind them.

Zack then realised a door with a broken lock wouldn't be much good at keeping demons out. The house was quiet, apart from their heavy breathing for a moment.

"We're hiding?" Mindy asked quietly.

"Best case scenario, yeah," Zack replied.

"Let's block the doors and windows," Graham suggested.

For a few frantic minutes they tried moving a small brown couch to hold the front door shut. Just as the couch was wedged against the door Mindy, who was watching the road out the window, hushed them.

"Shhh, they're coming."

Zack lifted the frilled window netting slightly as he peered out the lounge window. It reminded him of his Grandma's house. Zack and the others watched the road for a few seconds. Scarkin started to scamper down the road. Zack lowered his head hoping they wouldn't see him. The first Scarkin continued past the house, quickly followed by several more. A flicker of hope that they didn't see them washed over Zack. Then just as quickly it was extinguished.

The whole horde of demons suddenly turned and headed towards the house they were hiding in. Screams of their group pierced the air. Zack's heart pounded. James readied his branch. Graham pulled his baseball bat from where it was tucked under his backpack.

"Oh God, oh God..." Rebecca kept saying.

Beth leant her weight against the couch holding the front door. Mindy and Cynthia soon followed.

A loud gunshot and shattering glass stung Zack's ears. Mrs Gunderson was firing her pistol through the window into the oncoming demon horde. Zack tried to yell at her but his voice was lost in the gunfire. Zack glimpsed outside to see demons being violently thrown backwards by the impact of the bullets. However after precious little time they got up again, unhurt.

Mrs Gunderson fired off as many shots as she could before the pistol made a telling clicking sound. Zack could now hear her yelling profanity at the top of her lungs. Beth, Mindy, Rebecca and Cynthia screamed as a tide of demons smashed into the front door. Zack desperately prayed for help in his mind.

"Dear God, help me."

The sound of breaking glass behind him spun Zack around.

"They're inside!" James screamed.

The Scarkin that had just jumped in the kitchen window was skidding in broken glass over the ground. Zack ran in and crushed it with his Bible-club. He immediately decided it was a vast improvement to just holding the Bible in his hand.

The windows in the lounge shattered behind Zack as more demons flooded into the small house. Mrs Gunderson fell over as she was fumbling in her handbag for something. Graham and James fought them back as best they could, but it seemed for each demon they killed two more made their way inside.

Zack continued to swat demons in the kitchen. With each swing of his weapon another demon would fall to the floor in a bubbling pile of muck. Zack could hear James and Graham smashing their way through many demons in the lounge. The sound of breaking pottery and furniture falling over confirmed the lounge was getting smashed too.

Several desperate minutes of fighting passed. The front door then burst inwards in a shower of splinters. The couch holding it skidded backwards and sent all the girls flying. Cynthia was slammed around the corner of the hallway. As the others fell on top of her, her neck was twisted around the doorframe and broke. Cynthia died instantly.

At that moment a large Mortkin smashed its way through what was left of the front door. It roared like a wounded bull as more Scarkin skittered inside through the hole it had made.

"Front door!" Zack yelled as he found himself moving towards the breach.

His mind was trying to convince him to run away. He shook those thoughts from his head as he charged into the demons yelling at the top of his lungs. He was convinced that if he were to die he would go down fighting.

Zack swung his weapon through the masses of Scarkin, smashing his way forward. Graham and James continued fighting the demons in the lounge that kept coming in through the windows. Beth and Mindy pulled Rebecca into the kitchen, who had suffered a concussion.

With a roar, the Mortkin swung its large right arm, knocking away several Scarkin and knocking Zack to the floor in a single swipe. Zack's head smacked into the wall. The Mortkin stomped forward and brought its spiked arm down to crush Zack. Before the killing blow landed Zack managed to bring up his Bible weapon between them. The Mortkin's hand smacked into it and knocked it into Zack's face in the process. He felt like he had been punched by a boxing champion.

However, the Mortkin's hand could not withstand the purity of the Holy Bible. Its hand buckled and broke off, bubbling dark ooze spitting from its wound. Zack was still reeling on the ground. A series of stab wounds into Zack's leg loosed a scream from his lungs. He brought his weapon across the skull of a Scarkin and struggled backwards across the ground.

The large demon kicked a few Scarkin out of its way as it made its way again towards Zack. Zack flailed his weapon in front of him, trying to swat away the oncoming demons. With each swing he would kill another small demon, but suffer yet more cuts and stab wounds in the exchange.

The Mortkin again stood over Zack ready to kill him. Then a series of kitchen objects flew across and hit it in the head. The girls in the kitchen were throwing anything they could get their hands on at it. Beth kicked a small demon, surprisingly accurately at it, too.

The Mortkin moved its focus to them and moved towards the kitchen doorway. Zack swung his weapon and hit it in the back, dislodging a prime cut of demon meat. It spun around and knocked Zack to the ground again. Rebecca threw a toaster at the beast but was standing too close. The Mortkin stepped forward extending out its arm and stabbed her in the stomach.

Screams of pain filled the air. Rebecca held her stomach and fell backwards on to the floor, bleeding profusely. Mindy went to help Rebecca. Beth took a kitchen knife in each hand and tried stabbing the large demon with a flurry of strikes. It shook her off and threw her to the floor.

Zack stood once more and rained down repeated hits on to the back of the Mortkin's head. It burst and dissolved into a stinking pile of evil. It was finally dead. A Scarkin jumped on to Mindy and started slicing up her back and arms. She shrieked and tried to throw it off. Zack landed a solid kick and sent it across the room. He then finished it with his Bible club. Zack stood in the kitchen, bodies, blood, demon muck and debris covered everything. He could hear screaming coming from the lounge and rushed in to help.

Graham and James had been killing many Scarkin but had suffered many injuries as they did so. Mrs Gunderson had been overwhelmed by the demons and lay dead in a pool of blood at the back of the lounge. Still more demons came inside through the front door and lounge windows. The three men fought them with every drop of their remaining strength.

After several more brutal minutes of fighting a single Scarkin remained. Graham swung his baseball bat and crushed it against the wall. They rushed back to the kitchen to check on the girls. Beth and Mindy were injured but alive.

"Oh Beth!" Graham said as he rushed over to hold her in his arms. He kissed her. Zack looked out the window across the front lawn. He didn't see any demons. Shattered, he slumped to the floor exhausted. James dropped to one knee panting and holding a deep cut in his right arm. The back of Zack's head throbbed with pain.

"Are you okay Mindy?" Zack asked.

Mindy looked at him with tears flowing from her face. "Rebecca is dead."

He looked at Rebecca; she looked pale, a panicked expression was frozen on her face. Zack looked away. Winston emerged with Bradley in his arms from somewhere else in the house. Both had some minor injuries but were otherwise okay.

The surviving members of the group took stock of their losses and tended to their wounds as best they could. James took Mrs Gunderson's death particularly hard. Although they had not known Cynthia and Rebecca long, the whole group mourned their deaths.

James took Mrs Gunderson's pistol and a single magazine of ammunition he found buried at the bottom of her bloodied handbag. They ate what they could find in what was left of the ruined kitchen.

"We must go straight to the church that Brother Christopher mentioned," Graham stated.

Everyone agreed.

After taking all they could practically carry from the broken house, they slowly set out. Zack's head hurt. He didn't know how to process the emotions he was feeling so he just bottled them up inside.

"James, can I have that gun please?" Beth asked.

"What for?" he replied.

"What do you think?! You guys all have your weapons; I want something I can use."

"Okay, okay, have you fired a pistol before?"

"No, but I'm sure if Mrs Gunderson could do it I can too."

"Good point."

James spent some time showing her the basics of pistol handling as they walked. Mindy looked on quietly.

"We really need some more of that blessed wax. If we put that on the bullets, I'm sure that would kill those demons," Mindy said out of the blue.

"Brilliant idea," Graham said. "Let's get some more when we get to the church. It sure made my bat worthwhile."

Graham scraped a small amount of the little remaining pale blue wax on his bat and gave it to Beth.

"Hopefully that's enough for a few shots."

The group walked slowly across the front lawn of the battered house. They had left the bodies of their fallen friends with blankets covering them. They intended to return to bury them, but they never did.

"I think the fastest way there will be up North Street and across Sandling Road," Graham said, pointing.

"Sure, sounds good," replied James.

The group slowly made their way through the suburbs. Zack prayed they wouldn't encounter any more demons on the way. He checked the makeshift bandage on his arm. It was already bleeding through. They rounded a bend in the road, which had been winding up a small hill.

"We should be able to see the church from up here," Graham called back from the front of the group.

They looked over the city; it looked like a war-zone. It was a war-zone. Plumes of smoke were rising from numerous fires. Large fissures from the earthquake split the ground, leaving many buildings in piles of rubble. There was a large smouldering bomb crater where a church once stood.

"Oh No! It's gone! Just gone," Zack said in disbelief.

"Not that one Zack, this one," Graham said, pointing in the another direction.

"Phew! Oh right, of course."

Zack saw St. Thomas Church in the distance. It was still in one piece.

"I guess the Government isn't coming then," James said. "There is no military; I can't hear any sirens, no helicopters, nothing."

"It's just us," Graham said.

Zack opened his Bible to where Brother Christopher had marked and read out a passage.

Matthew 21

[21] Jesus replied, "Truly I tell you, if you have faith and do not doubt, not only can you do what was done to the fig tree, but also you can say to this mountain, 'Go, throw yourself into the sea,' and it will be done. [22] If you believe, you will receive whatever you ask for in prayer."

A few members of the group said "Amen".

"We'll make it through this," said Mindy.

Zack nodded in agreement.

They continued towards the church. After about an hour of walking they made it to the long road that had their destination on the far end.

"Nearly there guys, hang in there," Graham said with a pained look badly hidden on his face.

The sound of breaking glass from behind them drew everyone's attention. Zack surveyed the houses around them. His eyes found a house with glass scattered over the front steps. Out stomped a Mortkin. It roared and started to run at them. Zack froze. He was so sore from his last encounter he doubted his ability to fight.

Gunfire rang out as Beth fired her pistol into the creature. Large holes bored through the demon as the blessed wax did its job. In a few seconds the demon was dead. Beth was standing with her legs shoulder-width apart, both hands on the grip just like James had shown her earlier. She was still pulling the trigger despite the empty clicking sounds.

"It's okay, you got it, you did great," Graham said, lowering the pistol with a gentle hand.

A few moments later two men wearing 'School Patrol' high visibility vests came running down the road from the direction of the church.

"Are you all okay here?" one of them called. He was carrying a spade of some sort.

"Yeah, just killed a demon. Are you two by chance from St. Thomas Church?" Graham asked.

"Why yes. My name is Adam and this is Malcolm. Please come with us, we can offer protection from the demons."

"We heard. We met Brother Christopher and he told us we should come. We had many more in our group. But... they... well... didn't make it."

"I'm sorry for your loss. It's very dangerous out here, you've done well to make it this far."

Malcolm spoke up. "How did you kill that bigger demon?"

Malcolm had a mohawk haircut. He was very muscular and strong looking. Zack thought he must have been a body builder or a boxer. Malcolm wore dirty brown pants and a tatty white T-shirt. His school patrol vest only just made it over his broad shoulders. He was carrying a large hammer in each hand.

Beth answered, "I shot it."

"Really? I have not seen a demon killed by mere bullets before."

"The bullets had blessed wax on them, from Brother Christopher."

"Oh brilliant, I had not thought of that. Anyway, we should get you inside, follow us."

They followed them for several the minutes walk up the road.

"What's with the school patrol vests?" Zack asked.

"Just so we can be easily seen, and we are on patrol around the school and church perimeter. But mainly because I always wanted to be on the patrol when I was a kid, but I didn't make the team," Malcolm said with a smile.

They arrived at the gates and Adam and Malcolm left to continue their patrol. Zack looked at the Bible pages wrapped around the fence line.

"Check it out," he said to Graham, who nodded.

Sandy opened the gate for them and welcomed them in.

"Hi, I'm Sandy, welcome!" she smiled and shook their hands.

After tending to their injuries, introductions and a brief chat they were given a tour of the church and school. While they were walking through the school grounds, a lady ran up to them.

"Sandy! Please, we need you."

She gave her apologies and left in a hurry.

"Please make yourselves at home; I'll see you all later," she called back to them.

"What do you make of this place?" James asked.

"Seems legit to me," said Zack. "They have demon proof fence."

"Do you think they will have enough supplies for everyone?" James continued.

"I'm not sure."

Bishop Kephas walked out of a nearby classroom and introduced himself.

After some talking he commented on their weapons.

"So, I take it you have seen some fighting?"

"Yes, plenty," Graham said.

"Would any of you like to volunteer for combat duty?"

"We've only just arrived," said Mindy.

"I'm sorry; I don't mean to pressure you. But I'm sure you are familiar with the situation out there. And I must be upfront with you: I don't think we will be safe here permanently."

"Oh, why not?" Beth asked.

"I just don't expect our enemy to give up is all."

"I'll volunteer," Zack said.

As much as he wanted to stay safe behind the walls, he felt like this was right for him.

James, Graham and Beth volunteered too.

"Thank you all." Bishop looked at Mindy; he noticed the first aid kit peeking out of her bag. "Ah, would you like to join our healers?"

"Would that be like how Brother Christopher healed us?" she asked excitedly.

"Yes indeed. It's hard work, but I have a feeling you'll be great."

Later that day Kephas was in his office pouring over scrolls when Deon walked in.

"Good to see you Bishop," he said as he walked in.

"Ah Deon! You made it back safe and sound I see? I knew you would. How did it go?"

"I went to all the locations you showed me on the map, but most of them were destroyed before I got there. I encountered many people on the roads but it's worse than I thought."

"I see. From what I've learnt so far the bombers are called the 'Sons of the Snake'. I don't know much about them, but I know they serve the evil one."

"What will we do?"

"I'm still working on that."

"Is Will and Brother Christopher back?"

"Will is, but not Brother Christopher yet."

They looked at the map on the table. It now contained many red 'x's over places where they were hoping to find survivors.

"Okay, let us wait for Brother Christopher to return, and then we should have a good idea about the state of all Brakenside."

Zack, Graham, Beth, Mindy and James had settled in. They had two meals a day of rationed food. They slept on the floor of one of the classrooms at the school. The community slept in shifts, as there was no longer a distinction between night and day. They ensured a few people were always on patrol.

Brother Christopher stopped in to see how they were going upon his return. Zack saw how everyone contributed in some way to keep everything going. He and his friends watched the walls of the school in shifts. When their shifts allowed everyone attended the daily church service. One passage that was read out stuck in Zack's mind.

Psalm 23

¹ The Lord is my shepherd, I lack nothing.
² He makes me lie down in green pastures,
he leads me beside quiet waters,
³ he refreshes my soul.
He guides me along the right paths
for his name's sake.
⁴ Even though I walk
through the darkest valley,

I will fear no evil,
for you are with me;
your rod and your staff,
they comfort me.

Zack had enjoyed the privilege of combat training with Bishop Kephas. Zack couldn't believe how skilled he was. He assumed correctly that he must have been training his whole life. Zack and the thirty or so others in combat duty trained in the church car park for hours everyday. They were trained in basic weapon techniques and kept fit with exercise and strength training. They would regularly escort the water collection team to the river and back. Zack was thankful that there had not been any large-scale demon attacks lately.

Weeks flew past in what felt like a moment.

One day while escorting the water team, a pack of Scarkin attacked, but with a full guard of trained combatants they were quickly put down. Zack had seen how some other fighters had custom blessed weapons like what Brother Christopher wielded. Zack thought that would be much better than his Bible club weapon.

"Excuse me, how do I get a spear like that?" he asked Brother Christopher one day after training.

"Go and see the Smith in the school workshop, he may be able to help you out. Though be aware, he is struggling to keep up with our demand."

"Great, thanks. I will."

Zack ran off to the school in search of the workshop. As he did so, he imagined he had a new blessed weapon and swung it around like a child would.

"Still practicing, Zack?" Mindy asked walking around the corner of a classroom.

"Oh hey Mindy. Oh me? Yeah," Zack said awkwardly. "Anyway, how are things with you? I haven't seen you in while."

"I'm okay thanks. I've been learning so much listening to the others. Did you know the Bishop can heal without leaving any scarring?"

"Oh, really?" Zack looked at the scars on his arm where Brother Christopher had healed him.

"So Mindy, have you healed anyone yet?"

"Um, not yet, but soon I hope. I've been learning first aid things too. Speaking of which, I have to get going. Catch you later Zack." She walked past him and touched his shoulder gently as she passed.

Zack waved and held his shoulder after she went around the corner. His heart fluttered. The thought went through his mind of telling her how he felt. Then thoughts of what he had done rose to his mind.

"She would never go near me if she knew," he said to himself quietly.

He pushed all thoughts from his mind and walked down the path to the school workshop. Zack could hear clashing metal and hammering as he approached. He opened the door and walked in. Jacob was working at the front desk on what looked like a sword. Two other men were watching him closely and occasionally going back to their benches. Memories of his own time at school entered Zack's mind. He recalled when he made a lunchbox.

"Can I help you?" Jacob asked.

"Oh, yes please. I was hoping to get one of those new weapons you are making there."

Zack eyed the sword on the table.

"Do you now? I'm flattered. But I'll be straight with you: everyone wants one of these. We have to try and put these weapons in the hands that will do the most good with them. Are you a fighter?"

"Yes, I am Sir, I'm in the combat duty."

"How many demons have you killed?"

"Um, I haven't really been counting. Lots?"

"Prove it."

"What? How would I prove it?"

"You pull out their little eye that looks like a gem. Did no-one tell you?"

Zack remembered he had taken one from the first Scarkin he killed at the old hotel. He fished in his pocket and pulled it out and set it on the bench.

"There you go," Zack said proudly.

"Okay, that's a good start. But did you have that in your pocket? That is like the essence of evil kid, keep your future ones in this," Jacob handed him a small pouch.

"It has been blessed and whatnot. You don't want to be carrying around evil with you uncontained."

"Ok, thanks. So please may I have that sword you are working on?"

"No sorry, but I tell you what: I like your attitude, you can have this," Jacob reached under the bench and pulled out a small knife in a sheath. It looked like a diving knife to Zack. He took it thankfully and pulled it slowly from its sheath. The shiny blade had been carefully etched with the simple but holy words:

"Jesus Christ is Lord."

It was not the size Zack was hoping for, but there was no doubt it was masterfully crafted.

"Thank you very much Sir."

Zack started to slowly walk away.

"Oi! Don't leave that demon crystal here. Chuck it in that barrel of holy water."

Zack nodded and picked it up and dropped it in. He watched the gem bubble and quickly dissolve into nothing.

"Bring back as many of those as you can and I'll have some better kit for you."

"Sounds good, thanks again," Zack said as he left.

Zack ran off to show Graham his new knife. After checking their classroom he went to the training area. Graham was crossing the street between the school and the church.

"Oh good, I was coming to find you Zack; the Bishop is calling all fighters for a mission."

"Oh, what mission?"

"I'm not sure; briefing is in a few minutes."

"Ok good. You can check out my sweet knife on the way there."

"Where did you get that?" Graham said, inspecting it.

"From Jacob the Smith. Oh and we need to collect proof of our demon kills."

"Nice knife man," he said, handing it back to him.

Zack explained further as they walked to the church car park.

A few minutes later Kephas addressed the fighters assembled there.

"Thank you for coming. This will be the first mission for many of you so I wanted to make sure everyone is prepared. Be warned: your lives will be at risk, but for good reason. Today we will try and find more food. I suspect the local supermarket will have more than we need, but last time we scouted it, it was defended by armed men. Let me be clear: even though I have given you all weapons training, under no circumstances will I condone killing people. We will try and talk with them, and failing that we will look elsewhere. We will need to keep searching until we find some food so be prepared for staying outside the walls for as long as it takes."

Zack looked around; many fighters looked concerned, some looked confident. Zack was sure that as long as the Bishop was with them things would be fine.

Kephas continued. "I've been informed that we have a very little blessed wax left so if you need some please see Deon after this. Everyone will need another form of sanctification when this runs out. Are there any questions?"

A middle-aged man raised his hand as he spoke. "Do you expect we will meet heavy resistance?"

"Yes I do."

The man gulped down his fear.

Kephas prayed over them all in Latin. Zack felt more confident as he heard the holy words wash over him.

"Sounds like last rites to me," said James quietly.

"Whatever man, I'm coming back to my cosy classroom," Graham replied.

A few chuckles broke the serious atmosphere.

The group spent some time readying their gear. Zack had a small backpack with two small water bottles, a small bag of food and some makeshift bandages that looked to be made from old curtains. Zack opened the bag of food. It contained just a single apple and three lollies. Zack was suddenly aware how desperate the food situation was.

Zack took his Bible off the branch and secured it around his left forearm like a small shield. He felt ready. Beth was handed a machete with some blessed wax still remaining on it. Graham and James readied their weapons.

Deon walked through the fighters wrapping some white tape around each person's upper right arm. Zack concluded that it was to identify each other in combat. He hoped it wouldn't get that frantic.

The group set off at a brisk walking pace with Bishop Kephas leading the way. The further they got from the safety of the compound the more on edge Zack became.

"Stay alert," one of the fighters ahead of them said unnecessarily.

Zack's eyes scanned the windows, doors and rooftops of all the houses they walked past. The group made steady progress towards the supermarket. Soon they had made it to the same corner of the building where David was shot. Zack saw a pool of dried blood on the ground and wondered whose it was.

Kephas stood out in the open and called out to the men at the supermarket.

"Hello! I am unarmed. Please, I just want to talk," he stood with empty hands and slowly turned around, showing he didn't have any weapons.

There was no reply.

Kephas called out for a few more minutes with no response.

"Okay, we're coming in. We mean no harm," he called.

Kephas walked across the car park to the front doors of the supermarket.

"Everyone, let's go," Deon called as the rest of the fighters followed Kephas.

Zack quickly made his way across the car park looking at the rooftops as he did so. After a few tense moments everyone had made it to the supermarket front doors, out of line-of-sight from the snipers previous position.

Zack looked around the inside of the supermarket. It was a mess. There was broken glass scattered all over the floor. Some of the display cabinets had fallen over, food and packaging was all over the place. The smell of rotting meat assaulted Zack's nostrils. He and other fighters gagged.

"I guess that means the freezers have had no power for a while," Graham explained.

"Oh that is rank!" said Beth, covering her nose.

"Tinned food it is I guess," Zack added.

Kephas signalled the group to move into the supermarket.

"Grab a trolley everyone, get as many non-perishables and supplies as you can," Kephas called.

Zack holstered his knife and pulled out some trolleys from the trolley bay and passed them to everyone. The fighters then made their way through the seemingly empty supermarket filling their trolleys.

"This is fun!" said Beth as she filled her trolley with anything and everything she wanted. The mood of the group lightened as it seemed they would not be fighting for these supplies. Zack couldn't shake a bad feeling he had in his gut. Laughter rang out through the supermarket as people found food items they thought would be long gone. It had been a long while since Zack had heard that sound.

"I found some chocolate!" Beth said happily.

"Oh good work honey," Graham replied as he gave her a kiss on the cheek.

Zack didn't share their mood. He slowly wheeled his squeaking trolley along the aisles looking for what he should take. He reached the baking goods aisle and loaded all the flour into the trolley that he could. Others took what was left of the tinned goods, medical supplies, sanitary items, dried foods and bottled water.

Zack walked into the next aisle. Blood splattered on the floor caught his eye. He followed the trail towards the checkouts. There he saw Kephas walking up the steps to the second story offices. It seemed he was following the same trail. Zack could see blood sprayed across the inside of the office windows. He left his trolley and followed Deon, who was starting to walk up the stairs.

They entered the office to see the bodies of two men strewn over the ground. The office was trashed, like the dead men had fought for their lives and lost. There were bullet holes in all the walls and blood covered the floor. It looked like the two men died from a huge number of cuts. Zack recognized the wounds inflicted by Scarkin.

"They are all dead," Deon said passing Zack a rifle he pried from one of the bodies.

"Very dead," Zack replied. "Hey, where did Kephas go?"

The Bishop climbed in from an external window leading to the part of the roof where the men had set up position earlier.

Kephas was carrying another rifle and a large knife.

"Two more bodies on the roof. I'm confident demons killed these men. I imagine from all the spent bullet casings they fought long and hard, but without any sanctified weapons they could not stand against them."

"I agree. Did you find any ammunition?" Deon asked.

"Just a little. Okay, let's get what we can back to the church and school. I know there are hungry people waiting."

"Yes Sir," Zack replied.

Zack walked down the steps and brushed his hand past the many bullet holes in the wall. He put the rifle into his trolley.

"Everyone, prepare to move out," Kephas hollered.

After a few minutes of hurried packing the group of fighters pushed their trolleys out the checkouts. They had returned to the front doors of the supermarket when the people at the front of the group stopped.

"Bishop!" Deon called in a panicked voice from the front of the group.

Kephas ran between the trolleys to meet with Deon. He looked to where Deon was pointing. Zack tried to peer past the people in front of him to see what was going on.

"Weapons ready!" Kephas commanded. "Leave your trolleys and get out here."

Zack's heart kicked into gear. Everyone shed the bags they were carrying and drew their weapons. Zack joined the other fighters making their way through the front door. Then he saw them. On the far side of the car park a horde of demons were emerging from behind several buildings. The horde was made up of countless Scarkin and a dozen Mortkin.

Zack had been feeling pretty confident since he had received combat training, but he didn't expect to go up against such a large group. He looked at Kephas. He was striding forwards towards them. He drew two sharpened metal battle crucifixes from the inside of his custom coat. After a few steps he turned and addressed the scared fighters quoting Holy Scripture:

Psalm 121

¹ I lift up my eyes to the mountains—
where does my help come from?
² My help comes from the Lord,
the Maker of heaven and earth.

"But there are so many," one wavering voice called from amongst the fighters.

"I understand your fear and I will not force you to fight. I only ask you to think of all those people you hold dear. Who will protect them from this evil if not us? My faith is steadfast in the Lord God. And my enemies will break upon me like waves on the bow of a ship. Come with me now and we will crush them with divine wrath!"

A loud cheer rose up from the fighters. Zack felt like he was in a part of some great historical battle with his army behind him.

Kephas turned towards the approaching enemy and held his weapons high. The fighters did the same. They roared a loud battle-cry in unison as they ran forward to meet the demons. Kephas yelled a holy battle chant over the din. Zack felt a tingling sensation all over his body. He felt strength fill his body. He rushed forward with the others.

The demons screamed their own battle cry as they crossed the car park. Just prior to the demons making contact the Bishop dropped to one knee. He held up the crucifix in his right hand and with it drew the shape of a cross in the air in front of him.

His voice boomed loudly.

"Testantur Sanctam Dei!"

Kephas had translated it from one of the scrolls from the cathedral. It meant 'Bear witness to the holy light of God'.

A searing bright light burst forth from him in the shape of a large cross. Zack squinted his eyes and felt a wave of pressure slam against him. It felt like someone had fired a cannon close by. The holy light utterly vaporized the front rows of demons and sent many stumbling backwards to the ground.

"Let none escape!" Kephas commanded.

Zack loved his confidence.

The line of fighters smashed into the demons like a bowling ball into tenpins at a bowling alley. The Bishop leaped forward onto a Mortkin and cleaved off both its arms before decapitating it. Zack charged into the fray, smashing away a Scarkin with his Bible-shield and stabbing another with his holy etched knife.

The battle was all consuming. Zack heard his friends fighting alongside him. But every demon he slew gave room for another to attack. Zack frantically swung and stabbed with all he had.

"Duck Zack!" Graham' voice shouted from behind him.

Zack dropped to the ground and turned just in time to see a lethal swing of a Mortkin go over his head. Graham swung his blessed baseball bat into the back of its head, dislodging muck and sending it reeling. Zack scrambled to his feet and repeatedly stabbed it in the face with his knife. The demon burst into a shower of murky liquid.

"Thanks!" Zack called between more Scarkin attacks. Some he didn't dodge in time and they cut deep into his flesh. Zack choked down the pain and continued fighting.

Zack heard Kephas bellowing amid the fighting. It provided him needed encouragement. To be fighting the demons in some strange way felt good. Zack felt like he finally had a purpose and that's what he was made for. Zack received yet more injuries in an exchange with another demon. That part did not feel so good.

A distinctive scream from behind him entered Zack's ears. It was Beth. She had been knocked over and was scrambling for her weapon. A panicked look shot from Graham's face to Zack. They both forced their way through the fighting towards her. Both of them earned several more cuts from demons in the process.

Beth was struggling to hold the multitude of demons back. Graham's face showed his pain whenever his love gained another injury. James broke through from behind some nearby demons and kicked the Scarkin off Beth. Graham and Zack arrived moments after and helped her up.

"Mate," was all Graham managed to say to thank James.

James nodded.

Beth was angry and slew two Scarkin with a single enraged swing of her blessed machete. The four of them now stood back-to-back in a small circle. They continued fighting with all their strength. Occasionally Zack heard a loud scream suddenly cut short. Some part of his mind knew that his comrades were dying.

The ground became slick with a horrific mix of spilt human blood and demon remains. The four young fighters did their best to support one another. The density of demons started to gradually decrease and Zack drew in a hopeful breath. Through the fighting he saw his fellow fighters in similar circles trying to defend each other. Zack caught glimpses of Kephas leaping through the fighting. It seemed like he was focusing on slaying the Mortkin.

Zack killed another Scarkin and to his surprise another demon did not immediately take its place. Zack stepped forward and stabbed a demon in the back, which was attacking another fighter. Zack's circle expanded as each fighter found more targets. Zack could hear rousing shouts from the others.

"We got this!"

"Kill them all!"

Zack's tight defensive circle became a roaming kill squad, running between other fighters slaying demons as they went.

Zack encountered a large Mortkin facing away from him. He ran up to it and landed a flurry of stabs in its midsection. It turned and knocked him to the ground. Fighters piled onto it from all sides, rending it in to bloody pieces. Zack was helped up by another fighter and they kept slaying.

The demons fought furiously down to the very last. The last Scarkin was pierced by many blessed spears. Then it was over.

Zack and the others looked all around them for more threats. None remained. Zack fell to the ground exhausted, breathing heavily. Others followed suit.

The Bishop, Brother Christopher and Will rushed around checking on the wounded fighters. They placed a hand on the heads of the wounded and closed their eyes. Zack watched as Kephas prayed the holy words of healing over a fighter who looked like he had been put through a blender.

To his surprise he promptly opened his eyes and sat up. Zack watched on in awe. The man wiped blood from his face. The cuts that were there before had now vanished.

Kephas went straight to the next fighter lying on the ground. Zack watched him close his eyes and hold his hand on the man's head. He stood and proceeded straight to the next fighter. Zack realised that man must have died. He lay just a few steps from where he was. The fact that could have easily been him was not lost on Zack. At the same time his blood loss took its toll and he fainted backwards, hitting his head.

"We made it buddy," Graham said as Zack opened his eyes.

He saw Will stand up from his side, who had just healed him. Zack never got used to that feeling.

"Thank you," Zack called to Will.

Will smiled back at him.

"Our little squad made it through alive," Graham said, smiling, answering Zack's next question before he asked it.

The dead were counted. From their original thirty fighters, eight had died. Considering the odds that they faced in battle, it was an impressive result. Yet the deaths of their fallen weighed heavily on each fighter. The dead were laid side by side with their eyes closed. Their bags and weapons were taken and loaded into a supermarket trolley.

Kephas stood atop a car.

"We still breathe! We have had a small victory today. With our fallen soldiers' sacrifice, we can now feed our starving people. They have gone to be with the Lord God, where there is no more suffering. One could not hope for a more noble death than fighting to protect others. Let us pray that we shall do their sacrifice justice."

He continued in prayer. "God our Father, Lord Jesus Christ, please accept the souls of these fallen soldiers into your presence in Heaven. They died doing your will. May we always remember them. Thank you Lord God that you have granted us the ability to defeat these evil spawn this day. May this food that we have paid for in blood nourish your people to live lives towards you. Amen."

All the fighters echoed back a solemn "Amen".

Kephas continued. "I know many of you would stay to bury these fallen men and women. However, right now we must get this food back to the community. We are not clear of danger yet."

The fighters returned to the supermarket and checked their loaded trolleys.

"Put two fighters guarding the front and two at the back," Kephas directed as they prepared to move out.

They pushed as many trolleys packed with food as they could across the bloodied car park. Zack grabbed some food from the checkout as he pushed his trolley past. With each swallow his stomach felt a little better.

"What are you eating Zack?" Beth asked.

"Some chocolate nut bar. Want some?"

"Sure, thanks."

Zack passed bars from his trolley out to his friends.

"You guys really saved me out there," Zack said thankfully.

"Me too," said Beth.

"I think we all fought well," Graham added.

James agreed.

They continued pushing their trolleys from the car park onto the footpath. It was slow going with lots of broken ground proving difficult for supermarket trolley wheels.

"Excuse me Bishop, can I ask you a question?" Brother Christopher asked.

"Yes, what is it?" he replied.

"How did you cast that holy flare earlier?"

"Yes, that proved quite effective, didn't it?" he said smiling. "As you know I've been pouring over those scrolls and what you saw was the results of my study. As you could probably tell it wasn't something I wanted to practice in my office. Now that I am confident I understand, I will teach you when we have time."

"Thank you Bishop."

"Have you been able to heal without feeling exhausted afterwards yet?"

"Yes, I think I have made lots of progress in that regard. It was as you said. It takes some getting used to."

"Good good, have you been able to heal any injuries and leave no scarring?"

"Just small superficial ones."

"Oh, that's great progress, I'll have you learning the holy flare soon."

The group of fighters made their way back through the streets towards St. Thomas' Church. Upon reaching an intersection about halfway back Kephas held his hand high to signal a stop. Kephas was looking intently around the houses in front of them. Everyone tried to see what he was looking at. Zack could not see past the people in front of him. He readied his knife.

"Demons!" Deon shouted pointing to the backyard of one of the houses.

A dozen Scarkin cambered over the fence and made their way towards the group.

"Weapons at the ready!" Kephas shouted.

The fighters left the trolleys and prepared to fight. The demons quickly made their way over the road and attacked. A loud battle-cry rang out as the fighters charged. The dozen demons were quickly destroyed. Several fighters received injuries that were promptly healed.

"Ok, let's move," Kephas called.

Again the food convoy set out. They made it back with no more demon encounters. As they pushed the trolleys up the street of the church Zack could see the few fighters patrolling the fence line. He saw people start to run up to the gates and fence. Zack could see the hunger in their eyes.

Zack felt like a returning war hero. People were waving and cheering. Zack and the others pushed the trolleys inside the church gates. A great crowd of people swamped around them with happy looks in their faces.

Kephas prayed a blessing over the food.

"God our Father in Heaven, thank you for this precious food. May it strengthen us to do your will. We remember those who died and we commend their souls to your care. May God bless us all. Amen."

Everyone said "Amen" and ate their fill.

A lady in the crowd tapped Zack on the shoulder.

"Yes it's you. This is the hero of Eastlands!" she declared.

She waved her arms and tried to get the attention of those around her. A horrid feeling swelled up into Zack's throat.

"No, you must have me confused with someone else," Zack said firmly.

"Oh don't be like that; I recognise your face from the news. It's definitely you. I never forget a face."

More people turned and stared at Zack.

"Yes, it's him alright," someone said.

Zack wanted to disappear, but he was surrounded with people.

A bunch of people started clapping for him. That was all Zack could handle. He turned and ducked and weaved his way through the crowd as fast as he could. He ignored the calls from behind him and made his way over to the school. Feelings that he thought he locked deep away inside him bubbled to the surface. His eyes started to leak; he wanted to be alone.

He wanted to die.

Chapter 7

Meadows Peak

Some time later Graham found Zack sitting on the top of the school playground.

"There you are. I've been looking everywhere for you!"

Zack was rolling his knife around in his hand.

"I just needed some time to myself."

"Are you okay?"

"I don't know."

"Well suck it up man. We have a new mission."

"Oh?"

"Yeah, we are going on a rescue mission to that old folks' home out of town."

Zack continued to play with his knife.

Graham continued: "It's just going to be six of us. You, me, Beth, Mindy, James and someone called Tom."

Zack ears pricked up as Mindy was mentioned.

"Oh okay. I thought Mindy was doing her healing thing?"

"Yeah, that's why she'll be coming with us. You really should have been at the meeting dude."

"Yeah, yeah. Who's this Tom guy?"

"He was with us at the supermarket fight. Come on now, the others are waiting."

"Are we leaving now?"

"Yes, come on."

Zack jumped down and followed Graham to where the others were waiting by the church office.

"Hi Zack," Mindy said with a smile on her face.

"Hi there. How did your healing lessons go?" he replied.

"Really good thanks. It's pretty exhausting but I should be able to keep our little team going."

"Awesome. Thanks in advance."

A tall man walked out of the church office. He had short black hair and stern looking face. He wore black pants and a dark green jacket. Both were speckled with mud and what looked like blood.

"Hi, you must be Zack. I'm Tom. I'll be leading this little rescue party."

They shook hands. Zack felt Tom's grip was unnecessarily hard. He reminded Zack of the deputy principal at his high school. Zack didn't like him for some reason he couldn't yet identify.

"Nice to meet you," Zack replied.

Tom continued: "Okay everyone, if you haven't already done so, go and see Jacob at the school workshop and get some kit. We leave in thirty minutes from the church gates."

"Sure thing," Graham said.

Tom walked off in search of Sandy who was organising food for their mission. Zack and his friends walked over to the workshop and talked with Jacob. Jacob and his two helpers had been building as many blessed weapons as they could. With each iteration they managed to improve the quality of the weapons.

"Okay, you lot should know the drill. The best kit goes to the best fighters. Nothing personal. I've labeled this gear with how many evil gems you need to purchase each different item," Jacob explained.

"What?" Mindy asked.

"It's a proof of kill thing," Zack added. He dug into his pocket and pulled out a handful of gems that he picked up after the battle at the supermarket.

"My shout guys," Zack said with a smile.

"Wow, you lot must have seen a lot of combat," Jacob said looking at the pile of gems.

"You could say that," said Graham as he added his to the pile.

Zack chose a small shield. It was wooden construction with metal reinforcing. Graham picked a solid looking mace with metal studs embedded in the violent end. James chose a converted fire axe. Beth chose a pair of hunting knives.

With some encouragement Mindy picked up a double-bladed spear. Each weapon was covered in deeply etched holy words. Zack noticed that the etching had ink set inside it this time so the words were more visible. Zack's shield read:

Psalm 18

² The Lord is my rock, my fortress and my deliverer;
my God is my rock, in whom I take refuge,
my shield and the horn of my salvation, my stronghold.

Jacob plopped the evil gems into the barrel of holy water and they all watched as they sizzled away to nothing.

"Thanks for ridding us of those things. I hope these tools will help," Jacob said.

"They have literally been a life saver. Thank you Jacob," said Zack.

Zack looked at a sword that looked to be still under construction behind Jacob on the table behind him. Jacob saw him looking.

"That one might be ready by the time you get back."

"Okay. Thanks again."

The group made their way back to the church gate to meet Tom. He was standing next to eight plastic bags.

"This will be our food and water for our mission. We need to make it last. I am not exactly sure how long this rescue may take and I expect we will need to share it with those we bring back with us."

Tom handed out a bag to each person. Zack knelt on the ground and packed it in to his backpack. He smiled as he peeked inside and saw a chocolate nut bar.

"Okay gather around, this is our plan." Tom took out a hand drawn map and pointed as he spoke.

"This is us, this is the edge of town and over here is Meadows Peak. This is where we are going. I want us to go on foot on the way there and keep a low profile, then hopefully obtain a vehicle for the way back. Any questions?"

"Just one. Who are those other food bags for?" Zack pointed to the two food bags remaining.

"The Bishop and one other are going on a separate mission. Those are for them," Tom replied.

Tom picked up a sanctified sledgehammer leaning on the side of the fence and swung it up onto his shoulder.

"Okay, let's get this done."

They departed at a quick walking pace behind Tom.

A few moments later Deon and Bishop Kephas walked out of church with Brother Christopher.

"I'm leaving this place in capable hands," Kephas said.

"I'm grateful for your confidence Bishop," Brother Christopher replied.

"We hope to be no more than a few days, but as you're well aware with the dangers out there we may not return. Keep these people safe in our absence."

"I understand, God willing we can do so together on your return."

"May the light of our Lord Jesus Christ shine upon you, bless you and protect you."

"And you as well Bishop."

Deon picked up the two food bags and packed them into his backpack.

"Are you sure you want to come with me on this one Deon?"

"Yes Bishop, you'll need my help."

"Yes, I will. Thank you."

Bishop Kephas and Deon walked out the church gates and down the road in the opposite direction to Zack and his friends. The two men walked past the men in the school patrol vests.

Malcolm called out.

"Good hunting Bishop."

Kephas waved back to him.

They kept walking and soon they were well out of range of the school patrols. Deon felt vulnerable, but drew confidence with the Bishop at his side. Kephas had a determined look on his face. Deon wondered what he was thinking about.

"We need a motorcycle," the Bishop said.

"There is a biker bar on Custom Street that is bound to have motorcycles. Or I think the car dealership by the central park has some."

"I see, which is closer?"

"The biker bar by a long way."

"Let us go there then. Lead the way."

They walked down to the end of the street. As Deon was deciding which road would be faster Kephas called out.

"Weapons ready!"

Deon readied his axe and Kephas drew his battle crucifixes.

The sound of a screaming woman rang out through the suburbs. Kephas sprinted towards a nearby house and vaulted over the fence. Deon ran after him. As Deon approached he could see blood and demon innards being sprayed over the fence. He climbed over and saw Kephas standing in a pile of bubbling Scarkin carcasses. Deon saw a woman laying against the side of the house covered in deep cuts. She had short blonde hair and wore a blue top and black pants.

Kephas approached her slowly.

"I can tend to your wounds."

She nodded.

Kephas prayed the holy words of healing over her and she stood up.

"What magic is this? Am I hallucinating?"

"This is very real. But let us explain somewhere away from here."

Kephas flicked the guts from his crucifixes on to the ground and put them back under his coat.

"I'm Deon, this is Bishop Kephas. What's your name?"

"I'm Michelle. Thank you for saving me."

They hurried down the street, keeping an eye out for more demons.

Deon talked to Michelle all about the church, school and how they got to where they were.

"How can God be real with so much suffering in the world?"

Kephas spoke. "God gave us freewill, and many of us choose to do the right thing. Sadly many choose not to. This results in much suffering. The Devil has influence on the earth causing even more pain. Yet this does give opportunity for courage, and standing up for what's right to exist. Jesus Christ suffered greatly when he paid the price for our sin. Although we suffer for many hours on earth, how can we compare that to an eternity in heaven with God?"

"That just doesn't wash with me."

"That's understandable; I'm not expecting to convince you immediately. Please let us continue to talk more when you're ready."

"Okay fine," she said.

It wasn't long before they had arrived at the biker bar 'The Road Hog'. Unfortunately, it was on fire. The three of them approached cautiously but saw no one around. No demons either.

As they got closer they saw the bar must have been burning for some time. Already many parts of the roof had collapsed. The surrounding car park had been scorched and tiny bits of burning embers drifted in the air. The smell of burning plastic, wood and flesh permeated Deon's nostrils. He peered amongst the building to confirm his fear. He saw a human hand burning beneath the rubble inside the bar.

"What happened here?" Deon exclaimed.

"More tragedy," said Michelle.

Kephas nodded. "I was hoping to find survivors here. But now we must carry on with our mission. Michelle, you are free to come with us or we can give you directions back to the church. I am sorry but both options will be very dangerous."

"So I can head back to safety alone or trek with you two out into the wilderness?"

"Unless you have any other ideas?"

"I guess I'll stick with you two. You are heading back to this safe place eventually right?"

"Yes we will. Okay, let's see if we can find a couple of working motorcycles."

They spent some time looking for keys then eventually succeeded in hotwiring two motorcycles that were in front of the burning bar.

"Did you hear that?" Kephas asked.

Deon and Michelle strained their ears. After a short silence they heard the roar of a Mortkin.

"Let's get going quickly," Deon suggested.

Kephas and Deon climbed on a bike each. Michelle climbed on the back of Deon's bike and held him tightly. Deon realized it had been many years since he had rode a bike. He prayed that the cliché was true that one does not forget how to. Kephas' bike revved into life, shortly followed by Deon's bike. They started to slowly pull out of the car park as Deon saw a dangerously large pack of demons scampering their way down the road. Michelle held on even tighter.

"Follow me," Kephas called.

Deon gave him a thumbs up signal.

They sped away from the demons down the road in the opposite direction. The demons started to give chase but were soon left behind.

"I think they're gone," Michelle said to Deon.

Deon nodded with relief.

The two bikes were ideally suited to the broken and blocked roads through town. They weaved their way through abandoned cars and rubble. Soon they had left the suburbs and were making good progress on rural roads. Kephas slowed down and stopped at the side of the road. Deon pulled in behind him.

"Deon, what's this place?"

Kephas pointed down a side road, which slowly wound its way up a small hill. Deon looked and saw many construction vehicles, piles of building materials and a large sign. It was too far away to read.

"Oh, I think that's going to be the new prison, it was in the news a while back."

"Let's check it out," Kephas said as they headed down the side road. Kephas called out to see if there was anyone around. There was no reply.

They slowly made their way around the complex. It was still a long way from being finished, but many structures were completed. The administration building looked to be in good condition, with just paint and finishings needed on the inside. There was a building in-progress next to it that was now just a collapsed pile of timber framing on a concrete foundation.

"What are you looking for Bishop?"

"A plan 'B,'" he said with a knowing smile.

Deon followed him around slowly on his bike wondering what he was up to.

"Is this the place you two are looking for?" Michelle asked Deon.

"No, I'm not sure what Kephas is thinking, but I'm sure it's for a good reason," he replied.

Behind the administration building the cellblocks were largely complete. Kephas hopped off his bike and peered through the windows. Deon could see him nodding to himself. They continued throughout the complex with Kephas occasionally checking on something. There was even two watch towers mostly built with a clear view over the complex.

"Let's check the perimeter Deon and we'll be off," Kephas called.

They took their bikes onto the grass and assessed the walls. Tall, thick concrete rectangular slabs had been set-up around the perimeter of the prison. They had only partially completed wall construction with about thirty percent of the perimeter having no walls. There was a pile of slabs for the wall that had yet to be erected by the construction supplies left near the entrance.

"Yes this will do nicely," Kephas said quietly to himself.

He then shouted out to Deon. "Okay, let's get going."

Deon nodded and they sped back to the main road. They continued on for another hour. Kephas slowed and turned into another side road.

After a few minutes they drove up to the historic cemetery. They hopped off their motorcycles and walked into the lines of gravestones. Deon looked around; several trees bordered the cemetery, which was filled with all sorts of old graves. Some tall and ornate, others just a simple stone with rough etchings in the ground. The place seemed to have a thin film of lichen over everything. The scheduled annual cleaning seemed to have been months ago.

Kephas searched for something amongst the gravestones. After several minutes he called Michelle and Deon over to him. To Deon's surprise it was not one of the big tombs like that of a long dead king. Kephas leaned over a small tombstone laying flat on the ground. It looked to be truly ancient with many of the markings worn off over the decades. A large cross was still clearly visible in the centre of the stone.

"Why did we come all the way out here to pay respects to someone long dead?" Michelle spat.

Deon looked on expectantly.

Kephas replied: "Give me some time; trust me this will be worth the trip."

The Bishop carefully touched the gravestone all over with his hands.

"I know it's here somewhere," Deon heard Kephas mutter.

"Ah!" Kephas said loudly, clearly relieved.

He pulled out his combat crucifix from his jacket and placed the hilt into a small recess in one of the markings. He pushed the crucifix down a small way into the stone.

Nothing happened.

"I think it must be broken," said Kephas.

He started to dig away at the dirt around the edge of the stone. The more he dug out the more stone he uncovered. Deon knelt down next to him and helped him dig. After several minutes of digging, they had uncovered a larger stone buried slightly beneath the surface stone.

"Okay, we just need to pry the hatch off," the Bishop said.

"Hatch?" Michelle asked.

"Yes. Please can you both give me a hand?"

Kephas wedged his weapon into a small crack under the gravestone.

"I'll pry, and you two push," Kephas directed.

They heaved and pushed until there was a loud cracking sound. Deon fell backwards onto the grass. The top stone slid off a small opening in the ground. They all peeked into the dark hole. Cold, stale air steeped out into their noses. Deon saw some type of old locking mechanism around the hole. One of the metal links looked broken, but it had otherwise faired well over the years.

The Bishop spoke a quiet and reverent prayer then reached his arm down into the hole. He pulled out what looked like a handful of human bones. He carefully piled them up next to the hole.

"What are you doing?" Michelle demanded.

"I know this looks profane, but underneath these bones there is something we need."

Kephas slowly pulled out what looked to be a largely complete human skeleton out of the small hole. Deon looked in and saw nothing left in the hole but dirt. Kephas started to dig again into the dirt beneath the bones. Then finally he unearthed a small handle. He pulled with all his might and the dirt loosened its grip on a long metal case. Kephas stood and pulled it out of the hole and laid it on the ground alongside the bones. He brushed off the dirt around the hinges and lid, then pried it open.

A treasure trove on ancient artefacts lay inside. A strong smell of incense was liberated from the case. The three of them stopped and smiled at each other, happy that their toil was for good reason.

Inside the metal case lay many parchments and scrolls, many of which had red wax seals imprinted with an insignia from Kephas' Holy Order. Kephas carefully removed them from the case. He passed each to Deon, who placed them into his pack. Beneath the parchments lay several small containers of holy oil. Each was made of metal and had fine engravings on them. A few of them were glass underneath a metal casing. Deon could see a liquid inside that looked like olive oil. Kephas carefully handed each to Deon.

The case now lay bare, apart from a few small pieces of parchment scattered about. The Bishop lifted the case and slowly turned it around in his hands. He placed his fingers near one of the hinges and pushed until there was a satisfying click.

A false bottom of the case fell out, followed by two swords and a strange stone tablet. The first sword was smaller than the other and Deon recognised it as a Roman Gladius. Deon felt happy with himself that watching the history channel seemed to have been useful. The sword was very simple and looked to be thousands of years old. The Bishop picked it up but he fumbled and dropped it on to the gravestone. As it landed the handle broke and came away from the blade.

"Crap!" Kephas said angrily.

Deon and Michelle looked at each other then cracked up laughing. The Bishop let a smile escape as he apologised for his language. He wrapped the broken weapon in a durable looking cloth then handed it to Deon.

"This blade is the Gladius of Saint Peter; I'm hoping our talented Smith can repair it."

"Oh I knew it. But do you mean 'the' St. Peter?" said Deon.

"Yes, the same."

"Wow…" Deon said smiling.

The Bishop turned his attention to the second sword. This one had a much longer blade, like one wielded by knights of old. It was also in much better condition. Kephas unrolled the decaying material from over the blade. Deon was impressed how the blade still looked clean and shiny. The blade itself looked worn but well cared for. There was the occasional nick in the blade but it looked to be in serviceable condition. Along the center of the blade was masterfully engraved writing, which looked to Deon like Latin. The handle and pommel were ornate but sturdy looking. This was a sword built for battle, but with Biblical purpose.

"Wow," was all Deon could think to say.

"Great, another big knife. Next you'll tell us that this belongs to Saint George or something," said Michelle.

"Why yes. It did belong to Saint George."

"What? No way. That is just a kid's story."

"Yes, the common folklore around Saint George and a Dragon is just a story. However it has some truth based on the actual events. Let's just say this sword is well suited for the task at hand."

Kephas stood and drew the sword upwards into a combat stance. He took a running start and then swung the mighty blade into the trunk of a small tree. Kephas' swing followed through the other side of the tree. The tree toppled over at the point where he had cut it down with a single strike. As it fell, small branches smacked Kephas in the face. This ruined his otherwise very stylish move. Michelle muffled a laugh.

"I thought I was the gardener," Deon said with a chuckle.

Kephas laughed.

Kephas inspected the sword and swung it around a bit.

"Yes, this will be very useful," he said.

He returned to the last item in the case. It was a small rectangular granite tablet. There were writings cut into it, which Deon didn't recognize. The markings covered both sides. It looked to be the oldest item from the case.

"Is that Latin too?" Deon asked.

"No, this tablet is written in ancient Hebrew. And it's why we came all this way," Kephas moved his fingertips over the words slowly.

A quiet minute passed.

"So? What does it say?" Michelle asked impatiently.

Kephas let out a big breath. "I have no idea."

"Wait, what?" Deon said.

"I can't remember. I was able to read Hebrew back in my day, but the late Father Andrew had been responsible for this sort of thing for years. I can recognize many of the words. But that will just not do."

"What will we do now?"

"I was hoping seeing Hebrew again would jog my memory. But since that's not going to work we will need someone else to read it for us."

"I suppose you have an expert on ancient languages hanging around somewhere, do you?" Michelle said sarcastically.

"Actually I hope so. I've already sent a team to Meadows Peak, where Sister Paula has been spending her retirement. God willing she is alive and can read it for us."

"Okay then, where to next for us?" Deon asked.

"Let's get back to the church. I'd like to spend some time looking over these scrolls and I'm sure Michelle would like a hot meal."

They spent some time to re-bury the ancient bones. Kephas said a prayer as they finished. They packed up and hopped on their motorbikes.

"Let's try to avoid any combat if we can help it on the way back," said Kephas.

"Sounds good to me," Michelle replied.

After hours of riding they made it back into Brakenside. They slowed down as they entered the suburbs due to the narrow broken roads and abandoned cars. Occasionally they would see a few Scarkin approach, but they always managed to out-pace them. One demon leaped at Kephas from behind a car as he drove past. The demon was met with swift fist to the face, which sent it reeling backwards.

They drove up slowly to the church gates as the school patrol was walking past.

"How went the hunt bishop?" Malcolm called out.

"Very well. How has it been here?" Kephas replied.

"Strangely quiet. Just a few demons killed on the far side of the school."

"Good work. Do you know if the other team has come back yet?"

"I don't think so. Check with Sandy, she'll know."

"I will. Thanks Malcolm."

The three hopped off their bikes and walked in the gates. Sandy appeared and after a brief conversation she showed Michelle where to find some food. Deon followed Kephas to the church office where Brother Christopher was studying holy scrolls.

…

Zack and his team had been walking through the suburbs when Tom motioned everyone to stop. Tom held his hand up in a fist. Zack thought he'd just seen that on some action movie and had no idea about actual military tactics. Zack was right.

"Get down," Tom whispered loudly.

They dropped down behind the hedge they were walking past. Tom leaned past the end of the hedge and looked down the road. At the far end of the road were several Scarkin. He pulled his head back without getting seen.

"Demons. Far end of the road. Let's back up and cross the road," Tom suggested.

"Okay," whispered James.

They cautiously made their way back way up the street then crossed over to the grass on the other side. Tom led them down the grass verge into the small river. They walked along the shallow parts at the river's edge. Rubbish littered the banks of the stream. Zack's feet were wet again. He hadn't taken his shoes off in days, and didn't expect to find them healthy when he eventually did. However, he would much prefer to walk in a river than confront more demons.

The group walked slowly out of the suburbs. Ahead of them Zack could see the industrial and commercial areas of Brakenside. They trudged their way through a large culvert underneath one of the larger roads above them. It reminded Zack of going for adventures with his friends when he was young. He wished he could have a bag of lollies and a soft drink to enjoy like he did back then.

"Hold up," Tom stopped everyone in the culvert with another fist signal.

He pointed to his ears then to above them. Zack was sure it was going to be nothing. A few tense seconds later the long claws of a Mortkin reached over the top part of the culvert. It then dropped into the stream with splash and a roar.

"Attack!" Tom yelled rushing towards it with his weapon held high. The others joined him rushing the creature as several Scarkin dropped down on the other side of them.

"Behind us!" James yelled.

Tom, Graham and Zack fought the Mortkin as the others fought the smaller demons. The Mortkin stomped forward and swung at Zack with its clawed arms. Zack managed to block with his shield in time. The demon yelped as its evil flesh slammed into the blessed shield. Zack followed up with a few quick strikes with his knife into the beast's left arm. Tom and Graham took the opportunity while it was distracted to wail on it with their weapons. In its final thrashings it managed to clip each of the three men before it was destroyed.

The three returned to help the others on the other side of the culvert. Zack saw Mindy thrust her spear into the head of an oncoming demon with impressive accuracy. After a few minutes of fighting they had put down the last of the demons.

"Is everyone okay?" Tom asked.

He was met with several out-of-breath nods. Mindy put down her spear and placed her hands on Beth's wounded arm.

"Accipere professio medendi spiritus Christi," she spoke the holy words reverently.

Mindy closed her eyes and breathed slowly. The expression on Beth's face changed from one of pain to that of profound relief.

"Thank you Mindy," she said happily.

In turn Mindy healed each of their wounds. Zack looked on in amazement. Mindy came to Zack next.

"Allow me to see those cuts Zacky," she offered. Zack loved the sound of her voice. She placed her gentle hands on his bleeding arm and shoulder. For a moment it felt like it was just the two of them.

"Hey. What do those words mean that you say?" said James as he barged his way into their moment.

"Oh, it means 'receive the healing breath of Christ,'" said Mindy as she took her hands off Zack.

Zack and James thanked her. Zack looked at his arms. He had accumulated an impressive number scars.

"Ok let's get moving. Remember people are waiting to be rescued," Tom announced.

Mindy looked exhausted and Beth helped her as they walked further downstream. After several minutes the stream had become too deep and the banks too steep to easily travel. The group climbed their way up the grassy banks and found themselves in the industrial part of town.

Zack looked around. He thought back a few years ago when he was driving through this part of town on a public holiday. There was no-one around. Yet as he looked, he was reminded he wasn't on holiday. There were abandoned crashed cars, smoke billowing out of a nearby building, and blood sprayed over walls like graffiti.

There were several large warehouses and factories around them. Some of them had broken windows and doors. A large split in the ground from the earthquake cut the road in two. Someone had been unlucky enough to drive into it as it happened and their dead body remained trapped in their car. The surrounding buildings had high rooftops, which seemed to Zack like a good vantage point for Scarkin.

It was eerily quiet. They walked down the road maintaining an active watch for demons.

The sound of smashing glass drew the group's attention. On the far side of the road was a large industrial complex. It had a two-story building at the front of the property and many warehouses behind it. Remnants of the second floor windows were raining down on the pavement below. Zack saw someone fighting a demon through the broken window. Then a Scarkin was thrown out through the window and landed heavily on the concrete below.

"Let's help them out," Tom commanded.

The demon shook itself off and ran back inside through the smashed front doors.

"Help is coming!" Tom yelled up at the second floor as they entered the office building.

The place looked like a dollhouse that a toddler had picked up and shaken. Broken glass, smashed equipment, office supplies and blood spatter was everywhere. Zack found the staircase and pointed it out to the others. They rushed through the mess and made their way up.

As Tom climbed the stairs a Scarkin jumped onto his back. He struggled and cried out as it stabbed its claws into his flesh. Tom lost his balance and toppled backwards down the stairs. Zack was directly behind him and managed to smash the demon with his shield as they all fell. Graham and Beth helped them back to their feet. James ran up the stairs past them.

"Hang on," he yelled.

Zack could hear the fighting continuing upstairs. Mindy went to lay her hands on Tom's injuries.

"Not yet, let's save these people first," Tom insisted.

The group followed James up to the second story of the building. A body lay in the hallway; it was covered in deep cuts. A large puddle of blood was soaking the carpet around it. Another crash from down the hall drew Zack's attention. He ran down the hall closest to him.

The others followed and they soon all entered a large meeting room. It had been utterly trashed. A man stood covered in blood in the center of the room. He was grappling with a small demon. James ran up and hacked the demon off him. Another man and a woman were cowering behind a barricade made from the meeting table. Both were badly injured. One of them was holding a bloody table leg as a weapon.

Three more Scarkin scampered in the far meeting room door. Zack, Tom and James ran to meet them. The demons were cut down like evil wheat at harvest time. When Zack turned around Mindy was already healing the injured.

"Let's clear the rest of this floor," Tom called.

After a quick search yielding no more demons, they returned to the meeting room.

"How did you kill them?" the man holding the table leg asked.

He had a long black beard, a bald head and wore the remains of a grey suit.

"The short version, they are evil demons, these are holy weapons. Is there anyone else in here? Will you be okay?"

"Seriously?"

"Yes."

"Oh wow. Um, yeah it's just us three left. The others are dead. I'm Jason, this is Peter and Nikita. Thanks for saving us."

Tom introduced his team and everyone chatted for a few minutes.

"I don't mean to push it, but you don't happen to have any food in those bags, do you?" Peter asked. He had light blonde hair and wore a dark blue business shirt and black pants. He sat on the ground with his hands on his knees.

"Yes, we can afford to share some," said Tom, opening up his pack.

He offered some to Nikita. She had long bedraggled red hair and wore a black dress. She took the food and started to eat. Her eyes seemed to stare off into the distance.

"It looks like you have been through hell," he said to her.

She didn't respond.

"Nikita saw her colleagues killed in front of her. She hasn't spoken to us at all since," Jason explained.

Tom handed out some more food. Others in the team shared their supplies too. After they had time to eat Tom spoke up.

"We better get moving again. We have people counting on us."

He explained their rescue mission and gave the new survivors an option to make their own way to St. Thomas' or join them on their way to Meadows Peak. They looked at each other then Jason spoke for them.

"We will definitely be sticking with you. We will keep up and help where we can."

"Okay, let's go."

Jason helped Nikita up and they all made their way out of the building. They walked out onto the street and made their way through the industrial part of town. Occasionally a solitary Scarkin would screech from somewhere close by. Each time, the group would stick closer together.

After much walking they approached the edge of town. Fields lay behind the last warehouse in front of them for as far as they could see. On top of a large hill in the distance was their destination.

Meadows Peak was a retirement village and hospice. It was built twenty years ago and was initially a very expensive establishment with only the wealthy being able to enrol. Over the years, cutting of maintenance budgets resulted in a bad customer experience. This resulted in a price drop and a further drop in maintenance. Despite it being run-down it had well loved gardens and caring staff.

The group continued their long walk out of town towards Meadows Peak. Zack was puffing hard by the time they neared the top of the hill. Many of the group were now walking very slowly.

"Come on everyone, we're nearly there," Tom encouraged.

Zack stopped and put his hands on his knees for a moment to catch his breath. He turned as he stood back up and something caught his eye in the distance.

"What's up?" Graham asked.

"I'm not sure, look over there tell me what you think that is," Zack replied.

Zack watched him squint his eyes. He looked back at the blurred mass in the distance. As he stared he saw it was slowly moving. He wondered if it was a flood of dirty water washing out between two buildings at the edge of town. At once his brain made sense of what he was looking at. It was a terrifyingly large horde of demons. They looked to be heading their way.

"Oh no, no, no!" Zack said progressively louder.

"Demons!" Graham yelled.

The others spun around to look where they were pointing.

"We gotta get the people out now!" Tom commanded as he ran up the last part of the hill.

Thoughts of just running away flickered through Zack's mind. Graham ran past him following Tom. The rest of the group followed. They ran up the short driveway at the top of the hill. The carefully shaped hedges blocked the oncoming horde from view.

The property had numerous large trees and many gardens. The two-story brick building looked tired, with much of the paint peeling off around the windows and doors. The front doors were wide open. Zack could see a little inside the dark hallway. A body in a toppled wheelchair lay on the floor. Zack's heart sunk. He prayed that the people they were coming to rescue were not already dead. Tom ran up to the front doors and turned around.

"Graham, Beth and Zack, you must hold them off at the front doors. Mindy, James and the rest of you, help me search the building," he commanded.

"We'll do it," Graham said confidently.

"Ok," said James.

Zack watched them rush inside looking for survivors. He turned his gaze to the driveway and watched the way they came in. Soon demons would be flooding in. Zack was scared.

"We got this," Graham assured.

"Yeah," Beth replied.

Zack nodded.

A few nervous moments passed. Then the howls of the demons approaching could be heard. The three slowly backed up towards the doors. The first demons made their way around the perimeter hedges. Zack saw three Scarkin come around the hedge. He readied his shield and knife. He saw Graham patting his mace on his hand. Beth stood with a fierce look on her face with her knives ready at her sides. Zack closed his eyes and remembered something he read in his Bible earlier that day.

Psalm 27

¹ The Lord is my light and my salvation—
whom shall I fear?
The Lord is the stronghold of my life—
of whom shall I be afraid?
² When the wicked advance against me
to devour me,
it is my enemies and my foes
who will stumble and fall.

Zack felt ready. The three watched more demons flow onto the driveway. Zack drew in deep breaths starring down his enemy running towards him.

"God damn you!" Zack yelled as he ran forward into the demons.

Zack heard his friends yell and join him in battle. Zack shoulder charged a Scarkin to the ground then followed up with a few rapid stabs. Another demon from behind him leaped at him, but Zack managed to roll out of the way. He stood up as another demon swiped its claws past his face. He swung his shield into it and the demon bounced off onto the ground. Zack fought for his life. After far too short of a time, the three were starting to lose ground.

"The doors!" Graham yelled.

The three of them broke off from combat and ran back to the front doors. Graham and Zack stood side by side blocking the front doors with Beth just behind them in the foyer. They looked at each other and understood without using words. They had to hold the demons back, no matter what.

A few seconds later the demons crashed into them again. Zack was constantly blocking and stabbing what seemed like endless Scarkin. Guttural roars announced that the Mortkin had made their way up the hill. Zack wanted to hear some encouraging words from Graham but he was too busy fighting to stay alive. He heard nothing from the searching team yet either.

A few moments later the first of the Mortkin smashed its way in to the front lines. A wild swing of a clawed arm narrowly missed Zack's throat. He dropped back a step and lunged forward with all his strength as knife pierced through limbs and into the Mortkin's chest dropping it like a sack of potatoes.

Graham and Zack fought bravely but as more and more Mortkin made it into battle they bitterly moved backwards into the foyer. A large Mortkin roared and charged into them, knocking them both over onto their backs. Zack's head hit the floor.

The large demons stood over them about to land killing blows when gunfire erupted. Beth emptied the clip of her pistol into the front lines of demons. The blessed bullets tore through multiple demons, felling many Mortkin. Zack didn't know where Beth had found more ammo but was thankful that he continued to draw breath.

Zack and Graham stood up and continued fighting. As the demons pushed their way into the foyer Beth had room to join in the fight. Zack saw one of her blades burst through the demon in front of him. He would try to remember to thank her for that if they made it out alive.

"We got her! Backdoor now!" Tom's voice rang out like a school bell to signal lunchtime, and Zack was famished.

Tom rushed down the stairs to join their fight in the foyer. He swung his sledgehammer into a Mortkin's head, dropping it in a single blow. Zack stood back to avoid getting hit. Tom swung his hammer back and forth with surprising speed. For a moment they seemed to have gained a little ground in the battle.

Zack could hear the others rushing down there stairs behind him. He didn't see the many old people he was hoping to save. Sadly most of them had already died.

"Go, get outta here! I'll hold them off," Tom commanded.

As much as Zack didn't think one person could hold off so many demons alone, Tom was doing a great job swinging that big hammer. The three of them hesitated and kept fighting.

"Now! The rescue comes first," Tom yelled.

Beth ran back towards the others followed by Graham and Zack. With the extra space Tom swung his sledge all the harder dropping more demons with each swing.

Running out the back door Zack saw the others making their way through the back gardens towards the city in the distance. Their group was helping the few elderly people escape. He saw a frail old lady in a pale blue nightgown being carried by James. She was singing. It reminded Zack of a choir singing in a great church. Zack somehow felt energised by the holy words. He now understood how James had the strength to carry her and run at the same time.

"Get going!" Tom screamed.

Tom had retreated to the backdoor and was keeping the demons from getting out and following his team. Zack thought of staying to help him fight, but saw the look on Tom's face. His mind was made up. This was his fight. Zack ran with the rest of his team down through the beautiful gardens towards the back hedge. Jason had reached there first and had broken a few branches to make a way out. He pushed himself through shortly followed by the others.

Zack cast one last look at Tom. He realized that even though Tom liked to order people around, he would be happy to sacrifice himself for the lives of his team. Zack decided he wasn't a bad guy afterall. Tom was standing on the back porch swinging his sledgehammer like it didn't weigh anything at all. However more and more demons were pouring out of the rest home.

Zack tried to swallow the lump in his throat and pushed his way through the hedge. Zack knew Tom would die protecting them. The survivors ran down the hill with an impressive pace. Zack should've been exhausted but Sister Paula's singing somehow kept him going.

Tom stood surrounded by demons. He had been substantially wounded but kept swinging. He knew he would not make it out of this fight alive so poured everything he had left into each strike. He had a strange moment of clarity between swings. Tom thought that if he was to give his team the best chance of escape he'd try and kill all the faster moving Scarkin. Then if he was still alive he'd kill as many Mortkin as he could.

A claw ripped across his face snapping him back into the fight. Tom struck the demon with the handle of his hammer then swung the business-end around into the demon's head. Tom fought with much more skill than he had in the past. He didn't know Sister Paula was praying for him.

Tom fought for what felt like hours, slaying demon after demon. However with each injury he began to lose strength to a growing puddle of his blood beneath his feet. His team had made it back to the outskirts of town when the fatal blow drove into Tom's chest. Tom fell to the ground and quickly died.

"Do you think Tom will be okay?" Mindy asked quietly.

Zack looked at her, unsure of how to answer. His silence told her what she feared.

The group was making good progress through the industrial area of town. They decided to take a more direct route back to the church. With the demon horde somewhere behind them they needed to cover as much ground as quickly as they could.

"So I hear you young ones need me to rescue you?" Sister Paula asked.

Zack thought she must be senile. Graham spoke before Zack could think of what to say.

"It's okay, you're safe with us now. We will look after you."

"I have all my marbles Sonny! Your man Tom told me specifically that he wanted my help, a matter of life and death. And he mentioned an ancient tablet."

"Wait, what?"

Zack looked at the little old lady trying to determine if she was serious.

"You heard me lad. I'm rescuing you."

CHAPTER 8

THE SIEGE

Zack kept thinking about what Sister Paula said as they made their way back to the church. He was sure someone would explain it all on their return. On the way back the group encountered a small pack of Scarkin but managed to destroy them with only minor injuries. Mindy healed the wounded and they carried on. The group walked back through the suburbs and met the school patrol on the way into the church.

"You all okay? Where's Tom?" Malcolm asked.

Graham shook his head slowly.

Malcolm understood and his face fell. He drew a small knife and made a small notch in the handle of one of his hammers. Zack talked to him later to learn that each notch on the hammer, which he carried in his left hand, represented a fallen comrade. Each notch on the right hammer was a demon that he had killed. Both handles were nearly full.

"Here we are," James said as he lowered Sister Paula on to the ground in front of the church gates.

"Thank you young man. Hold my hand until I can find something to use as a walking stick will you?" she asked.

"Sure thing."

Sandy met them all at the gates and directed her helpers to show Jason and the other new survivors around.

"The Bishop would like to see you in his office if you please Sister," Sandy asked.

"Yes, yes, take me to him," she replied.

"The rest of you please take a well deserved rest. Thank you for putting your lives on the line for us," Sandy said.

Zack and his team started to walk off to their classroom for some sleep.

"Zack, please can I have a minute?" Sandy asked.

Zack was surprised she knew his name.

"Yeah?"

"I know you've only just got back, but please could you make a trip to the supermarket when you can? We're running out of these items," she said, handing him a list.

"Sure. Is it okay if I have some sleep first?"

"Of course. Thank you again."

Zack wandered back with the list in his hand. He felt good that someone asked for his help, even if it was just supermarket shopping.

They made it back to their classroom and found some floor space to lay down. Others in the room lent them some blankets as they left. Zack was exhausted. As soon as he lay down and wriggled a bit to get nearly comfortable, he fell asleep.

Four hours later he woke. The others around him were still sleeping. Zack decided he'd rather keep himself occupied than struggle with his nightmares. Zack slowly stood up and quietly made his way out of the classroom.

"What's up?" James asked quietly.

"I'm just going for a walk."

"Ah, can't sleep? Me too."

James got up and they walked outside.

"What are you holding?" James asked.

"Oh, a list of stuff Sandy needs," Zack passed it to him.

James had a look at it.

"Alright let's go."

"Go?"

"Yeah, to get this stuff."

"Now? Just the two of us?"

"Sure, it's not that far from the patrols and we cleared out the demons already. You said you wanted to go for a walk didn't you?"

"I did, didn't I? Okay let's go."

Zack hadn't known James all that long but they got along like old friends. Zack was glad James was with him. They grabbed their weapons and walked out the school gates and onto the road leading to the supermarket. They only encountered a single Scarkin on the whole way there and between the two of them they had no problem killing it.

James grabbed a shopping trolley and Zack walked alongside with the list. They slowly made their way through the battered supermarket collecting supplies.

...

"I'm so glad you made it out alive Sister. I had feared the worst," Kephas said as Sister Paula walked in to the church office.

"Good to see you too Kephas," she replied.

She made her way slowly to the desk and sat down. She had been given a broom handle for a walking stick by one of the congregation. She placed that next to her.

"So what's all this about?"

Kephas spent some time discussing all that had happened and explained his knowledge of demon slaying.

"I see. I had wondered about some of the details of your stories you told of your missionary work, but I didn't expect anything like this."

"Oh?"

"I was at a few of your talks in the cathedral and I just thought your memory was showing it's age."

"*My* age?" Kephas said smiling.

"Anyway, where is this tablet? What do you expect me to read from it?"

"Here." Kephas pulled the ancient stone out of a drawer in his desk.

"It's been too long since I've read Biblical Hebrew. I just know that it's what the Order of Salt and Light planned to use in times such as these."

"I see. It's been a while for me also but I think with some time I'll be..."

Screaming from outside interrupted their conversation.

"Stay here," Kephas said as he rushed outside.

Deon was running up the path towards him.

"We're under attack! We've lost a few patrols already."

"Take me there," Kephas replied.

Members of the church were running everywhere in a panic.

"Get inside all of you and pray," the Bishop commanded.

Deon and Kephas ran towards the school.

"Where are our fighters?" Kephas asked.

"Some are out getting supplies; the rest should meet us there."

They ran between the classrooms and on to the backfield of the school. Deon ran up to the guard on the fence line.

"Where?"

"Through there," he replied as he pointed.

Deon looked through the fence to see demons coming up the once secured street. Several fighters arrived at the fence line.

"We still have the fence," one of them said.

A line of fighters now stared at the approaching demon horde. Deon assessed that there were a lot more demons than at the supermarket battle. This time they had a fence but fewer fighters. Deon was scared. The demons made their way up to the sanctified fence.

A bold Scarkin snapped its jaws at part of the fence with a sparing amount of Bible pages attached to it. The closest fighter ran up to it and stabbed it in the head with a blessed spear. Soon more and more demons were snapping at other weak points in the fence.

The fighters tried to keep a safe distance and stab what they could. The fence line was now completely surrounded with demons. Many Mortkin had now made their way up into the ranks. The fence was keeping them out but only just. A single Scarkin managed to climb a tree on the far side of the fence. It then jumped over the top of the fence and landed inside the schoolyard.

"Get that demon!" Kephas yelled.

On seeing that demon's success other Scarkin scampered up the tree to do the same. The Mortkin roared. Deon made it to the demon on the inside of the fence first and sliced it down the middle with his axe. The bishop ran up to the fence line closest to the tree and knelt down.

Kephas cast the holy flare that Deon had seen at the supermarket battle. The bright white light burst through the fence and incinerated the demons, climbing the tree and all those around it. Deon was knocked back a step with the pressure wave it generated. The ground was covered in the muck of defeated demons. A horrible smell permeated the air. More and more demons kept pouring in to reinforce those snarling at the fence line.

It was not long before more demons had climbed the tree and were launching themselves into the school. Kephas, Deon and the other fighters were kept busy trying to kill them before they made it further. They continued to fight as more demons waited for their opportunity to attack.

Brother Christopher ran up from behind them holding a molotov cocktail. He lit the rag and threw it over the fence into the tree the demons were climbing. It burst into flames as the molotov broke in its branches. The demons were burnt by the holy fire. They screamed and crackled as they burnt like cooking evil popcorn. Many Scarkin bumped into other demons spreading the fire to them. A loud cheer rose from the fighters.

"How?" Deon asked.

"I put some holy oil in the bottle," Brother Christopher replied, happy his idea had worked.

"Great thinking, that should keep them out," Kephas commended.

The tree was well ablaze now. It seemed they were safe from that avenue of attack for a time. The fighters continued to attack any demons that got too close to the fence.

"How are the other sides of the school and church?" Kephas asked Brother Christopher.

"This whole side of the school looks swamped from what I saw. We have spread out our fighters around the perimeter as best we can. I haven't seen how the church fence is doing in a while."

"I see, please can you go and check it for me and report back? Also can you ask Sandy how long we can survive in here with our current supplies?"

"Yes Bishop," Brother Christopher said as he ran off.

"Okay Deon let's keep patrolling these sides of the school. It seems that's where most of the demons are concentrated,"

"Sounds like a plan," Deon agreed.

The ground beneath them started to tremble. It was barely noticeable at first but increased in intensity until a few fighters fell over.

"Earthquake!" one of them yelled.

Deon steadied himself and looked to Kephas. He had a deathly pale look on his face. It initially confused Deon as he didn't think that a little shaking would unsettle such a battle-hardened man.

Before Deon had the chance to speak the ground outside the fence burst upwards in a rush of dirt and rock. The earth fountain shot high into the air as if explosives were detonated underground. Deon looked on in shock. This was not an earthquake.

"I can't believe it, a Magnukin, here." Kephas said with a wavering voice.

"A what?"

"No time Deon, run and find Sister Paula. Tell her she needs to read that tablet right now!"

"Yes Bishop."

"I'll try and hold it off," Kephas said. He drew his combat crucifixes and stood ready at the fence.

Another explosion of dirt which was twice as large as the first sent dozens of demons flying into the air. The house closest to the now gigantic hole was bowled over. Huge clods of dirt rained down in all directions. One large chunk landed on top of a fighter, crushing him instantly. A deep intense roar like that of a ship's foghorn mixed with a dying cow reverberated through the air. Deon fell over and held his ears. Kephas dropped to one knee and tried to fend off the incoming rain of rocks and chunks of broken pavement.

Two giant arms as thick as a human is tall emerged. They were covered in protruding sharp bone spikes. Bloodworms writhed all over its flesh and spilled onto the ground all around the massive demon. The Magnukin slowly pushed itself up out of the ground.

"Deon! Run, get everyone to run!" Kephas screamed.

Deon stumbled to his feet and dragged the closest fighter with him.

"Get everyone inside the church!" Kephas yelled after him.

Kephas stood alone against the demon horde. He struggled with himself not to run away for a split-second. But his faith and fortitude was strong. The Magnukin resembled the other types of demons except on a giant scale. Like its brethren the Magnukin had two forearms splitting at the elbows. Its giant hands had huge claws the length of a human. Its head burst out of the ground with an ear-piercing howl.

Kephas dropped to both knees and prayed as hard as he could. He drew in all the spiritual strength he could muster, every ounce of his very soul.

The giant creature pulled the rest of its body out of the hole it made. It unfurled a set of huge wings sending a shockwave across the school. The wings, though large, looked stunted and damaged. In comparison to the size of the beast it didn't look able to fly. Kephas chanted a prayer with all the volume he could manage.

Isaiah 41

[10] So do not fear, for I am with you;
do not be dismayed, for I am your God.
I will strengthen you and help you;
I will uphold you with my righteous right hand.

However Kephas was barely audible next to the Magnukin. Even the screams of the people fleeing to the church could hardly be heard. When Kephas was at his limit, he shouted the holy words to cast the Searing Light of Christ. A marvellous flash of blinding light burst out, evaporating rows of demons.

Before the light could hit the Magnukin it smashed its arms into the ground, sending up a wall of dirt and dust. Kephas poured all he had into that attack. Despite him killing fifty demons in a single moment he had failed. After the dust settled the Magnukin shook off some of its charred flesh and continued forward towards the meagre fence.

Kephas slowly stood up. He was exhausted. The Magnukin dug its hands into the road and pulled up a giant chunk of dirt and concrete. It then hurled the giant projectile at the fence. The blessed fence was promptly flattened like an empty cardboard box. The horde of demons rushed in through the breach. The Magnukin lumbered on behind them.

Kephas stood up just in time to be set upon by numerous demons. He chanted his holy battle rites and fought them back with all his strength. He was a whirlwind of death. Each blow found its mark, each strike on target. His weapons flung demonic blood in wide arcs, felling any that came close.

A few short moments passed as the Magnukin made its way into the school field. It approached the mess of ruined demons where Kephas was and threw up its arms. Kephas saw its hulking arms above him and knew he needed to get out of there. He used his weapons like mountaineers climbing pick axes and scrambled his way out of the demons surrounding him.

As he did so the massive arms of the giant demon crushed the whole area. Many demons were driven deep into the ground. A large crater remained. Kephas was breathing hard; somehow he had managed to dodge the lethal attack. But he knew this was a battle he couldn't win. He prayed that the others were working on something.

Kephas stood up on the edge of the crater and started to move away from the Magnukin. Several Scarkin were already upon him raining down numerous strikes with their sharp claws. Kephas struggled to remove them from his back. He skewered one demon with his crucifix and managed to throw another to the ground.

But he was too late. The Magnukin had already lined up another swing of its right arms. Kephas cleared the Scarkin from him just as a giant arm smacked into him. He and a handful of other demons were thrown high into the air. He flew through the air and landed on top of one of the classrooms.

Upon landing he broke his back in eight places. Many of his ribs were broken, with one puncturing his left lung. He suffered multiple breaks in both of his arms. He had massive internal bleeding and a mild case of indigestion. He lost consciousness without delay and began to die.

Deon heard loud thumping on the rooftops around him as he desperately tried to empty the classrooms of people.

"Go now! Everyone to the church," he yelled.

The first ranks of Scarkin scampered between the classrooms sending up screams of terror. Deon and the few other fighters went to their defence. Deon swung his sanctified axe through many demons as he and

Adam battled between classrooms Seven and Eight. This bought valuable time for others to escape to the church.

The Mortkin had now made it into battle and were swatting aside the smaller demons to get their turn at fighting. Only a few strikes into the fight with Deon and Adam, and a large clawed arm had slashed through Adam's throat. Adam dropped his weapon and began to fall to the ground as more blows from the larger demons killed him.

Deon cried out. More demons flooded in behind each demon that was slain. Deon wondered where Kephas was. Deon fought with all he had, desperately trying to keep the demons back. The Magnukin had made it across the field and was shredding the classrooms on the edge of the field so it could continue advancing.

Brother Christopher ran into the school courts behind Deon with many other fighters. Reinforcements had finally arrived.

"Over here!" Brother Christopher yelled, directing his fighters to help Deon.

"Adam is dead," Deon delcared.

"We may not be far behind at this rate. Where is the Bishop?"

"I don't know,"

Another wave of evil crashed into them. The reinforcements proved significant and they carved up many demons. For a moment they felt like they had started to push the demons back.

"That massive one is getting closer, we should pull back," Brother Christopher yelled amidst the din of battle.

Deon nodded and signalled the other fighters. They were just about to make their retreat when Mindy came running up behind them.

"Help! The Bishop is dying," she screamed.

Deon ran to her. "Where?"

"Follow me."

"We'll keep the demons off you," Brother Christopher declared.

Mindy lead them to the classroom where Kephas had landed. They arrived and saw Graham killing a few Scarkin that had slipped past. Deon saw the bishop's broken body laying in a pool of blood on top of the roof. His eyes were closed, one of his hands was still tightly gripping his weapon. His other hand was broken and mangled.

"I've only had time to heal him a little, he's in really bad shape. But there are demons everywhere!"

"We need to get him out of here," Deon said.

"What do we do?" Graham asked.

Deon's mind was panicking. He couldn't think. His heart thumped in his ears. He remembered something Kephas liked to quote.

Psalm 31

²Turn your ear to me,
come quickly to my rescue;
be my rock of refuge,
a strong fortress to save me.
³Since you are my rock and my fortress,
for the sake of your name lead and guide me.
²Turn your ear to me,
come quickly to my rescue;
be my rock of refuge,
a strong fortress to save me.
³Since you are my rock and my fortress,
for the sake of your name lead and guide me.

Deon drew in a deep breath. He noticed the curtains on the inside of the classroom windows and had an idea.

"Okay, help me out," he said confidently.

Deon smashed out the windows with his axe and ripped the curtains out. He then threw them on the ground earning confused looks from the others. Deon climbed up the side of the building and on to the roof next to Kephas.

"Mindy, please heal as we move him. This will hurt."

She nodded and started to pray.

Graham readied himself beneath the edge of the roof. Deon started to roll Kephas' body next to the edge of the roof. He then rolled him off on to the ground. Graham and Brother Christopher did their best to catch him. But it was a painful experience for all involved.

Mindy shrieked as she saw him lowered so crudely. But as more screams rang out around them she was reminded of the need of urgency. Mindy got straight to work healing him as the three men pulled him on to the curtain.

"He's close to death, let me stay here for a bit with him and heal him," Mindy pleaded.

"We have to go now. Trust me. We'll all be dead if we wait for that giant demon to get here," Deon replied.

Mindy nodded and healed what she could while they got ready to drag Kephas away.

"One, two three, go," Deon said as he and Graham pulled Kephas up the path towards the road. Mindy followed close behind with her spear in hand.

A couple of Scarkin jumped off the roof next to them as they made their way through the school. Mindy managed to impale one as it leaped towards Kephas. The other demon inflicted yet more injuries on Graham and Deon before being stabbed by her holy spear. Mindy prayed that she'd have the opportunity to thank Zack for giving her the encouragement she needed to wield a weapon. She prayed that she would live to see him again.

They made it to the school gate. Across the road was the relative safety of the church fence. Between them was a large pack of Mortkin.

"Wait," Brother Christopher called out.

Deon stopped pulling the curtain for a moment and held his weapon tightly. Graham did the same. Deon waited for the fighters that were behind them to show up. They didn't show. Deon knew they must have been killed.

Deon looked at Graham and Mindy. It was the look one gets when he knows he will die. The Mortkin ran across the road towards them from where they were poised outside the church fence. They roared loudly and charged. Just as they did so the largest of them screamed in pain and fell to the ground. Malcolm was standing behind it and pulled his hammer out from its carcass.

"Go! I'll hold them back!" he declared loudly.

Deon nodded thankfully. A few seconds later Malcolm had felled two more Mortkin. His fighting style showed he must have years of martial training before the world fell into darkness.

Graham and Deon grabbed the curtain and dragged Kephas across the road through the fighting. Malcolm sprung to counter every attack that went their way. Mindy managed to gouge a hole in the back of a Mortkin that didn't pay her the focus she deserved. Brother Christopher carved a path through the demons ahead of them. They finally made it through the open church gates.

"Malcolm!" Deon yelled.

He yelled back an acknowledgement and miraculously made it through the demons. He jumped past one demon and rolled between two others and in the gate. The scared people inside slammed it shut after he made it through.

Mindy and others thrust their weapons through the bars, stabbing the demons that got too close. Mindy turned her attention to healing Kephas who lay ground just inside the gate. She closed her eyes and lay her hands on his shoulder.

"He's still alive, just."

There was a combined small sigh of relief. Sandy ran out from the church to meet them.

"I've got as many people as I can fit into the church. We'll be safe there right?"

Brother Christopher and Deon looked at each other. They both thought of the Magnukin.

"No," they said simultaneously.

"Wait, what? What do we do?"

"I don't know," said Brother Christopher.

Kephas spat out a mess of blood. It sounded like he was trying to speak. His eyes were tightly shut and he looked to be in intense pain. Deon dropped to the ground and put his ear close to Kephas' head. Mindy fervently continued to heal him. But he lapsed into a coma.

Deon stood up. "He spoke."

"What did he say?"

"I think it was...'Bee.'"

"Bee? What does that mean?" Sandy asked.

Deon rattled his brain to try and come up with the answer.

"Oh that's it! 'Plan B'!" Deon exclaimed.

Deon explained the prison construction site they had come across earlier.

"How will we get there?" Sandy asked.

"On foot I guess."

"With a demon horde behind us we'll never make it," Brother Christopher said.

There was silence for a moment as everyone tried to come up with a solution. The administration building of the school was torn to pieces by the Magnukin, making a loud destructive noise. This reminded everyone they didn't have time to think.

"That thing is nearly upon us," Sandy said in a panic.

"Half of the fighters stay and fight, the other half of us escort the people to this Citadel you mention," Brother Christopher declared.

Initially there were rumblings of protest as staying and fighting would surely be a death sentence. However, it was soon apparent that if they didn't do something fast they would all be dead.

Brother Christopher continued.

"The demons seem to be strongest on the school side, so let's try and punch through on the furthest side of the church and flee from there. Sandy, please try and get word to all our fighters. Let them choose if they want to stay and fight or escort people out. Have all evacuation team start to clear a way out behind the church. Send all fighters who want to stay to assemble at the church doors."

"Yes Brother Christopher," Sandy said as she ran off to get word around.

"I'm going to stay. I'll buy you time to get the people out." Deon said.

"How will we find this place if you don't come with us?" Brother Christopher asked.

"There is a lady, Michelle. She knows where it is, she can lead you there."

"Okay. Thank you Deon, I look forward to catching up with you for a coffee in Heaven," Brother Christopher said with a smile.

The two men shook hands.

"Sounds good," Deon replied.

Brother Christopher entered the church and a few seconds later he emerged with the procession pole with the crucifix on the top that the priest is lead into the church behind during mass.

"Graham, Mindy will you help me escort the people?" Brother Christopher asked.

"But what about the Bishop? I haven't had time to heal him," Mindy asked.

"I'm sorry, but we can't drag him all the way there, and there won't be enough time to heal him here. Please I'll need both of you with me."

Mindy thought hard.

"It's okay, I'll take care of the Bishop," Deon assured.

Another loud crash signalled the Magnukin had nearly cleared enough buildings to make it over to the church.

"Let's go," Graham said.

Mindy nodded and they followed Brother Christopher as he made his way to the back fence behind the church. People flooded out of the church to follow Brother Christopher. He was like a shephard leading his flock of terrified sheep.

Once they had left, Deon dragged Kephas into the church. He saw sister Paula had remained inside still pouring over the ancient tablet.

"I think we've ran out of time for that thing," Deon said to her.

"Nonsense! This will save us all."

"Really? Have you translated it?" Deon said hopefully.

"Not completely, but there is some really encouraging words I've made out."

Deon's heart sunk again.

"Thank you Sister, but please make your way out while you can."

"No, I'll get this done. Have faith boy," she said smiling.

Deon hoped that he'd be a smiley old person like her. He'd seen too many elderly people who always seemed to have a grumpy look on their face. Sister Paula seemed to always be happy, even at the end of all things. Deon then realized he probably wouldn't live long enough to get old.

He nodded and stood outside the church doors. A few more fighters assembled around him including Jamie and Sandra. Deon took a deep breath. The Magnukin was picking up chunks of buildings it had demolished and throwing them onto the blessed school fence. It then ploughed its way through and made its way across the road. Deon looked up at it in horror.

Mindy was following the others to the back side of the church. She was eager to see if her friends were already there. A team of people had started to remove part of the fence when a pack of demons rushed in.

"Mindy!" Beth called out.

Beth was at the fence line stabbing demons with her twin blades.

"Beth!" Graham rushed towards her slaying demons as he went. Mindy followed behind healing Graham as soon as he suffered injury. A few desperate minutes of fighting later and they had killed enough demons to start evacuating people. Beyond the fence was the back yard of a few houses.

Brother Christopher led the people out between the houses and on to the road. He was kept busy with demons attacking from all sides. Many people were killed with the small numbers of fighters struggling to keep the demons back. They gradually made it up the road with fighters circling around the main group trying desperately to keep as many alive as they could.

...

Meanwhile Zack and James were casually walking around the empty supermarket trying to find all the items on Sandy's list.

"I think that's just about it," James called as he dropped some batteries into the trolley.

"I'll just get some disinfectant and then we'll go," Zack replied.

Zack found what he was looking for after a brief search and dropped it into the trolley as they made their way out. As soon as they were outside Zack didn't feel right. He couldn't identify the cause of the feelings he had.

"Is that smoke?" he pointed to a fresh plume coming from the direction of the school. The tree that Brother Christopher had set alight was still burning.

"Yeah, it's smoke. So what? You've seen the whole damn city is burning as much as I have," James replied.

"Yeah, I know. I just have a bad feeling about it is all," Zac replied.

Zack tried to dismiss it, but the feeling hung around in his mind. They walked back pushing their trolley slowly through the ravaged suburbs.

"I thought we would've seen some demons by now," Zack said.

"Yeah, I was expecting at least a sighting of a few," James replied.

They gradually got closer to the school and approached the boundary of where the school patrols would go. Zack stopped and looked up and down the street. He didn't see any patrols. It was easily possible that they happened to be patrolling down another street. But Zack was concerned.

"What's that noise?" James said holding a hand up to his ear.

Zack strained to listen for something. Then a scream was heard in the distance, faint but distinct. It was coming from the direction of the school. They looked at each other, left their trolley and ran ahead at full speed.

Deon drew smokey air into his lungs. He could now smell the giant demon approaching the feeble church fence. The Magnukin smelt like burnt flesh with a dash of rotting blood. Deon watched as the beast lumbered across the road. Deon held his sanctified axe tightly in his hands. He couldn't think how he could kill a demon of that size when even Kephas had failed.

The Magnukin drove its huge clawed hands into the rubble left from the school administration building. It then hurled it at the church fence.

"Take cover!" Deon yelled as he dove to the ground. The air was filled with flying debris and broken fence fragments. Jamie was hit in the head by a large chunk of metal that bowled him over.

The Magnukin roared as demons charged into the church grounds.

"Get up! Fight for your very lives!" Deon screamed.

The few fighters left scrambled to their feet as the first wave of demons crashed into them. The fighting was brutal. They quickly lost ground against the demons. The air was permeated in a sound Deon didn't expect: singing. The people who had chosen to remain in the church were singing the holy words of a hymn.

Deon felt somehow rejuvenated by the sound. He kept fighting with increased vigour. The demons close to the church started to steam and sizzle as if they had been sprayed with boiling water.

"Die you damned creatures!" Malcolm yelled as he cleaved his way through numerous Mortkin.

A flicker of hope ran through Deon's heart. Then the lung trembling roar of the Magnukin drowned out the singing. The battle quickly turned back to the demons favour. The massive demon picked up a small car left on the road and held it high and prepared to throw it.

Inside the church Sister Paula was pouring over the ancient tablet. She had nearly understood what the Holy words meant. She mouthed words beneath her breath but was stuck on the final verse.

The Magnukin threw the car with its immense strength into the church. It smashed into the church roof sending tiles and bricks flying in all directions. The church remained standing but there was now a large hole in the roof. Debris rained down on those inside the church killing many and permanently silencing the singing.

Sister Paula lay bleeding on the floor with a beam from the roof crushing both of her legs. She saw a pool of her blood leak out from underneath the debris. With the sight of her blood she finally understood the last words of the Holy tablet. She closed her eyes, clasped her hands and poured her last breaths into the Holy prayer with everything she had left. Outside the Magnukin had picked up a large truck to finish off those left alive in the church.

Zack and James rounded the corner of the road that the church and school were on. Zack nearly fell over in shock. His eyes soaked in the horrific details. He saw the enormous demon standing in the street holding a truck over its head. Dead bodies and demons were everywhere. The school had been utterly obliterated. He saw the church fence was down and demons were fighting at the church doors. He was lost for words. He felt saturated with the guilt that he had failed. He dropped to his knees.

"God, please!"

The last words of Sister Paula's prayer left her lips. Then she coughed quietly and died. Deon and Malcolm were the only ones left alive from the fighters who chose to stay. Deon saw the truck sail through the air. He knew he was moments away from death.

A glorious bright light shone all around. Everyone had to try and shield their eyes. A huge gust of wind blasted the entire area. A Holy

Angel from Heaven had appeared from nowhere. It was covered in blue and white holy fire. Beneath its radiant glow it resembled a human with large wings, similar to how Angels were depicted in old paintings. It was gigantic in size, slightly taller than the Magnukin as it wasn't hunched over as the demon was.

Zack somehow knew within himself that this creature was an Angel. It wasn't the fluffy white winged timid creature he had seen in the movies. This was a hardened soldier. It looked like moments ago it had been fighting, with marks over its body that could've been injuries. It held something in its right hand that Zack could only think to describe as a sword made from lightning. In his left hand it held the truck that the Magnukin had thrown at the church. The Angel had somehow caught it mid-air.

The Magnukin roared at the Angel, and then charged towards it. The Angel threw the truck into the hordes of smaller demons at its feet then spread its glorious wings and rose slightly above the ground. It shouted some holy words that Zack couldn't comprehend. Whatever they were, it caused the majority of Scarkin and some Mortkin to detonate like they had explosives inside their heads. The Angel flew straight towards the Magnukin with its sword held outwards. The two giant creatures clashed in a titanic struggle. Zack could only look on in awe.

The Angel swung its mighty blade and severed the Magnukin's right arm. Before the demon had time to react, the Angel spun around and decapitated the giant foe. Zack's eyes were struggling to keep up with how fast the Angel moved. The Angel jumped over the Magnukin's headless body, slicing through its spine as it did so. It landed behind the Magnukin and stabbed its sword into the fallen demon's head that was rolling on the ground. It exploded in a massive spray of muck and gore.

Zack covered his face just in time before all around them was dosed in demon remains. Zack looked back and saw the Angel had disappeared as quickly as it had arrived. The Magnukin's body slumped to the ground and started to slowly rot away.

"Now is our chance!" James yelled.

Zack ran with James towards the church. The demons that remained seemed dazed. Zack and James felled several Mortkin as they ran across the road towards the church.

"Deon!" Zack yelled as they approached.

Deon killed the final demon that was at the church doors.

He waved back still a little bewildered that he was still alive.

"I never thought I'd live to see an Angel of the God fighting right in front of me," Malcolm said in disbelief.

"Astounding!" Deon exclaimed.

The church door burst open and Sandy rushed out. She had blood over her top and a deep cut on her head.

"Help, the roof is coming down!"

They followed her inside the church. It looked like a war zone, with debris, bodies and blood everywhere.

They tried to pull as many people out of the wreckage as they could. Zack saw Winston and Sister Paula had died. He then saw Kephas lying on the floor not moving.

"What happened to the Bishop?" he cried.

"That big demon happened," Deon replied.

"Help me lift this," Malcolm called.

He and Zack lifted a broken pew off Denise.

A large chunk of tiles and wood fell from the church roof and landed with a crash. Luckily it didn't land directly on anyone that was still alive.

"We gotta get out of here!" Sandy yelled.

They risked a few more minutes to get the rest of the survivors out and then sat down on the grass outside the church.

"We can't stay here," Sandy decided.

"I agree, the demons will be back soon," Malcolm added.

"Where did everyone else go?" Zack asked looking around fearing they were dead.

"Most escaped to somewhere out of town," Malcolm replied.

Zack looked to Kephas but he was still unconscious. Then Deon came around the corner of the church pushing a wheelbarrow.

"We have to get to the Citadel," Deon said, using the word coined earlier. Deon thought it sounded much safer than a rural, partially complete prison complex.

Deon continued: "There is no point in staying here. Come on, help me lift him."

Malcolm walked over to Deon and helped him lift Kephas into the wheelbarrow.

"Let's spend a minute to gather what we can, then let's go," Deon said.

Zack looked around for something worth carrying. He saw Mindy's yellow ribbon, which she always kept in her hair lying on the ground. He ran over and picked it up. There was a little blood on one of the ends. The others around him quickly gathered any supplies they could find. Thoughts of Mindy being hurt or killed filled Zack's mind, rendering him useless. He couldn't bear to think that they had literally gone through Hell and he still hadn't told her how he felt about her.

"Demons!" James yelled.

Zack stuffed the ribbon into his pocket and looked where James was pointing. On the far side of the road a large horde of demons emerged from the smoke and debris.

"Follow me!" Deon called.

The survivors filed out the back of the church through the hole in the fence that the previous group had made. Deon pushed Kephas in the wheelbarrow leading the way. They moved as quickly as they could, but in their weary state this was not very fast.

Zack swallowed the lump in his throat as he saw numerous bodies on the side of the road. He recognized David's dead body still clutching his pickaxe. They made their way along the road constantly looking behind them to see if the demons were following.

A few moments passed and Zack thought for a second they had got away safely. Then a swarm of Scarkin poured through the fence followed by many Mortkin.

"We have to move faster!" Malcolm called. The survivors' pace quickened but it was clear that they would not be able to out-run the demons.

Zack thought of all those who had died for him thus far. He thought about Matthew and Tom. He admitted there were many other fighters he didn't even know by name. Zack thought of his friends. He knew that he had to do something. He now understood the look in Tom's eyes when he made a similar decision. Zack stopped running. James stopped too.

"What are you doing?" James asked.

Zack turned around to face the oncoming demons. He held up his blessed shield and knife.

"I'm going to hold this evil back if it's the last thing I do," he declared.

James stared into Zack's face trying to confirm his fortitude.

"I'll stand with you. You can't do this alone," James said adamantly.

He stood next to Zack and turned to face their approaching enemy.

"What's going on?" Malcolm called back.

"We've got this. Hurry and help the others escape," Zack yelled.

Malcolm looked back at the size of the demon horde. He understood what they were doing.

"I'll make sure they make it out safe," he assured.

The first of the Scarkin were now getting close.

"Thanks for everything, James."

"Yeah, you too Zack."

Zack tried to think of some inspiring Bible verse, but his mind was blank. James looked at Zack, who nodded back at him. They understood each other.

They both started running towards the demons. They yelled a battle-cry at the top of their lungs as they crashed into the demon horde. James swung his blessed axe with all his strength, lopping off demon limb and head alike. Zack used his shield to shoulder-charge deep into the demonic ranks. The Holy writings on it loosed multiple pained screams. He furiously stabbed his blessed knife in every direction; with each thrust he punctured another evil creature. They held their own against the Scarkin, only suffering the occasional slice.

However the longer the battle continued the more demons arrived. The first of the Mortkin now entered the fray.

"Watch it," Zack called as he saw the bigger demons approaching.

James nodded and continued to hack away at the demons. Zack was finding he had less and less room around him as more demons closed in. He was quickly getting surrounded and caught several slashes across his back. He struggled to fight his way closer to James. Soon they were fighting back-to-back, hopelessly surrounded by tightly packed demons. Many Mortkin now filled their ranks.

The seriousness of the situation was not lost on Zack. He was still resolute in his decision to fight to allow the others to escape. But staring death in its snarling face everything seemed quite different. Zack had thought perhaps they could kill all the demons if they were really lucky. But between slashes and dodging incoming attacks he saw that even more demons were making their way down the road.

Zack thought of his friends. He kept fighting with all he had. More and more demons fell to their hands. The ground became slick with demonic muck. They were now surrounded in a wall of large Mortkin demons, with the Scarkin either killed or squeezed out by their larger kin.

A sharp cry escaped James' lungs as a Mortkin's attack cut deep into his shoulder. Zack turned and tried to help the best he could but the blows did not stop raining down on him either. James swung his axe furiously, but it gradually lost speed. A Mortkin thrust its spiked arm into the James' back and he dropped to the ground dead. Zack heard the telling noise and spun around to see his friend die.

"No!" Zack screamed.

He became charged with a fury and killed demons with dizzying pace. However, being surrounded by demons one can only last so long. A Mortkin's thrust got past Zack's shield and pierced his chest.

He fell.

CHAPTER 9

THE LIAR

Deon pushed the wheelbarrow with Kephas' unconscious body down the broken road as quickly as he could. He was getting tired. He knew it was still a very long way to the Citadel.

"I haven't seen any more demons behind us," Malcolm called as he ran up from the back of the group.

"I guess those two are keeping them busy. Long may it last," Deon replied.

Deon tried to think about what he could say about Zack and James getting out alive. But he couldn't think of how they could. Malcolm looked at Deon. From the look on his face Deon could tell he was thinking the same.

"Here, let me take a shift on the barrow," said Malcolm.

"Thanks Malcolm, that'd be great," Deon replied.

Malcolm pushed the wheelbarrow and Deon went ahead of him with his axe ready.

They continued through the suburbs without any demons in sight for an hour or so. Then a familiar howl cut the air.

"Everyone, stay close!" Deon called.

The group drew closer together and quickened their pace. It was unclear what direction the demons would be coming from. More howls came from other directions in quick succession.

Deon closed his eyes and prayed.

"God almighty, please help us. Help me get these people to safety."

Deon opened his eyes and hoped that another Angel would appear. Instead Deon found his eyes drawn towards a sign on the side of the road. It read 'Central Middle School'.

Deon thought of an idea.

"Everyone, follow me," he called.

They made their way as quick as they could down the short driveway to the school car park. They came to a stop and Deon frantically looked around. Just as people were starting to get nervous, Deon signalled them to follow him once more.

"Everyone in," Deon pointed to a school bus parked at the back of the car park.

He jumped on and wondered how difficult it would be to hotwire a bus. Deon looked at the ignition and his face lit up in a big grin. The keys were in it. There was even petrol in the fuel tank.

"Thank you God," he prayed silently.

Deon sat in the driver's seat and started the engine. The bus roared into life. Deon heard more demonic howls nearby.

"Hurry hurry!" Sandy pleaded.

Malcolm picked up Kephas and climbed into the bus behind everyone else. He lay Kephas down on the last spare seat. The bus was packed with people.

"Let's go," Malcolm said.

Deon pulled out of the car park just as a pack of Scarkin made their way down over the roof of the neighboring building.

They drove out onto the road. Deon did his best to avoid the major holes in the road and abandoned vehicles.

"Hold on!" he yelled as he smashed aside a small car blocking the road. He drove on the footpath until he made it to the end of the street. The bus collected several letterboxes and destroyed a few fences, but they made it through.

After they cleared the suburbs he had much easier drive, only occasionally needing to go off-road. Deon let out a big sigh of relief when he saw the road sign that the Citadel was on.

...

It was a bright sunny Monday morning and Zack was sitting at home, watching television. His mobile phone rang. He answered it.

"Yeah?"

A familiar voice was on the other end. It was Zack's boss Stanley.

"Hey Zack, you are going to owe me big time. I got you that shift you wanted."

"Serious? Oh Stanley you're a star. Thank you!"

"Yeah I'm great. Just don't let me down Ok. Be here as soon as possible."

"I've got this. Sure, see you soon. Thanks again."

Zack felt this was going to be a good week.

He was wrong.

Zack stood up and turned off the television. He walked into his room and found his uniform in his closet. He pulled out the dull grey shirt with the 'Gold Star Security Services' emblem on it. He put it on, followed by his black work pants. Zack had been trying to get a shift in the bank security division of his company for months. When he was first hired he enjoyed his role as a security guard, but it didn't take many weeks for boredom to set in.

Some of his friends had always known what they wanted to do after they finished high school. Some went to university, others had jobs lined up already. Zack had no idea. The school guidance councillor was of no help to Zack. When school finished he lived with his parents for a few months tidying up the place. This typically consisted of an hour or so of cleaning or painting the roof. Afterwards he'd spend time with his friends or watch television for the rest of the day.

Both he and his parents were keen for him to find something else to do. So when Zack saw the glossy advertisement for a job with Gold Star Security Services he applied. He wasn't expecting to be offered the job, but was glad he was. A few weeks later he moved into a small flat with his best friend Graham. He really enjoyed the freedom of being out from under his parent's wings. He also was more than happy to spend all of his earnings each week on whatever he felt the need to.

Yet inside, Zack felt there must be some other deeper purpose for his life. He just didn't know what. He even read a motivational book or two, yet he didn't feel any different afterwards. Zack would just live day to day and not ponder anything too deeply. He avoided staying up with current affairs and news, as he felt helpless to change what was going on.

Zack walked into the bathroom and looked at himself in the mirror.

"Maybe this bank security will be my thing," he said.

He thought for a few moments about that. Then he hoped that wasn't true. He felt like he was destined for something big. Maybe even become famous. He still didn't know how though.

He shrugged it off.

Zack quickly made some toast for breakfast and walked out the front door after he finished eating. The blazing sun shone into his eyes as soon as he stepped outside. He remembered there was some report on the news about an increase in UV radiation over the past few years. But Zack didn't remember or care about the details. He put on his sunglasses and walked to the bus stop down the far end of his street. He amused himself with his mobile phone while he waited for the bus to arrive. It arrived late.

"Just what I need today," he thought to himself.

After a short bus trip he arrived at his stop. He hopped off and ran down the road to the Gold Star Security Services offices. They had a large office building and warehouse on the edge of town. The building was modern and very expensive looking. It was only a year old and had won an architectural award. They had armed guards on patrol constantly. The nice building was probably the major factor that lead Zack to apply for the job. Unfortunately for him he was rarely on-site. He'd often be on the far side of town guarding industrial warehouses.

"You're late Zack!" Stanley yelled from the garages.

"Sorry, the bus…"

"Yeah, yeah get in."

Stanley was sitting in one of the many company armoured trucks. He was a large balding man with a small but well manicured beard. Stanley wore the same uniform as Zack but he actually ironed his. The truck was black and dull grey with a large gold star on the side. Zack ran across the parking lot and jumped in the passenger side.

"Don't make me regret this boy," Stanley snapped.

"I won't. If we leave now we can make the pick-up in plenty of time," Zack said.

Stanley just looked at him.

"Sorry."

"Okay, let's get this done."

Stanley backed up the sturdy vehicle and drove down the road towards the first bank scheduled for pick-up. Brakenside banks would regularly send transfers to their larger branches in the nearby large city of Doverton. Today was one such collection day.

Zack had heard from other staff that these shifts were amongst the best you could get. Bank shifts entailed spending a good portion of time in a near-new air-conditioned vehicle driving around town. Zack drew in a deep breath in through his nose. It still had the faint scent of new-car smell.

Gold Star had recently bought more armoured trucks when they won all of the bank contracts for Brakenside. The trucks had only been on-line a few months and were well cared for by staff.

"So do I get to carry a gun too?" Zack said as he looked at Stanley's holstered pistol. Zack was currently only permitted to carry pepper spray and a baton. Neither of which he had reason or desire to use.

"No. Get your safety procedures manual signed off like everyone else first. Afterwards we can look at getting you on the next set of drills."

Zack remembered the intimidatingly thick safety manual he still hadn't gotten around to reading. Zack rolled his eyes.

"How about just for today?" Zack said with a pleading smile.

"Nope."

"Can't blame me for trying," Zack replied.

"I guess. Listen Zack, I want you to pay close attention to what I do today. If you do just as I do, in few months you could get regular rostered shifts."

"I understand," Zack said.

Stanley nodded and turned on the radio. It played some old-fashioned music that Zack didn't know or like. Zack looked out the window. He looked up into the bright blue sky, peppered with small fluffy white clouds. He started to daydream.

A short drive later and they approached their first stop. Zack looked at their schedule; the first entry of the five was 'Douglas & Douglas Bank'. The truck came to a stop directly outside the bank.

"Okay just remember to act like a professional."

"Yes, I got this," Zack said assuredly.

Zack climbed out of the truck and walked to the back of the truck to help Stanley with the money trolley. Zack pushed the empty trolley around towards the front of the bank. Stanley locked the truck rear doors behind him.

Zack looked up to see a man outside the bank. He wore a white scruffy T-shirt and blue jeans. His hair was brown and wild and he was carrying a rifle. He wore a crazed look on his face. Zack's body flooded with adrenaline. He froze. The man looked Zack in the eyes. Zack looked back at him. The gunman then aimed his rifle at Zack and fired.

The bullet drove through Zacks chest and knocked him over backwards. The concrete bit down hard into the back of Zack's head. His chest erupted in pain. Zack spat a fountain of blood out of his mouth. His eyes closed.

Zack jumped up off the ground like he had just awoken from a deep sleep. It took him a moment recognise his surroundings. He didn't seem to notice his injuries. Stanley was screaming at him from behind. The gunman grabbed a lady frozen in panic next to her expensive-looking car. She wore a black business dress. The lady had long, black hair neatly tied back in a ponytail and was clutching a bright red handbag like her life depended on it.

"Give me your keys!" the gunman screamed. His voice was strained and hoarse. He grabbed her hair and tried to get her handbag.

A vengeful anger rose up inside Zack. Zack knew this man was everything wrong with the world. He was worse than scum. The gunman got frustrated with the lady and aimed his rifle at her.

"Eat dirt!" Zack suddenly blurted out as loud as he could. Zack charged at the gunman in a fury. The gunman was taken by complete surprise that Zack had managed to stand after taking a bullet, let alone attack him.

Zack closed the gap between them quickly as he sprinted at him. The gunman raised his weapon just as Zack grabbed the barrel and pointed it to the sky. The rifle fired.

The two men exchanged a series of punches as they fought. Zack saw his foe up close. He had unkempt facial hair and bloodshot eyes. Zack thought he must be a drug addict. The rifle discharged several more rounds randomly into the surroundings.

"Zack! Get out of the way!" Stanley yelled.

Stanley had his pistol trained on the gunman but hadn't yet taken a shot for fear of hitting Zack. The gunman landed a punch into Zack's stomach. Zack couldn't help but loosen his grip on the rifle slightly as he struggled to stay standing. That opportunity was all the gunman needed. He aimed the rifle at Stanley and pulled the trigger. The bullet smashed into Stanley's head. He was dead before he hit the ground. The lady at her car screamed even louder and cowered on the floor.

Zack saw Stanley fall and became even more filled with rage. Zack spat blood into the gunman's face and followed up with multiple head butts. The gunman's nose started to bleed profusely. Zack's head would've been hurting if he didn't feel numb all over. Zack managed to land an elbow to the gunman's face. The gunman yelled some profanity and punched Zack again in the stomach. This time Zack was determined to retain his grip. They spun around as they struggled with more bullets flying in all directions.

Zack stepped backwards slightly, bringing the gunman off balance. He followed up with an uppercut to the gunman's jaw. Zack could hear his foe's teeth breaking. Zack grabbed the rifle and aimed it at the gunman's head and pulled the trigger. The gunman managed to land a desperate kick just as the rifle fired. This caused the shot narrowly miss his head, pierce his right ear and fly off towards the supermarket behind the gunman.

Zack trained the rifle again to his head and pulled the trigger. The rifle made a distinctive clicking sound. Zack pulled the trigger several more times before he realized what was happening. The gunman stood to continue his attacks. Zack smashed the rifle butt into his foe's face.

The impact knocked him back to the ground. Zack dropped the rifle and set upon him with a flurry of punches. The gunman's jaw broke in three places and he fell into unconsciousness. Police sirens slowly increased in volume as they approached.

Zack stood over him for a moment, breathing heavily. His bloodied fists were quivering.

"You saved me!" the lady called to Zack.

He turned to face her.

She gasped at the sight of him. Zack looked down. He saw he was drenched in blood. He had a large gunshot wound in his chest. The injury looked fatal. The numbness he had enjoyed lapsed and he lost consciousness.

What felt like a few days later, Zack awoke in hospital. Pain coursed through his entire body. He felt like he had been run over by a steamroller. He could hear hospital sounds around him and some people talking. He tried to open his eyes. They seemed fused shut. At last he opened his heavy, swollen eyes and light rushed in. He squinted.

Zack could see Graham and Beth playing a board game on the small table on the far side of the room. They hadn't noticed he was awake yet. Zack tried to talk but his mouth felt horribly dry. He gagged on the tubes going into his nose and mouth. He coughed and spluttered. Graham and Beth spun around.

"He's awake!" Graham exclaimed.

"I'll get the nurse," said Beth.

Graham rushed over to his side.

"Are you okay buddy? You gave us all such a scare! We thought you were a goner," Graham smiled. But Zack could tell he was stressed out.

Zack tried to talk again but couldn't manage it.

"Hey, slowly does it man. You're supposed to be in a coma. Don't try to talk just yet. Take it easy."

"Stanley?" Zack asked.

Graham shook his head.

Zack's heart sunk.

Beth came back into the room followed by a nurse. She examined Zack and had a surprised look stuck on her face.

"Everything looks okay. You are such a lucky young man. The doctors couldn't understand how you managed to still be alive after losing so much blood and suffering such serious injuries."

Zack looked down at his chest. He very slowly raised a weak hand onto his chest and felt the sting of a line of stitches down his chest.

"Sorry, I never paid attention in biology," Zack said in a quiet and raspy voice.

Everyone laughed.

They talked for a few minutes, then Zack showed signs of getting tired.

"Rest up Zack, we'll talk again soon," Graham said.

Zack nodded, closed his eyes and lapsed into unconsciousness again.

Zack awoke the next day when he heard talking in his room. He opened his eyes and saw a policewoman talking to the nurse.

"He really needs to rest," the nurse insisted.

"I understand that but I need to get his statement as soon as possible."

Zack spoke up. "It's okay, I can talk."

The policewoman and nurse exchanged looks. The nurse nodded then left the room.

"Hi, I'm Sergeant Wilson from the Brakenside Police Department. I'm here to get your statements on the events of Tuesday the 15th of March. And to be honest, to thank you."

"Oh?" Zack said quietly.

"Yes, we've already collected eye witness statements that are all in agreement about what happened that morning. This visit is more of a formality."

"Okay..."

"Mrs Featherston has asked me personally to pass on her thanks and asked if she could visit."

"Sorry, who?"

"Mrs Featherston was the lady you saved that morning."

Zack nodded.

"Sure, she can visit."

"Thanks, but I'm getting off topic. Let's discuss the events as you remember them."

Zack told the Sgt Wilson all about that morning and she took notes.

"That's all I need, thank you. And just between you and me I expect you'll get a visit from the mayor too. You're a hero!"

"Cool, do I get some solid food?"

She smiled.

"Sure you can."

She stood up to leave.

"Did you catch him?"

"Oh sorry, I thought you knew. Yes, Mr Jones will be spending the rest of his life in prison for two counts of murder."

"Two?"

"Yes, your co-worker Stanley McGregor died at the scene. But also Eric Peterson died from gunshot in the supermarket across the road from the bank. The bullet matched Mr Jones' rifle. It seems he was just unlucky."

Zack was filled with guilt.

"I see," Zack said in a tiny voice.

Zack distinctly remembered firing the shot at the gunman's head that went through his ear. Zack now remembered the supermarket was behind his target. Zack was responsible for Eric's death. Zack went pale.

"I can see you need a rest. Take it easy Hero."

Zack couldn't manage to say anything. He struggled with himself whether he should admit to firing the bullet that killed Eric. But before he could decide, Sgt Wilson had closed the door behind her as she left.

Zack lay in his bed weeping. After many hours he finally fell asleep.

He awoke again to see Mrs Featherston smiling through a narrowly opened door.

"Can I pop in?" she asked.

Zack blinked his eyes and nodded.

"I really just wanted to personally come and thank you for saving my life. I'd be dead without you."

"Sure thing," Zack replied.

"If there is anything I can do to help just let me know."

"I don't need anything, but Stanley's family might."

"Oh yes, I've been to see the McGregors. I'll make sure they are looked after."

"Thanks."

"This whole thing is just a tragedy really. I heard that this Henry Jones fellow lost all his savings due to a banking system error. He has a terminally ill wife. Agnes was her name, I think. When he tried to make a withdrawal for payment of her treatment, the bank said he'd already spent the money. He just flipped. I heard that the bank later admitted fault."

"Oh really?"

Zack had found it so easy to hate the gunman. He didn't think about whether he had family or not. Zack felt more and more responsible for the deaths of that day.

"I think I need to rest," he said weakly.

"Yes, the fact that you are recovering from that wound is amazing. You're just amazing all around! Thanks again."

Zack forced a smile. He closed his eyes. He just wanted all of this to go away.

Zack stayed in hospital for what felt like months. Zack missed the funerals for both Stanley and Eric. Eventually he returned to work. He forced himself through a ceremony where the Mayor gave him a medal. For a while people stopped him in the street to congratulate him. Zack hated it all. Zack told no one of the truth that he had killed Eric.

Graham told Zack of a boat trip that he was setting up as a holiday for the four friends, Graham, Beth, Mindy and Zack.

Zack was looking forward to it.

...

Zack awoke with the foul aftertaste of sin in his soul. He lay on his back amongst a pile of demon remains. He wasn't dead like he expected. There wasn't a horde of demons standing around him. He wondered what happened as he spat out some blood.

Zack grabbed his chest where he remembered getting stabbed. He pulled up his shirt to see a painful but shallow wound. He saw the scar on his chest from the gunshot he received from the gunman at the bank. He ground his teeth. Zack gulped down the lump in his throat. He decided it was finally time to admit he killed Eric.

"God, I am sorry. I killed Eric. It was all my fault," he prayed loudly. Zack successfully remembered some Bible verse that he had been trying to memorise.

Psalm 51

[1] Have mercy on me, O God,
according to your unfailing love;
according to your great compassion
blot out my transgressions.
[2] Wash away all my iniquity
and cleanse me from my sin.

Zack closed his eyes and drew in a deep breath. For the first time in a long time he felt alright in his own skin. He looked up at the gloomy sky. Zack thought about what he'd do next and realized he didn't know where the Citadel was.

"God, what do I do know?" he asked, looking up at the sky.

"Zack!?" A voice called from nearby.

Zack sat bolt upright and looked around for God. He didn't see God, he saw a man. It was Ronald.

"What are you doing laying in the filthy street?" Ronald asked with a smile.

"Come join me, the water is fine." Zack splashed around in the demon sludge like he was swimming.

They both laughed.

"How did you find me? Where have you been?" Zack asked.

"I could ask you the same questions."

Zack noticed the assault rifle Ronald was carrying.

"Nice hardware."

"Oh, yeah thanks. I found it on a dead soldier. I thought about what Brother Christopher had told us and I scratched the word 'Jesus' into each bullet. It drops demons quick smart. However I think I only have a couple of bullets left after felling that lot."

Ronald pointed to the demon remains Zack was sitting in.

"Oh, did you save me?"

"You must have really hit your head hard. Did you not hear the gunfire?"

"No? I guess you're right."

Zack felt the back of his head. His hair was matted down with blood.

Zack stood up and rushed across to James' body. He looked very dead. Ronald walked over to him.

"I'm sorry for your loss."

Zack gently closed James' eyes.

"We can't leave him in the middle of the street. Help me lift him."

Ronald bent over to help Zack lift but couldn't think of where they would put him. They carried James to the side of the road and lay him down underneath a tree.

"I guess that's better. Do you know any words we should say?" Zack asked.

"I'll try. Dear Lord God. Please look after our friend James. Help him get to heaven. Amen." Ronald prayed.

"Amen. Thanks Ronald. Here, you take his axe; he would've wanted you to have it."

Ronald took it and looked over it in his hands.

"Wow, this thing looks like it's done some miles. Etched holy words too."

"Yeah. Have you got base or something Ronald?"

"No, I was on my way to come to your church, the one Brother Christopher told us about."

"Sorry, that's been destroyed, we only just made it out alive."

"Oh crap. Where to then?"

"Most of us have gone to this defendable place in some rural area. I heard it called the Citadel. But I don't know where it is."

"Ok, that sounds good. What sort of place is it?"

"A prison that's still being built, I think."

"Oh, the one on Boundary Road?"

"You know where it is?"

"Yes. It backs on to my friend's farm."

"Fantastic news! Let's go," Zack said happily.

"Sorry to bust your bubble kid, but it's a long way from here. I don't think walking is going to cut it. And I'm sure this axe and your knife is good, but if we meet another big pack of demons we're done for."

Zack thought hard for a moment.

"Let's go to Gold Star. It's got guns and armoured trucks we can use."

"Where?"

"It's the security place I used to work at; it's not too far from here."

Zack pointed the general direction.

"Okay that's the opposite way we need to go, but like you say, if we can get supplies there it'll be worth it."

They started walking at a quick pace towards Gold Star Security Services. Zack looked back at James' body. He promised himself that when all this business with demons was finished he'd come back and bury his friend.

He never did.

Ronald and Zack made their way through town. As they got closer to the Brakenside city centre they slowed to a stealthy pace. Zack felt exposed. They approached the older part of town and there was a long street filled with shops. In the centre of the road was a large pack of Mortkin.

"Wait up," Zack cautioned.

Ronald looked around as they stood by a tree at the far end of the street. Zack tried to think of a way past them. The street had signage and awnings over each shop for almost the whole way along.

"I think we could use the rooftops and those shop front overhangs to get over without them noticing."

"Okay, fine. There are more demons coming up the road behind us," Ronald said in a hushed voice.

They made a stealthy dash towards the back of the first shop on the street. Zack used a rubbish bin to climb on to the small storage room then made his way on to the roof. Ronald tossed Zack his axe and rifle and then carefully followed him up. They cautiously crept across the roof and made their way along.

More than once the roof would creak and buckle beneath their weight. Ronald hushed Zack frantically and told him to only walk on the riveting of the roof. Luckily no demon had heard them.

They had made good progress across the shop rooftops until they reached a large office building in their path. Zack had thought they'd just be able to climb up like they had previously done. But it seemed like this office building had graffiti problems in the past and had lined their walls and windows with barbed wire.

Zack tried to pull some of the wire down, but it was not like in the action movies he'd seen. He just cut his hand. Since they couldn't ascend, they had to drop down to be able to continue. Zack's initial plan was to move over the shopfront overhangs, but it looked too close to the demons for his liking now.

Zack pointed to Ronald their path forward. They were now close enough to the pack of Mortkin they had seen earlier they didn't want to risk talking. Occasionally Zack would hear a snapping of demon jaws or the sound of them moving around. He didn't want to peak to confirm, but they felt dangerously close.

Zack dropped to his hands and knees and slowly lowered himself down onto the shop overhang. He kept as far away from the edge as he could. Once he was down he waited for Ronald. Upon seeing him make it down Zack let a sigh of relief slip from his mouth. A flurry of activity was then heard on the ground level beneath them. Zack pressed his face flat onto the dirty metal. More grunting and movement sounds came from below him.

Zack tried to slow his panicked breathing. He could smell the demons now; they reeked of rot and blood. Zack closed his eyes, he wanted to be as small as possible. He waited. The first few minutes slowly dragged past. After ten minutes the movements from below seemed to quiet down. Zack tried to slowly drag his body over the roof. The roof creaked. It generated another eruption of grunting from beneath Zack. He gripped his knife and waited for the demons to attack.

The two men remained stationary for hours before the demons below them started to move away. Zack's leg had gone to sleep but he dared not try to move it. Zack heard the demons move away. He waited another ten minutes then slowly raised his head. Ronald gave him the thumbs up signal. Zack crawled across the overhang and onto the next one. Ronald followed close behind.

They made their way across until they reached the end of the street. Upon reaching the last shop in the block Zack turned to Ronald and risked talking.

"I think they're gone, shall we drop to ground level?" Zack said in a quiet voice.

Ronald nodded.

Zack made his way to the edge of the overhang and lowered himself down. He dropped to the ground with a thud. Ronald dropped his axe and rifle down to Zack and lowered himself down too. As he did so a piece of the awning broke and dropped to the ground with a loud crash.

"Go!" Zack yelled.

They sprinted between the buildings ahead of them and around the corner of the street. They continued running until they were completely out of breath. Zack dropped into a bush at the side of the road. Ronald joined him shortly afterwards. They both sat there catching their breath, thankful they had so narrowly escaped the demons.

After a few minutes rest Zack peeked out of the bush. He looked in every direction.

"All clear," he announced.

"Thank God," Ronald said sincerly as Zack pulled him to his feet.

"Just a long walk down these few roads and we should be there," Zack said.

"Let's get going," Ronald replied.

After a while they turned into the road, which their destination was on. They came around the corner casually as they had not seen any demons in a long time. Zack kicked a stone and it skipped down the road past an alleyway. It stopped at the feet of a pack of demons. Half a dozen Scarkin and a few Mortkin emerged just a short distance away. The closest demon hissed at him. All the others demons turned and charged.

Zack drew in a deep breath. Gunfire erupted from behind him as Ronald emptied the rest of his magazine into the demons. It ended all too quickly. However it did drop one of the Mortkin. Zack readied his shield and swatted one of the attacking Scarkin. He made a series of quick stabs into the Mortkin's side before dodging away. A Scarkin landed a deep cut on Zack's right leg and he dropped to a knee. He raised his shield just in time, blocking a heavy blow of the dying Mortkin.

Ronald swung his axe into it from behind, severing its head. The remaining Scarkin were soon dead but not before they dished out a few minor injuries.

Zack and Ronald caught their breath. Zack pulled some packing tape from his bag to dress their wounds. Ronald tore his shirt to make some makeshift bandages. Zack was reminded how easily he could die in the current times. He gulped down the fear rising in his throat.

"I killed him," Zack said.

Ronald looked over with an annoyed expression. "Yeah, I killed a few too."

"No, I killed a man. Eric Peterson was his name."

Zack felt some relief that he had managed to admit it aloud before he died, even if it was just to a confused Ronald.

"What are you talking about?"

Zack told Ronald all about the events at the bank and how he hadn't told the truth until now.

"I see," Ronald said as he thought.

Ronald was quiet for an awkwardly long time. Zack started to get nervous.

"Well?" Zack asked.

"Well what?"

"Aren't going to say anything?"

"Good on you for owning up kid, but killing someone is serious. You are going to need to do more than just tell some random guy who didn't even know about it. You need to talk to the Bishop and your friends about it at the very least."

"Oh sure, yes I plan to."

"Okay, good. Let's go."

A short time later they walked up the driveway of Gold Star Security Services. The building had managed to escape the earthquake relatively undamaged. Many windows were broken and a few cracks weaved up some of the walls. Otherwise it looked intact.

"Wow, nice place. You worked here?"

"Yeah, but mostly I was at other locations."

The front glass doors had been smashed. They walked in with broken glass crunching beneath their shoes. They looked around the lobby to see someone else had already looted the place. There was lots of deliberate damage inside.

"I hope there is something left," Ronald said.

"I'm pretty confident there will be," Zack said as he hoped this trip in the wrong direction was worthwhile.

They walked down the hallway and opened the door that lead to the armoury. A steel door blocked their way with a metal keypad on the wall next to it. The door seemed to have weathered a beating. There was a broken hammer on the floor. The walls around the door were also damaged.

"Looks like someone tried pretty hard to get in. How do you plan to get past where they obviously failed?" Ronald asked.

"Like this."

Zack entered seven digits into the keypad and a faint click was heard. Zack pulled the heavy door open.

Ronald looked surprised.

"I remember they explained to us on our induction course, our electronic locks have backups for backups and will keep working long after a power cut."

Ronald smiled as he nodded.

They walked in to the armoury. There were locked racks of various firearms on the walls. Locked cabinets were filled with all sorts of ammunition. Zack tried to open each of the cabinets, with no success.

"Those padlocks look pretty small. I think we could break them if we could leverage them with something," Ronald suggested.

They spent a while scouring the building for potential tools and eventually they succeeded in breaking the small locks. They now had a full armoury to themselves. Zack strapped a pistol to his thigh. Ronald slung an assault rifle over his shoulder and carried another one.

"Let's work on some ammo," Ronald said as he showed Zack how to etch holy words into the bullets.

They spent a few hours preparing enough ammo for themselves.

"I'm really hungry Zack. Does this place have anything to eat?" Ronald asked.

Zack was hungry too. He checked his bag and found no food.

"Let's check the staff room," Zack suggested.

They walked upstairs and found a large section where the roof had fallen in. The floor was covered in splintered wood, insulation, wires and broken tiles. They carefully made their way past to the staff room. They checked all the cupboards but found nothing. There was food in the fridge bit it had all spoiled.

"Over here!" Ronald exclaimed.

He had dug away some of the debris to find a fallen vending machine. They spent some time trying to break it open, with no success.

"Stand back," said Zack as he drew his pistol. He fired into the side-locking mechanism and it shattered to pieces. They now had a mostly well-stocked vending machine to themselves.

Zack opened some salted nuts and a bottle of juice. Each tasted so good. He tried to eat slowly, but failed. Ronald made lots of happy eating noises.

"There is much more here than we can carry. Do you have any ideas how we can take it all with us?" Ronald asked happily chewing some candy.

Zack thought for a moment then replied.

"Follow me."

They walked down the hall and Zack rummaged through a plain looking office desk. He pulled out the keys to an armoured truck with a big smile.

"Perfect!"

Ronald and Zack spent several hours packing all they could into an armoured truck they found in one of the garages. A couple of Mortkin surprised them on one trip, but they were quickly cut down with the ample holy ammunition.

They spent another few hours etching replacement rounds. Zack's fingers were starting to get sore.

"Remind me not to shoot any more than I have to next time," Zack said.

"Agreed," said Ronald as he nursed his bleeding finger.

Shortly afterwards they climbed into the truck and Zack drove them out onto the road. The nice smell of new car wafted into Zack's nostrils. Memories flooded in with it. Zack reminded himself he was different now. Ronald tried to get the stereo working as they drove their way out the broken city.

Chapter 10

Final Crusade

Zack followed Ronald's directions and eventually they arrived at the road that held the Citadel. Zack read the road sign aloud as they drove past.

"Boundary Boad. No Exit."

"That's the one, I think it's near the end of the road," said Ronald.

They slowly approached the complex and Zack was delighted to see people swarming around the gates. It looked like they had erected some fortifications. They had a patrol of familiar school vests at the front gate. Denise stood in the middle of the road and signalled them to stop. She walked to the driver's side and spoke to Zack.

"Who is the Lord of your life?" she asked sternly.

"Jesus Christ is Lord..." Zack replied awkwardly.

Denise smiled. She showed him the some scripture she had been reading.

1 Corinthians 12

[3] Therefore I want you to know that no one who is speaking by the Spirit of God says, "Jesus be cursed," and no one can say, "Jesus is Lord," except by the Holy Spirit.

"May Jesus Christ the son of God bless you," she patted Zack on the shoulder and signalled him to follow.

They pulled over and climbed out. Zack and Ronald unloaded the weapons and food from the truck into the grateful hands of the residents. Graham ran over from amongst the crowd and hugged Zack.

"I can't believe you're alive buddy! You just don't die huh?" he beamed happily.

"Yeah, man. It's really good to see you. Did the others make it?" Zack asked as he gripped Mindy's ribbon tightly in his hand.

"Beth and Mindy are just over there," Graham said pointing.

Zack looked to see them both rushing over to him.

Zack just stared at Mindy. She was so beautiful. Zack was like a sailor that had not seen land in months and she was the perfect tropical island. Mindy's face suggested she noticed Zack staring. Each of them hugged Zack.

"Good to see you made it out Zack," Beth said.

"I'm really glad to see you," Mindy said with a smile.

Zack gave Mindy back her yellow ribbon.

"Oh, that's really thoughtful. This was my mother's; I had thought I had lost it forever. Thank you so much."

"You're welcome," Zack said.

Mindy approached Zack for another hug.

Zack had been trying to prepare himself for this moment. He knew he had to come clean now.

"I killed that guy," Zack blurted. Mindy looked confused and stopped short of him.

"What?" she asked.

Zack spent some time explaining the truth about Eric's death in the bank shooting to his friends.

He eventually finished and waited for a reply. Everyone was silent.

"Why didn't you tell me?" Graham asked finally.

"I should have from the very start. I am deeply sorry to each of you."

"Well I guess this does explain why you acted like such an idiot getting that medal," Graham said with a smile.

"Yeah, pretty much."

They spent a few minutes more talking about James' death, Ronald and the armoured truck of supplies. Mindy didn't say much but listened to every word Zack said.

Zack walked around with his friends as they gave him a tour of the place. When people had been describing it as a Citadel, Zack had thought of a castle. He could see the similarities, but the name was very optimistic. Zack saw a bunch of people he didn't recognize and reasoned more people must've joined on the trip out. He looked for a few people he was hoping to see, but learnt from the others they had been killed in the siege.

Bishop Kephas walked around the corner of the building in front of Zack.

"Good to see you made it out," he said.

Zack couldn't help but show his confusion and relief.

"Ah yes, your friend Mindy healed me," Kephas explained.

"It took a long time, but eventually we got there, and I had help," Mindy said.

Zack wondered how long he'd been away for.

"Wow. That's wonderful."

The Bishop went to continue walking. Zack asked to talk to him and told his friends he'd catch up with them later.

"I really need to talk to you about something I've done wrong. I want to confess and seek forgiveness Bishop," Zack said.

"I see. Walk with me," Kephas replied.

Zack told Kephas all about Eric's death and Zack's involvement in it all. Zack felt a weight lift from his shoulders as he was able be honest about it all. The Bishop was a good listener and occasionally would ask questions to clarify.

When Zack had finished speaking he waited for the Bishop's decision.

"I understand if you want to throw me out of here," Zack added. He hoped he would get to stay, but was willing to pay for the consequences.

"We have two rules if you want to stay here with us. They come from Scripture:"

Mark 12

[30] Love the Lord your God with all your heart and with all
your soul and with all your mind and with all your strength.'
[31] The second is this: 'Love your neighbor as yourself.'
There is no commandment greater than these."

"Will you do these?"

"Yes I will," Zack replied.

"Then you can stay. But I'd like you to pray for Eric and his family. Jesus loved us and died for us while we were still sinners. How happy is a shepherd when he finds one lost sheep? You only have to come to Jesus and sin no more."

The Bishop quoted another Bible verse:

Romans 8

[38] For I am convinced that neither death nor life, neither
angels nor demons, neither the present nor the future, nor
any powers, [39] neither height nor depth, nor anything else
in all creation, will be able to separate us from the
love of God that is in Christ Jesus our Lord.

"I'd like you to talk and pray with me every day. How's 8am?"

"Yes Bishop, thank you."

Zack smiled.

The months seemed to fly past and before long the population at the Citadel had grown larger than the church and school survivors. They regularly made trips into Brakenside, bringing back more survivors and supplies. There were a few packs of demons that made attacks on the Citadel. The surrounding grass fields providing a clear line of sight and ample of sanctified bullets resulted in the demons being killed well before they could get close.

To Zack's delight Jacob had survived the siege and continued to make Holy weapons. Zack learnt that he had set up his workshop in one of the rooms at the back of the administration block. He decided to go and visit.

"Hi Jacob," Zack said as he walked in.

Zack was immediately impressed. Jacob now had four other people helping him and each one of them was busy crafting something. There were finished weapons hanging on the walls and Jacob was walking around providing guidance to his apprentices. Unfortunately the holy relic weapons that Kephas found in the cemetery had been lost in the siege.

"Oh, hi Zack. I'm glad you made it. I heard you helped many people make it out here?" Jacob said.

"James didn't make it. But it was thanks to your weapons that we held them back as long as we did."

"I'm sorry to hear that, he was a good guy. Let me show something I'm working on."

Zack followed him over to one of the benches. On it was a chest plate. It was made from beaten metal. It looked strong and durable. It was inscribed with Holy words. Black ink was set into the etchings to make them more visible. The edges of the metal were surrounded with leather of some sort.

"Wow, impressive work Jacob."

"Thank you, would you guess it was made mostly from and old car door? I used some of the upholstery from in the car to keep it comfortable too."

"Oh, nice."

"I've heard back from several of our fighters that the blessed weapons are doing the trick but they needed something for protection. I thought this armour would be just the thing."

"Yeah I agree. That will save a lot of lives Jacob."

"I hope so. I've got my apprentices working on a run of these. We'll have them ready before the mission to Doverton."

"Oh?"

"Yeah, go have a chat to Sandy or the Bishop. It seems after all this time there isn't much left in Brakenside so we're going there next."

Zack decided he'd go and try and volunteer for this mission.

"Anyway Zack, I've got something else to show you," Jacob added.

They walked over to another bench and Jacob pulled out a sword covered in cloth and laid it in Zack's hands.

"Here, you've earned this."

"Oh, I'm sorry Jacob," Zack replied. "I don't have any gems to pay for it. I didn't really expect to make it this far to be honest."

"Nonsense. This is a gift from the people you helped make it this far, and me. Free of charge."

"Are you sure?"

"I'm sure."

"Thanks."

Zack unfurled the cloth. It was the same sword that Zack saw Jacob working on at the school. Zack looked up at Jacob. They exchanged smiles. Zack lifted the sword up in his right hand. It was the length of an average short sword. It was designed to be used single-handily. It had a double-edged blade and was beautifully etched and inked in Holy words. Zack read out some aloud.

Psalm 3

[6] I will not fear though tens of thousands
assail me on every side.
[7] Arise, LORD!
Deliver me, my God!
Strike all my enemies on the jaw;
break the teeth of the wicked.
[8] From the LORD comes deliverance.
May your blessing be on your people.

Zack smiled.

"We even use a blessed ink in there just for good measure."

"It's a masterpiece. Thank you so much!"

"You're most welcome. Just kill a whole bunch of demons for me."

"With pleasure."

"Oh I almost forgot, take this too."

Jacob handed him a sheath to carry it in. It was clearly made from the remnants of a car seat.

"It's not pretty, but it works."

"This is perfect. Thanks Jacob."

One of Jacob's apprentices walked over to ask Jacob something.

"I'll let you keep working. Thanks again."

Jacob waved and Zack walked outside. Zack left to find Graham to show him his new weapon. He walked past the front gate as a team arrived back. A van slowly pulled in and six men got out. They all had long stubble on their faces and looked like they had been out a long time. Their clothes were torn and they had mud and blood stains all over them. They looked very fatigued.

Sandy came out from one of the buildings to greet them. Zack stood close enough to hear their conversation.

"I'm glad to see you made it back Will. How did it go?"

"Hi Sandy. Yeah. Not like we hoped I'm afraid. We lost Steve and Miri."

"I'm so sorry, " Sandy said as she put a hand on his shoulder.

"But there is more bad news. We searched everywhere. And there just is no food left. We did yet another run to clear the supermarkets. One has since burnt down from last time we were out. The others have been picked clean. We spent a few days going from house to house clearing out kitchens. This is all we could find."

Another fighter pulled out several rubbish bags filled with tins of food from the van. It was a good amount of food. But considering the amount of people at the Citadel it was clear from Sandy's face that it was less than they hoped.

"How about people, did you find anyone?"

"This is our third time out since we've seen anyone else out there. I'm sorry, nobody."

"We'll make this work. Thank you Will. You and your team have done a great job. Please take some time to rest while you can."

"Hey Zack!" Beth called from behind him.

"Oh hi Beth, what's up?"

"I heard a team is coming back soon… Oh, they're here. Have they got lots of food?"

Zack turned and pointed at the bags.

"Oh. Where is the rest?"

Zack shrugged.

"Oh, I see. Well, I'll have to think of something else. See you after your shift Zack."

"Thanks for reminding me. I'll head to the watchtower now."

Zack, like all people at the Citadel, had various jobs to do. He enjoyed watchtower duty. He would climb the steel ladder and look out over the dreary fields that encircled them. He had previously tried to keep his mind distracted when he was dealing with the guilt and shame of the lies surrounding Eric's death. It was quite refreshing for Zack to be happy to be alone with his thoughts.

Zack often thought how he'd tell Mindy how he felt about her. But he thought it best to give her some time to chew on the fact that he'd killed a man before he'd announce his undying love for her. Zack was deep in thought when he heard someone climb the ladder.

"I'm here to take the next shift," a middle-aged man said.

He had a short blonde hair and a long, wispy beard. He wore what was left of a black business suit and blue scarf worn like a bandana.

"Oh sure. Thanks," said Zack as he handed the man the watchtower rifle.

"You are that lad from the bank heist."

Zack's heart sunk again. However he didn't feel as terrible now that he was honest about it.

"I was there, you know. Hiding in my car anyway. We haven't met. My name is Salmon," he said with a smile.

"Hi," Zack said, trying to hide a grin at his silly name.

"Good, isn't it? I've decided to call myself Salmon to remind myself what's important."

Zack decided this guy was a loon.

"Ah, so what do you do?" Zack asked, changing the subject.

"I'm a lawyer. The top lawyer at my firm, actually. I had even received awards. I had a big house, with a pool. You know, I had seven cars at one point?"

Zack raised his eyebrows.

"And I had the whole limited edition series of platinum watches. I spent hundreds of thousands on those things. And you know what?"

Zack was already bored of listening to this man. As exciting as his story about how much he owned was, Zack wished he'd just stand away from the ladder so he could get down. Zack stood to the side of the watchtower to let him past. Salmon didn't notice.

"What?" Zack asked.

"They are all useless. Such a waste."

Zack started listening again.

"I had put all my time into getting as much money as I could. I then spent it to get as many things as I could. I had so many things. Junk!"

"Oh?"

"Yes. I was a fool. All those things are no use to me now. They certainly won't be of any use when I'm dead. Why did I devote my life to such empty treasure? I see the world differently now. You know, I hardly saw my family. I sent my children to boarding school. I divorced my wife because she bought a beach house. I didn't talk to my parents. I spent my time looking for the next investment. I thought my family would always be there and I'd spend time with them when I had enough. But I never did! Oh young man, don't be fooled by the material possessions of this world. Oh! I memorised this Bible verse too:"

Proverbs 11

[4] Wealth is worthless in the day of wrath,
but righteousness delivers from death.

"Ok..." was all Zack could say before he started again.

"I see it clearly now. Things of the spirit are eternal; things of the physical are just temporary. I had never cared to even look into God as I saw it as something not solid, not real. Oh how I was wrong. Spiritual investment, prayer, spending time with family and friends: that's my new portfolio. Oh I wish I had learnt this when I was your age."

"I'll try and remember that."

"Do you know why I call myself Salmon? It's because when I was young, I spent a summer camping in the woods with my family. We had no Internet, no modern conveniences, nothing. My father packed the food and we had tinned salmon every day. I hated the stuff. As soon as I left home I never ate it again."

"Okay, I'll not give you any salmon," Zack said with a confused look on his face.

"No, I was wrong! Now that I've had time to look back I've realized. That was one of the happiest times of my life. I wasn't surrounded with things. I didn't need them. Whenever I thought of salmon, I used to think of the physical yucky taste. Now I remember the time with family."

Zack thought of his family.

"You make a good point," Zack said.

"I wonder now if we should've seen these end times coming. When I was young there wasn't such brutal violence. We didn't need drug screening at school. There wasn't a new killing spree on the news each week. It seems evil has been growing underneath our noses."

"Yeah."

"I think my Aunty Elsie had it right. She had next to nothing to her name but she went to church all the time, and she always seemed happy. Even when she died at an old age. I remember she was smiling the day she died. At the time I thought she was an idiot. But now it seems I was the idiot, not her."

Zack smiled.

"Anyway it was good to meet you Zack. I better get on to keeping a lookout. Off you go."

Salmon finally walked away from the ladder and started to watch for any oncoming demons. Zack smiled to himself and climbed down the ladder.

"Oh how I miss the sun on my face," Zack heard him say as he made it to the ground. Zack decided Salmon wasn't so crazy after all.

"Zack! Check it out," Graham called.

Zack looked over to see his friend running over to him. Graham was carrying a new weapon. He held a large, steel mace in his hands. It looked very heavy and was covered with inked Holy etchings.

"Wow, impressive club man. It's nearly as sweet as my sword," Zack said with a cheeky grin.

"Whatever. Anyway it's a mace, not a club."

They swapped weapons and swung them around like little boys do playing with sticks.

"Oh, we are supposed to be on the next trip out. I hear we're going to Doverton."

"That must be why we get the new kit."

"Yeah, let's head over and see when it's due to begin."

"Okay."

They walked along a short distance then met Brother Christopher coming the other way.

"Good, I found you both. Please head to the gate. We have a new mission on."

"Good timing, we'll head there now."

When Zack and Graham arrived many others had already gathered at the gate. The bus that Deon drove out to the Citadel was being loaded with food and other supplies. A van, a ute and a dirt bike were also lined up next to the bus.

"Looks like a big one," Zack said to Graham, who agreed.

Zack looked around to see who he'd recognise. Jacob was there with his apprentices unloading something, just out of Zack's view. Amanda and Michelle were there too, doing something with a large pile of cloth. Zack saw Malcolm and was glad someone of his fighting skills was still around. The Bishop climbed up onto the roof of the van and addressed the people gathered.

"My family, my friends, we gather again here to venture out into our fallen world. As you will be aware our supplies here won't last much longer. We've confirmed that Brakenside has been bled dry, both in blood and supplies. We have no choice but to make a series of trips to the city of Doverton. As you know it's far larger than Brakenside and we hope that will mean more survivors and supplies. However we can expect in turn more demons on our path. I'm hoping for twelve volunteers to undertake this dangerous mission."

Many hands rose immediately. Zack raised his hand high.

"Thank you everyone. Please know we still need everything to run while we're away. To be completely open and honest, it is possible that none of us make it back. We really don't know how Doverton has faired in these end-times. Nor will we know how long it will take us to return. Please pray for us. We will be praying for you."

Amanda brought the pile of cloth closer to the Bishop.

"What is that?" Graham asked Zack.

Zack shrugged.

"Please come forward if you want to volunteer," Kephas called.

People started to shuffle forward and Zack and Graham followed. Beth and Mindy walked in behind them. Zack smiled at them and tried to look ahead to see what was going on.

Zack saw Malcolm lower his head as the Bishop placed a white poncho over his head. It had a large pale blue cross on it. Jacob then walked up to him and fitted a chest plate over the poncho. The Bishop held his right hand high and prayed over each person as they each had their turn getting a poncho and chest plate. The ponchos were all one large size so they fitted each person. It looked like Jacob had made a few different sizes and shapes of armour so that he had something to fit everyone.

Zack saw the man next to him had some sanctified brass knuckles.

"Nice knuckles man," Zack commented.

The large man turned around. He had seen a lot of battle with his face a mess of scars. He was bald and wore a tatty Hawaiian shirt and jeans.

"Thank you," a deep, booming voice replied. "You also have some fine gear," he said, pointing at the shield on Zack's back.

"Cheers. I'm Zack by the way."

"Call me Loko."

They chatted for a few minutes about all they had been through.

Soon it was Zack's turn. He bowed and had his poncho lowered over him. He wasn't exactly sure what the ponchos were for, but it made him feel like he was part of a team. That was a good enough reason for him. Zack decided he'd try and pay more attention, rather than talking with his friends next time. He heard the Bishop pray Holy words over him. Zack closed his eyes and absorbed them into his soul.

Next Brother Christopher handed out a vial of Holy oil to each person and a water bottle.

"This is holy water," he said, holding up one bottle. "And this is holy oil. Use this if you need healing."

"Come get ammo," Will called out in a loud voice.

Each person lined up and received about twenty rounds according to each person's weapon type.

"Get some food then put your packs in the bus," Kephas called.

After a bit more organization everyone was ready to depart.

Zack and his friends boarded the bus. Zack saw that it had been modified to better deal with the broken terrain. Reinforcing steel bars had been welded on around the sides of the bus and a small steel dozer blade had been attached to the front. Zack sat down in his seat and looked out the windows. He saw the other vehicles had similar strengthening. Deon climbed aboard the bus and sat in the driver's seat. He turned around.

"Everyone all set?"

Deon was met by nodding and 'thumbs up' signals. Zack saw the other members of 'the twelve' climb into the other vehicles. He watched Sandy attach a trailer to the back of the ute. She waved as the vehicles slowly drove down the road.

It was the last mission to ever leave the Citadel.

It was going to be long drive to Doverton and Zack hoped it would be uneventful. He looked out the windows and chatted to his friends. The convoy made slow but steady progress. Malcolm was riding the dirt bike and led the way, trying to find the best route for the heavier vehicles following behind. Several times they had to go off road as the road was completely blocked.

At one point they completely unloaded the bus to try and make it over a muddy verge on the roadside. They attached a towrope from the ute to the bus and drove very slowly. To everyone's delight the bus didn't get stuck. However they succeeded in getting sprayed in a foul smelling mud. Zack started to get hungry, but he knew he had to make their rationed food last as long as they could. The stench helped quell his hunger pangs.

After some more driving they arrived at a small petrol station on the outskirts of Doverton. They pulled the convoy over and completed a thorough search. They did not find any people but managed to scavenge a small amount of food. Zack saw Brother Christopher attach a poster to the front door of the gas station. It read:

"Safety! Come to Boundary Road outside Brakenside. May the Lord God almighty bless you."

Beneath the words was a small handdrawn map and a picture of a cross. Whenever they stopped Zack would see him leave another poster.

Finally they reached Doverton. Zack looked as far as he could into the murky distance. He could just make out the tall office buildings of the city. Many high rises had smoke billowing out from various levels. Zack was hoping that it was just Brakenside that was hit. But it seemed everywhere was affected by the demonic attacks.

The twelve approached on the main road that lead onto the motorway. Looking ahead Zack could see that it was filled with abandoned cars. Malcolm zipped ahead on his bike to try and find a way through. After a few minutes he returned and shook his head. They tried a few back roads and managed to get a little closer before they became too blocked to proceed. The convoy pulled into an empty car park at the side of the road. The Bishop climbed out of the ute and called out to the drivers.

"Park up here. We'll go in on foot."

It was decided to split up and search for two hours, then regroup at the vehicles. They started searching the suburb immediately surrounding the car park. They managed to find a veterinary centre that had some valuable medical equipment still intact. It was loaded onto the bus next to the food from the petrol station.

Zack was expecting to see many survivors in Doverton, but so far they had encountered none. Zack and his friends walked as a group searching and calling out in hope of discovering survivors. They entered numerous houses and found little remaining of value.

As Zack walked out from a house he saw someone jump over a fence behind the neighboring house and run away.

"Hey wait!" he called.

Zack ran after them. Graham followed some distance behind. Beth and Mindy returned with the little food they had collected to the car park. Zack jumped the fence and ran across the grass to the far side. He looked around and couldn't see anyone. Graham caught up to him.

"Why are you running off Zack? What did you see?"

"I'm sure I saw someone," Zack said, still searching.

There was a rustle in the bushes and a figure leapt out and scaled the fence to the next house. They wore raggedy clothes like they had been homeless for years, prior to the end-times.

"Hey stop!" Zack called.

Graham and Zack ran after them.

They climbed the fence and caught up with the person in the backyard of the next house.

"We have food if you need some?" Zack asked.

The figure stopped and slowly turned around.

The man had long brown dreadlocks, a mangy beard and bad teeth. He wore a well-used dirty brown jacket and dull blue, ripped jeans. He wore fingerless gloves and worn black boots. He held a small knife tightly in his hand.

"You'd just give me some food?" he said in a raspy voice.

Zack pulled off his pack and fished out a muesli bar. He tossed over to the man.

"Sure. Eat up."

The man caught the bar, examined it briefly, and then quickly scoffed it down.

"Truly you are strange," the man said. "Why would you give food to a stranger like me?"

"I thought you might be hungry, is all."

The man looked Zack and Graham up and down, trying to decide whether to run or not. His eyes rested on their weapons.

"We mean you know harm," Graham said.

"What's with the writing on your weapons? And why are you wearing sheets?" he asked.

"It's for killing demons," Zack replied.

The man chuckled.

"Killing those creatures? Not possible."

"I'm telling the truth. With all the crazy stuff that's been going on lately, are you sure you can so quickly decide what's possible?"

"Well said boy. Okay. I'm Bill. What do you want of me?" He put his knife back in his pocket.

"I'm Zack and this is Graham. We don't want anything of you. However you're welcome to come with us if you like. We have a place far from here, but it's a safe community. We can protect you from the demons."

"Okay…" Bill said, ponderously.

"What about the dead ones?" Bill asked.

Zack returned a puzzled look. He wondered if this guy was one some sort of drugs. His eyes kept flickering around and he seemed to be shaking.

"The skeleton things. You must have seen them?" Bill added.

Zack and Graham shook their heads.

"I saw them, in the cemetery. That evil one draws them out. You better stay away."

"Where is this place?" Zack asked.

Bill pointed. "Past Central Park."

"We don't know where that is. Can you show us?"

"Yeah, I might be able to show you, if you have some more food," Bill said with a cheeky look on his dirty face.

"Sure," Zack smiled as he reached into his pack and tossed him a small can of tuna.

"Okay, let's go. But be warned. I'm not going to get too close. You'll be on your own once we pass the park."

"Okay fine," Graham said.

They followed Bill out of the suburbs through back alleys and side streets. He obviously knew the place well.

"So are going to come back with us?" Zack asked as they walked.

"Me? No. You guys believe in God and stuff, don't you?" pointing to the blue cross on their ponchos.

"Yes. That's kind of the whole point," Zack said.

"Nope. That's not my scene. I've met a few 'holier-than-thou' types in my day. I know you're not interested in an addict like me. Nor is God."

"I understand where you are coming from. I too have met some people than do a poor job of acting like a Christian should. But these people are the real deal. I'd be long dead without them."

"I have done some bad things boy. I'm beyond saving."

"That's where you're wrong. Jesus died on the cross to pay for our sins while we were still sinners. He has given us the opportunity to come to him and be saved. You just need to say 'yes.'"

Zack never thought he'd manage to say anything like that and not feel like a fool. But he genuinely believed it now. Zack remembered a Bible verse he'd been trying to memorize:

John 3

[16] For God so loved the world that he gave his one and only Son,
that whoever believes in him shall not perish but have eternal life.
[17] For God did not send his Son into the world to condemn
the world, but to save the world through him.

"I dunno kid, you don't know me. I haven't always acted like the gentleman you've witnessed today."

"I've killed a man and I'm welcome at the Citadel. Jesus wants to save us all."

Zack finished his sentence with a gulp. He still wasn't used to admitting the truth.

"You? A killer? No."

Zack looked Bill square in the eyes. "Yes. It was my fault he died."

"Oh," said Bill quietly.

"If all this God stuff is real, why has he left me on the streets these past eight years then?"

"I'm sorry, I have no idea why God does what he does. But if it was just so that you met us and ended up spending eternity in heaven, that'd still be good deal right?"

"Ha! I'll think about. The park is not far from here."

"Thanks for listening Bill."

"Ok chatterbox, let's keep it quiet as we cross this road," said Graham.

Zack nodded and they kept low as they ran across the road where there was no cover to hide behind. They made it across the road then ducked down behind an empty car.

"I think we made it," said Graham quietly.

They moved from there between two houses towards the park beyond.

A shrill call pierced the air. Bill freaked out. Zack recognised it to be the noise made by Scarkin. Bill ran and hid under some rubbish then immediately got up again. He slipped as he did so and lay on the ground.

"Don't let them get me," he pleaded looking up at Zack.

"I'll protect you," Zack declared.

Zack looked at Graham. They both felt confident they could manage a few small demons. Before they had a chance to plan, a large Scarkin demon jumped up onto the roof of the house next to them. Zack noticed it was larger than the Scarkin he was used to seeing. Its hide was a darker colour too. It scuttled over the tiles and dropped down near them. It started to charge and Graham ran at it with his mace ready. With a swift right swing he pulverised the demon into the wall. Bill cheered with glee.

"Take that punk!" Bill laughed.

Several more Scarkin approached them from both sides. Zack heard a distinctive roar. Mortkin were coming their way. Zack nodded at Graham and they each took up positions either side of Bill. Bill heard the roar too and fumbled in his pockets trying to retrieve a hip flask. Bill looked around for a way of escape but more Scarkin had arrived blocking them in.

"We're going to die!" Bill hollered as he gulped down some whiskey from his flask.

"No. We will protect you."

Zack drew his pistol and held it in the hand that he had his shield strapped to. Zack was not scared. He recalled another bible verse he had been practising.

John 8

[12] When Jesus spoke again to the people, he said,
"I am the light of the world. Whoever follows me will never walk
in darkness, but will have the light of life."

A few Scarkin leaped forward triggering the rest of the demons to attack. Graham and Zack charged into the demons, swinging their weapons. Several Mortkin came around the corner and rushed into the fray. Claws and blades were spilling blood all over the place. Graham's mace thudded into demons with an almost rhythmic fashion. The Mortkin pushed their way up the ranks. Zack was ready. As soon as they were within striking distance he raised his pistol and emptied the clip.

Bill covered his ears at the sound of gunfire and tried to tuck himself into an even smaller ball. The blessed bullets made short work of the Mortkin. Zack was able to quickly drop all but one of them. When Zack heard he had ran out of ammunition he holstered his pistol and charged into the shattered ranks of the demons.

Zack was still getting used to the longer blade of his sword, but already he was finding it much more effective. Graham landed a heavy blow into the last standing Mortkin and he joined Zack on the offensive. Zack hacked his way through the demons pushing them back with righteous zeal. In a few short moments there were only a few Scarkin remaining. Bill finally stopped whining.

Graham batted a Scarkin across the lawn and Zack impaled the last demon. They stood for a moment looking for more threats. There were none.

"Haha! We did it!" Bill stood up and danced around. He kicked the piles of demonic remains. He then jumped into them like a child in a rain puddle.

"Yeah we did. Did you suffer any injuries?" Zack asked.

"Nope. I'm great!"

As the adrenalin slowly left Zack's system he was alerted to several wounds of his own. He saw a gash in his upper left arm and his right thigh was bleeding. Graham had received cuts to his arms and back.

"Have you got that Holy oil?" Zack asked.

"Yeah, good idea," Graham said as he fished it out from his pack.

Graham put some on his hand then rubbed it into his wounds. He tossed the bottle to Zack, who did the same. Relief flooded through them as the blessed oil stopped the bleeding and sealed the wounds. They would still need healing, but the injuries would keep until whenever that would be.

"Okay Bill, let's get going," Zack said as he reloaded his pistol.

"Yeah. Let's kill some more of those punks. Follow me," Bill said as he skipped away.

Graham and Zack hurried after him.

A short while later they had arrived at Central Park. There was no-one in sight. Zack had thought he'd have seen some more survivors by now. The park looked like it had been a battleground some time ago, but no clue was left as to what had happened. The grass was muddied and many of the trees burnt or broken. Zack saw several bloodworms wriggling around. He made a determined effort to stomp on them all as he walked by.

"We made it to the park. Have you got that food for me?" Bill asked.

"Sure, here you go," Zack said, tossing him his food bag.

"Thank you. Okay, go past that motorway underpass over there and then get to the roof of the car park building on the far side. You'll see the cemetery from there. Good luck."

Zack looked to see where Bill had pointed and saw the underpass. It had graffiti and rubbish everywhere.

"Okay where does this...?" Zack began. He saw Bill was already running in the opposite direction. "Hey wait!"

Bill waved but didn't reply as he ran off.

"It's okay, we know where to go from here," Graham said.

Zack nodded.

They walked off through the park towards the motorway. They both kept a watchful eye out for demons. They made it to the underpass and looked around. Zack saw remnants of what looked like a gathering point for homeless people. There was an abandoned car and several cardboard boxes that looked lived in.

"Hello? Anyone here?" Zack called.

There was no reply.

"Over there," Graham said pointing. "That's gotta be the car park he meant."

Zack looked across the road and saw the three-storey car park building. The large sign had fallen off and had made a big mess over the ground in front of it.

"Good spotting Graham," Zack said as they walked over.

Zack saw the earthquake had caused lots of damage in this area. Broken glass was everywhere as all the shop fronts had been smashed. The occasional building had collapsed in on itself, but most remained standing with a few deeply cracked walls.

They entered the car park building and started to walk up the driveway leading towards the roof. The car park building was largely empty, but a few cars remained. They made it to the roof and soaked in the view. The bruised and broken city lay sprawling in all directions around them. The highrise buildings of the central business district towered into the clouds on one side. Vast industrial and commercial areas covered the other side. Anywhere there was room, residential buildings packed in Doverton residents.

Zack looked around to see the earthquake damage was much worse than in Brakenside. There looked to be a gigantic crater the size of several city blocks near the high-rises. Deep fissures splintered through the city. Some large rubble piles were all that remained of many buildings. A thin mist of smog wafted up to the clouded sky, which hung stagnant above them.

"There!" Graham pointed towards what looked like a park. On further inspection they decided it was the cemetery they were told about. It was also a lot further away than they had hoped. Graham began rummaging in his bag.

Zack squinted his eyes to try and pick up any details. It was no use at such a long distance.

"Try this." Graham handed Zack a rifle scope from his bag.

"How did get this?" Zack asked, obviously impressed.

"Good aye? I was hoping it might come in handy."

"Perfect! Let's see what we can see."

Zack peered through the scope. He could see the cemetery clearly now. He could make out individual gravestones and even read the sign at the gate. Then he saw movement. Something ran behind a tree. Zack tried to steady the scope on the top of the car park. His eyes drank in the horror. He saw a human skeleton running by itself between the gravestones.

"Unbelievable!" he exclaimed.

"Give me a look?" Graham asked.

Zack handed it over and Graham had a turn. After a few minutes of searching he found what Zack was looking at. The skeleton was held together with a network of dark red gooey fibres that ran throughout like a circulatory system. Graham swore under his breath.

The dull red sinews flowed down to its fingers and looked to become solid and sharp. Each finger was now a long claw. The skull had been filled with the same dark red substance. Graham and Zack watched for a few moments in disbelief.

"Look there!" Zack pointed out a blur of movement coming from one side of the cemetery. Graham handed him the scope. Zack looked through to see a pack of Scarkin.

In the middle of the group stood a tall demon. It was approximately the height of one and a half humans. It resembled the other demons but looked like it was in charge somehow. It stood on two legs and held a staff in its right pair of hands. Like the other demons it had two sets of forearms splitting off at the elbow. Its right arms and hands looked like they had fused with the staff it was carrying. It was unclear where the staff ended and flesh began. It had a pair of tattered wings that it wore like a long cape. A long tail occasionally flicked out from underneath the cape. Small bloodworms wriggled all over its body.

The creature looked more evil than Zack thought possible. It had spines and horns over its back, shoulders and top of its head. It had three red dimly glowing eyes. It looked like it had crawled up through many layers of dirt and earth.

"What the hell is that?" Zack spat as he gave Graham the scope.

Graham looked where Zack pointed.

"I have no idea, but it looks bad."

"Agreed, we need to tell the others about it."

"Good idea."

A dark plume of smoke rose from the cemetery. Zack looked down the scope. It had not come from a fire but the staff of the strange creature. It stamped it on to the ground in front of one of the gravestones. It slowly raised its staff and Zack could see its mouth moving as if it was talking. Then a burst of earth and clods of grass erupted out of the ground where it had stamped its staff.

A dark smoke steamed out from the ground. A skeletal hand then sprang upwards from the dirt. It was followed by another, then a complete skeleton stood quivering in front of the creature which had summoned it. The evil creature then pointed the top of its staff at the skeleton and a dark red liquid sprayed out. It coiled around the skeleton and bound it. The skeleton was shaking as if it was trying to resist what was going on.

The Summoner walked forward and licked its head with a long forked tongue. Immediately the skeleton became still, its skull filled with the dark red liquid until it dripped onto the ground. The dark red sinews seemed to solidify throughout its body. The dead Husk was now under its complete control.

The Summoner pointed its staff quickly to its left. The Husk ran to where the staff was pointed. The Summoner tested it again, to which the Husk obeyed.

"Just when I thought it things couldn't get any worse!" Zack said quietly to Graham.

"Why are you talking quietly, man? It's not like they can hear us from here."

"Dude, I don't want risk it. You have to see what this Summoner can do."

"Oh?"

Zack watched Graham look through the scope for a few moments, then his mouth dropped.

"This thing raises the dead?"

"Yeah, I guess."

"Crap!"

"Yeah, crap is right."

They watched the Summoner raise several more Husks. Zack noticed that some graves it came across it didn't seem to be able to call the skeleton out from. The Summoner looked frustrated. Often it was gravestones that had a cross on them. A few times Zack saw it smash the gravestone with its staff. Zack made a mental note not to get hit by that thing. It made turning a granite grave stone to rubble look effortless.

"Okay, so what now? I think we've learnt all we can," Zack said.

"Yeah, okay. Pass me the scope."

Zack tossed Graham the scope. It was a poor throw and Graham fumbled the catch. He took a few steps and swiped it a few times with his fingertips. It then fell off the side of the building.

"Damn it," Graham said.

"Sorry," Zack added.

The scope smashed through a windscreen of a car below them, making a loud crash.

Graham and Zack looked at each other in alarm.

The Summoner pointed its staff in their direction.

Chapter 11

No Exit

Zack and Graham looked towards the cemetery. A flood of enemies rushed in their direction. They both sprinted back down through the car park building with a speed that can only be attained when running for your life. They kept the pace until they had made it out of the building and across the road to the underpass. Zack dropped behind a pile of rubbish for a moment, trying to catch his breath.

"We gotta keep going!" Graham said between breaths.

Zack nodded and they ran again through the park. Graham collapsed behind a tree, desperate for a small rest. Zack joined him.

"Do you think we've escaped?" Zack asked.

Graham peered out between the bushes. He pulled his head back in quickly.

"Nope. We have to move."

Zack's body protested. He then remembered the Holy water they were given. He dug in his bag and drank all he could. Graham wasn't too sure on this plan but he did the same. The cool water flowed down Zack's throat and with it rejuvenation washed over him. He immediately got up and started running again. Graham joined him.

They had made it to the far side of the park and Zack risked stopping for a moment to look behind them. On the opposite side he saw a pack of Scarkin scampering towards them. Behind them were the dead Husks. Zack turned and started sprinting even harder. They made it into the suburbs and weaved their way between houses, trying to lose their pursuers.

Eventually they made it back to the car park where they had left their vehicles. They saw the others there waiting for them. Several new survivors were amongst their ranks including Bill. Zack suddenly remembered they should've been back by now.

"Oh good, you two are back. We were going to..." Kephas began.

"We have to go NOW!" Zack yelled at the top of his lungs.

Everyone looked at him and saw the desperation in his face.

"What's going on?" Kephas asked.

"Demons and skeletons inbound!" Zack replied.

"Skeletons?" Kephas asked.

Before Zack had a chance to explain their enemies had found them. A few Scarkin scuttled around the corner of the car park. They were quickly joined by more demons.

"Get the survivors into the bus!" Kephas commanded.

Several fighters rushed to engage the oncoming demons. Others hurried the survivors into the bus. Bill was the last one on. The door shut promptly behind him however the demons had already swarmed into the car park. They blocked any way of the bus leaving.

Zack found himself surrounded in demons. He hacked away at them with his Holy sword. The twelve did their best to keep demons away from the bus, but through sheer numbers several Scarkin made it past. Screams could be heard from inside the bus as the demons tried to scratch their way inside. In a few short moments all the tires were slashed and many windows smashed. Zack and others fought towards the bus as best they could. Gunfire erupted as a few fighters let loose with their pistols.

The Bishop charged into the demons and cut down several with each swing of his battle crucifixes. After some savage fighting the twelve had managed to form a circle of fighters around the bus. Kephas and Malcolm stood amidst the demons, felling foes at an astonishing rate. Soon they had killed enough demons to push forward and stand side by side, meeting the demons as they entered the car park. Zack saw the first of the skeletons round the corner and charge into the battle. Many took a double take when they saw the Husks. Zack gripped his sword tightly and ran into the oncoming evil, alongside his fellow fighters.

A Husk ran at him and frantically tried to claw him to death. Zack blocked its attacks with his shield and swung his sword. His attack hit hard into the Husk's right forearm. The sound of breaking bones was lost in the din of battle to all but Zack. Despite losing a hand the Husk kept fighting. Zack blocked as many attacks as he could but suffered some deep cuts to his arms. Zack swung again and cut off the Skeleton's other arm. The Husk was still determined to kill Zack and tried to bite him. Zack took a side step and sliced his sword into its spine. The binding which held the skeleton together dissipated and it crumbled into a pile of bones on the ground.

Just as Zack thought they were gaining the upper hand the wooden fence at the rear of the car park was pushed down and even more Husks charged in. The Bishop cast the burning holy light attack Zack had seen earlier. The air reverberated around them. The evil sinews were blasted from their bones. A large group of Husks were sent flying backwards.

Gunfire again erupted amid the battle as many fighters desperately tried to keep their foe back. Zack watched many bullets pass between ribs or miss their targets altogether. It seemed other fighters realized that bullets were ineffective and the gunfire stopped. Mindy took the lid off her Holy water bottle and threw it into the Husks. It had no effect on the bones but melted off the sinews with ease.

Other members of the twelve followed suit and many Husks fell. Finally the Husks stopped flowing into the car park. Soon after that the twelve had banished them all. They stood amongst the broken bones, blood and demon muck, catching their breath for a moment. Then the roar of many Mortkin filled the air. Zack drew his pistol.

A few seconds later the large demons rushed in from two sides. Zack opened fire and perforated several of them. Every member of the twelve did the same and only a single Mortkin made it close enough to be dangerous. Malcolm charged and killed it with a single blow.

Zack looked around. He was panting. His mind notified him immediately that there weren't twelve people left standing.

Zack scanned the ground and approached the closet fighter body lying face down on the concrete. It was Loko. He was dead. He had a huge number of deep cuts all over him. Zack wondered how he'd managed to continue for as long as he did. Zack was confused that someone who looked so strong would fall. And yet somehow he had made it through alive.

Mindy and Will rushed around the fallen assessing injuries and healing everyone they could. Zack saw Kephas kneeling down in the muck. He had his hand resting on someone's head. He wiped it down over their face closing their dead eyes. It was Brother Christopher.

Zack ran over to him and pulled out his small container of Holy oil. Kephas held Zack's hand.

"I'm sorry, he's gone. That will do no good now."

Zack saw a tear run down Kephas' cheek.

"But, but..." Zack began.

Zack couldn't believe he was dead. Zack felt like if anyone had to die it should've been him. Kephas stood and went to the next fallen fighter. It was Ronald. He looked dead too. Zack's eyes welled up with tears. Kephas held his hands over him and began to pray the prayer of healing. Ronald spluttered out a mouthful of blood and opened his eyes. Zack thanked God he wasn't dead. Kephas needed to spend several more minutes of healing and applying Holy oil before Ronald could breathe normally.

Those of the twelve who remained able helped with the injured and took stock of what supplies they had left. The new survivors had thankfully all survived the attack, but the bus was no longer able to be driven anywhere. Ronald was eventually stabilized so that he could sit and talk. Both his arms were badly mangled. The healing he received had stopped the bleeding, but he'd need a lot more before he'd be able to fight again.

The dead were laid out next to each other and the Bishop said a prayer. Everyone knew they didn't have time to bury them. Zack walked up to Brother Christopher's body and laid his hand on his shoulder. It felt cold. Zack sat next to his body as they discussed what their next move should be. Zack and Graham explained what they knew about the Summoner and the Husks.

After some discussion it was eventually agreed that they needed to find and kill this Summoner before it made too many more Husks. Conversation then turned to how they would be able to keep the new survivors safe on such a dangerous mission.

Ronald spoke up.

"Let me guide these new survivors back to the Citadel. I can't drive but I can guide them back easily enough. I'm no use on the battlefield like this. We'll just slow you down."

"You make a valid point, Ronald," Kephas said. "But the bus is out of action?"

"Hmm..."

"You can take all the other vehicles. If you take the van and ute, and perhaps have some people riding in the trailer?"

"Yes, that'd work," Ronald replied.

"I'd feel better if another fighter went with you, in case you encounter more demons on the way back."

"I'll go," Mindy said, raising her hand. "That way I can keep an eye on his injuries too."

"Okay, Mindy. Keep them safe."

"I will," she declared.

"How will we get back?" Deon asked.

"There are plenty of abandoned vehicles in the city. We will find something."

"Okay."

Mindy came over to say her goodbyes to her friends.

"I'll see you soon," Beth said.

"Good luck," Zack said, despite all he wanted to tell her.

Graham waved.

"You guys be careful. See you back at home later on."

Zack realised how strange it was to use the term 'home'. But he liked the sound of coming home to see Mindy. He wondered if he should tell her of his love.

"Let's go," Ronald called.

"Coming!" Mindy called back as she waved goodbye to her friends.

Zack was adamant he'd tell her next time.

They helped Ronald in to the back of the van, which Mindy drove. Bill drove the ute with a trailer full of people towing behind. Moments later they had pulled out of the car park and were on their way.

"Zack and Graham, lead us to this cemetery. We will put this evil creature down," Kephas said.

"Agreed, follow me," Zack replied.

Zack, Graham, Beth, Kephas, Deon, Malcolm, Salmon and Will began their journey deeper into the city. Soon they had made it through the park and underpass and reached the car park building.

"We watched from there," Graham pointed.

"Very good. Lead on," Kephas replied.

They carried on through the devastated city. Surprisingly they encountered no demons or survivors. Soon they reached the cemetery. They cautiously entered with their weapons at the ready. However the Summoner was not there. The fighters searched the cemetery and found only broken gravestones and uplifted dirt where the Husks had emerged.

"It looks like it has cleaned this place out," said Deon.

"Agreed, where to next?" Malcolm asked.

"I don't know. We only saw it here," Zack replied.

"Is there any other cemeteries around here?" Beth asked.

Will spoke up. "The main Doverton cemetery is towards the inner city, near that big crater, I think."

Kephas agreed. "Yes let's head that way."

The group had only travelled a few city blocks in that direction before they encountered demon activity. They decided this meant that they must be on the right track. After a few hours of searching and a few minor encounters with Scarkin, Graham spoke up.

"Does anyone know exactly where this place is?"

"Sorry, I'm not exactly sure," Will replied. "I was just a kid when I came here last. I just remember seeing the high-rises close by."

"Let me get a look from the top of that building," Salmon suggested.

"Good idea," said Kephas.

The fighters formed a circle around the base of an office building as Salmon climbed up the fire escape ladders. When he got to the top of the four story concrete office block he removed the rifle from his back and used the scope to look around. After a few minutes he rushed back to the ladder and made his way down.

Everyone looked at him expectantly.

"Just a few blocks away from here is the edge of that large crater. There are those skeleton things everywhere, demons too. I'm pretty sure I saw the Summoner in the middle of them all."

"Good work," Kephas said. "How many?"

"A hundred maybe? It's hard to say. I didn't want to be seen."

"I see. Okay everyone, drop your backpacks here we will need to prepare," Kephas said.

Zack liked the way that, despite the huge odds, the Bishop wasn't discouraged in the slightest. Somehow he managed to focus on what they practically needed to do next – despite the recent huge emotional losses.

"Eat a little and drink, we will need all the energy we can muster for this fight," Kephas said as he passed out some food and Holy water from his pack. Zack, like many others, didn't feel like eating much. Zack wondered if this was going to be his last meal.

Everyone prepared as best they could. Weapons were reloaded and blades sharpened.

"Let us bring the wrath of God down on this evil filth!" the Bishop said as he raised his weapons high. There was a cheer from the fighters. Zack felt confident despite the odds.

They left their excess gear and walked off in the direction Salmon had pointed. They hadn't been walking long before they encountered more demons. Kephas and Malcolm were at the front of the group and killed the few demons with ease. More demons poured out from between the buildings. They all seemed to be larger than the ones Zack was used to in Brakenside. A few Husks also came into view.

"Form up and don't stop the advance!" Kephas called.

They closed ranks and pushed forward as one. Each fighter dealt with the foe immediately around them and left the others for other positions in their group. Zack was at the back of the group and was walking backwards to fight demons approaching them from behind. Their pace slowed to a slow walk as more and more evil foes joined in. The pace suited Zack but he didn't expect so many demons. After all they had not long ago managed to kill so many. Zack wondered just how many of these evil things there were.

"Keep formation!" Kephas commanded.

They tightened their group and drove forward one bloody step at a time. They eventually rounded the end of the street and saw the ground fall away into the giant crater.

The crater was as deep as a four-story building was high and was the size of a small suburb. The earth was broken and littered with debris. The buildings that once were there had just gone. In the centre of the crater was a deep hole. Thin smoke was wafting out from it. All over the crater were thousands of bloodworms. They seemed to be most concentrated at the crater's center. On the edge of the broken earth stood the Summoner. He was surrounded with Husks and large Mortkin. Zack nearly got stabbed in the face as he lost concentration for a moment as he looked.

Kephas spotted his target. He closed his eyes for a second, raised his right weapon in the air, then yelled in a deep voice.

"Testantur Sanctam Dei."

Holy light blasted outwards and obliterated a huge number of demons and Husks in front of them. The fighters struggled to maintain their balance as the shockwave hit them.

"Charge!" Kephas yelled.

They ran forward through the newly opened gap in enemy lines towards the Summoner. Malcolm ran ahead, clearing the way further for fighters behind him. The Summoner dropped down from a mound of dirt and rubble and stomped towards them. It raised its demonic staff and pointed it at them. Huge numbers of Husks seemed to pile in on them from all directions. The ground they had cleared was quickly filled again.

The Mortkin guards around the Summoner charged in to the fight. The Bishop chanted a battle prayer loudly over the fighters. Zack felt energized and somehow stronger. He swung his sword and cut an attacking Mortkin in half. He looked around and saw his fellow fighters had been reinvigorated too. The remanent of the twelve cut down Demon and Husk alike at a surprisingly fast rate. Zack saw Will smash his weapon through one demon and into another, which in turn knocked over a third.

"Attack!" Kephas commanded.

They pushed their assault deeper into enemy lines. They were nearly in striking range of the Summoner. Malcolm dove over the Scarkin in front of him and cut down the Mortkin guard behind it. He screamed a loud battle-cry and charged at the Summoner.

The Summoner moved its mouth and made some vile sounds that could've been demonic words. It lifted its staff and pointed it at Malcolm. A huge gout of black flame burst out of the end of the staff. Zack could feel the heat on his face even from where he was. The dark flames washed over Malcolm and the surrounding demons. Malcolm was engulfed and dropped backwards to the ground. A second later he was a smoking pile of ash. Zack couldn't believe that Malcolm was dead. He was adamant someone of his skills couldn't be taken down.

The Summoner turned his staff towards the fighters and let loose another deadly black flame attack. Salmon did not manage to evade in time and was burnt to death.

"Angelica testudinem!" Kephas shouted.

A bright white angelic shield wall of light materialized in front of the Bishop. It spread out like a pair of wings to either side of him, protecting their group. The black flames crashed into it with tremendous force but could not penetrate. The Demons and Husks could also not get through. The Bishop held his hands out to maintain the shield. Zack could see it was taking all his strength.

"We gotta kill that beast now!" Deon cried.

"I'll go right. You go left," Will called back.

"Covering fire!" Graham shouted. The remaining members opened fire with their rifles and pistols. A swathe of demons dropped, clearing the way for an attack on the Summoner.

Deon and Will ran out from each side of the wall of light to attack. The Summoner directed his staff towards Will and he was incinerated. Deon lunged towards him from the other side and swung his sanctified axe at its head. The Summoner spun around and managed to pull his staff in between them at the last moment. Deon's axe cut through the evil staff and dark bloody ooze sprayed out. The Summoner screamed in pain as it stabbed its other spiked arm into Deon's head. Deon died instantly.

Kephas dropped the wall of light and charged the Summoner. The Summoner flicked Deon's body on to the ground and turned to face Kephas. But the Bishop was too fast for the injured Summoner. Kephas stabbed one battle crucifix into its chest and then decapitated it with the other. The evil creature dropped to the ground dead.

A loud howl boomed outwards from the center of the nearby crater. Three more Summoners climbed out of the dark hole. Kephas dropped back to the remaining fighters.

"We must go!"

Zack's mind was still reeling at all which had just occurred.

"Now!" Kephas commanded.

The remaining four fought their way back through the enemy ranks as quickly as they could. Kephas blasted away another chunk of evil creatures with a burst of Holy light. It gave them enough room to run for short distance without needing to engage the enemy. Zack drew his pistol and unloaded it into the Demons ahead of them. Beth slung the assault rifle off her shoulders and did the same. Zack could see past his foe now. He saw the edge of the office building that they had come past on their way in.

"This way!" Zack yelled.

They ran past the building down the road, slaying Demons that approached them. The enemy ranks thinned out a little and the four were able to cover more ground. Zack used up all his remaining blessed bullets, clearing a path for them. They turned the corner at the end of the street. Even fewer demons were in view.

"Keep going," Kephas encouraged.

Graham used the last of his bullets, clearing the street. The roar of a multitude of demons could be heard from behind them. They kept running. They turned down another road. Thankfully this road didn't contain any demons.

"We need a car," the Bishop said.

They ran half way along the road and stopped by a blue sedan parked on the side of the road. Zack arrived first but he didn't know how to hotwire a car. A few seconds later Kephas arrived and smashed in the driver's window.

"Cover me," he said.

Beth reloaded her assault rifle. Zack checked his pistol and confirmed he didn't have any more ammo.

"I'm out," Graham said.

"Me too," Zack replied.

They readied their melee weapons and waited for the demons chasing them to catch up. Zack could hear the Bishop attempting to start the car behind them. It didn't sound like it was going well. A pack of Demons and Husks came around the end of the street and rushed towards them. Beth opened fire, dropping most of the Demons. She hit one Husk in the spine, dropping it. But the others kept charging. Graham and Zack ran forward to meet them and fought them back with all they had.

The sound of the car starting put a smile on Zack's face. Beth climbed in and the Bishop spun the car around. He reversed it at speed towards where Graham and Zack were fighting. The car ploughed over several demons and narrowly missed Graham and Zack.

"Get in!" Beth screamed.

She stood through the sunroof and lay down cover fire with her rifle. Zack and Graham scrambled into the car. The Bishop drove off with a skid of the tires. They sped down the road, smashing aside debris as they went.

After a few blocks they felt a little safer. Kephas slowed a little and made his way around the broken parts of the road. Soon they had reached the edge of the city. They left Doverton never to return again. Zack struggled with how many people they lost. He felt shell-shocked.

Beth sat down into the front seat. She felt like they were past the worst of it now. Yet she still clutched her rifle tightly, ready at a moment's notice.

"I can't believe we lost so many," Graham said quietly.

Zack looked to Kephas. He saw he had been silently crying.

"I'm reminded of a particular verse, though I never thought I'd outlive those that fell today."

2 Timothy 4

⁷ I have fought the good fight, I have finished the race,
I have kept the faith.

"We will see them again in Heaven," he added quietly.

They eventually made it back to the Citadel. When they drove in Zack saw many gathered at the gates watching expectantly for more vehicles following them. They returned with no supplies and they had lost what little they had in their packs. The blue sedan pulled into the complex and Sandy came out to greet them.

"Welcome back, are the others following you?" she asked.

"We are all that made it out," Graham said solemnly.

"Oh, I'm so sorry," she gave each of them a hug as they hopped out of the car.

"Did you manage to find any food?"

Graham shook his head.

"That's okay, we'll make do. We always have."

Mindy came forward and hugged each of them.

"I'm so glad you made it back," she said with a smile.

"How's Ronald doing?" Zack asked.

"He's okay. Moving slowly, but he'll be fine."

"I'm relieved to hear that. Thanks Mindy."

"The new survivors from the city you all saved wanted me to pass on their thanks," Sandy said. She reached into her bag and pulled out a block of chocolate.

"One of them asked me to give you all this. I guess it's your welcome home dinner," she said smiling.

They all ate some chocolate quietly. For a moment Zack closed his eyes and pretended he was back in his flat.

"Zack, are you okay?" Mindy asked.

"Yeah I'm okay," he replied.

Zack decided it was time. He drew in all his courage.

"Can I talk to you Mindy?" he said in an awkward voice.

"Huh? Sure, what's up?"

Zack lead her away from the others. Zack rattled his brains for the right words. With all the times he had daydreamed about this moment he couldn't think of anything that sounded right.

"I've been loving you," he suddenly blurted.

"Excuse me?"

Zack felt a surge of energy. He knew he was committed now so let his feelings flow out.

"I think you're wonderful Mindy. You're my dream girl. I just had to tell you, you are the most beautiful person alive. My heart loves you with all my heart."

Zack realized that sounded weird. He closed his mouth.

Mindy walked toward him. He couldn't read the expression on her face.

"I'm sorry if this makes it…"

She wrapped her hands around him and kissed him. Zack was thunderstruck. He opened his eyes and saw her beautiful eyes smiling back at him. Zack kissed her and she kissed him back.

"So you're cool?" Zack asked.

She giggled. "Cool? I feel the same about you, if that what you're asking."

"Why didn't you say anything?"

"Why didn't *you*?" she retorted. "You had to wait until the end of the world to tell me how you felt?"

Zack smiled. "Yeah, sorry I can't take you to a nice restaurant."

She smiled and they embraced.

"I had thought you weren't keen, and I didn't want to make it awkward between us," Zack explained.

"What? You didn't pick up on the subtle messages I was giving out?"

"What messages?"

Mindy thought for a moment.

"Well, me snuggling in to you when we slept in that barn for one."

"I just thought you were cold."

She kissed him.

"It's okay now. We have each other."

He kissed her.

"We do," he answered.

"Do you now? Beth asked with a frown on her face.

They both turned to see Beth and Graham standing there.

Zack suddenly wondered if they would be accepting of their relationship.

"Yeah?" Zack asked nervously.

Beth's frown melted into a smile. "We're all good with it. Just take good care of her, okay Zack?"

"I will."

"I'm happy for you both," Graham added.

Graham took out his wallet and handed Beth some money. It seems they had a bet going on Zack and Mindy's relationship.

The four friends had a long chat and updated each other on recent events.

Zack spent the rest of the day walking around the Citadel holding Mindy's hand. They were both getting hungry. Since their last mission didn't yield any supplies, food was scarce. Many people were constantly praying that they would soon find more food. Due to the lack of sunlight it was impossible to grow anything to eat. Slowly but surely their food reserves were running out. Zack decided to see what food there was left.

The new couple walked over to the administration building. They found a queue of people with the same idea. Zack could hear Sandy trying to reason with people at the front of the queue. Sandy was in charge of rationing and tried to do her best to make sure everyone had something to eat. This was not easy when people were going hungry. Eventually the people ahead of them walked away with a small ration and Zack and Mindy walked in.

"I'm really sorry but I've just given out the last of the food."

Zack's stomach protested loudly. He looked over to the empty supermarket trolleys where the supplies were kept and saw a single can of beans left in one of them.

"How about that can, may we eat that?" Mindy asked.

"Like I said I'm sorry, but I gave out the very last of the food. There is nothing left," Sandy replied as she busily went about double-checking a list she had written out.

"That one?" Zack said pointing.

Sandy looked up confused and looked over at the trolley with the single can of beans in it. She looked confused for a moment then she looked ecstatic.

"It's a miracle! Thank you God," she exclaimed earnestly.

Mindy and Zack traded confused looks with each other.

"What do you mean? Didn't you just miscount?" Mindy asked.

"I'm one hundred percent confident I didn't miscount. We haven't had beans for a few days now. Here look at this list. The last lot of items were all canned fruit." She showed them the list of food she had been checking off.

Zack walked over and picked up the can of beans. He rolled it over in his hands. It looked normal enough to him. Just a typical can like one would find in a supermarket. He brought it over and sat it on the table.

"I don't know, it just looks like normal beans to me. Nothing miraculous about them."

Sandy and Mindy inspected the can. Sandy started laughing. She pointed back to the supermarket trolley. In the trolley lay a single tin of spaghetti. Zack did a double take. He was absolutely certain that he had taken the only can left in the supermarket trolley.

Mindy walked over and picked up the tin of spaghetti. She shook the trolley then put the tin back in the trolley. She bent underneath the trolley and carefully looked over each part of the trolley. Zack joined her. They checked the floor, the roof and the other empty trolleys. Nothing could explain where the tin of spaghetti came from.

Sandy was so happy. She checked her food ration list and called to someone outside that they had some food left. Mindy asked Zack to hold the tin a tiny distance above the trolley and she ran her fingers underneath where the tin was sitting. Satisfied with their checking of the situation but still puzzled, Mindy picked up the tin of spaghetti and gave it to Sandy.

"I can't explain it."

"It's a miracle," Sandy said confidently.

Zack turned his back on the trolley for a moment then spun around to check it. He saw a can of peaches and laughed. Sandy picked up her Bible and read aloud:

Psalm 95

[1] Come, let us sing for joy to the LORD;
let us shout aloud to the Rock of our salvation.

² Let us come before him with thanksgiving
and extol him with music and song.

News spread around Citadel and everyone enjoyed a full meal. The blessed trolley seemed to somehow only provide just enough for everyone to eat in a day and not a can more.

Some time after everyone had eaten the Bishop called everyone together. Behind him Jacob was erecting large cross on the roof of the administration building.

"Attention everyone. We will need every single one of you for what will be happening next. Man, woman, child, old, young, sick, injured, new addition to us here or not. Our scouts have seen a demonic army marching towards this place. Escape is not a possibility."

A doomed groan rose from the crowd.

Someone called out. "How many?"

"Tens of thousands, probably more."

The crowd was silenced.

Kephas continued.

"We expect they will arrive in a few hours' time. This doesn't give us long to prepare. Everyone who can fight will be fighting at the gate. I need everyone who can't fight to be praying for a single fighter. We'll make sure each fighter has a team praying for them. You'll be using the sacred prayers of my Order that I was able to use in Doverton. Come see me after this. You will need some time before you can get it right."

Zack remembered how powerful he felt when Kephas was praying over their whole team. He wondered what would happen when he had a whole group of people praying for just him.

Everyone hurried off to prepare. Zack and his friends etched bullets and reloaded all the weapons they could find. Kephas dropped by with some Holy oil.

"Put some of this on each bullet."

"Yes Sir," Graham said.

Jacob sharpened everyone's blades. Sandy organised the teams for prayer. The Bishop taught them the Rite of Battle. Others painted holy words of protection on the walls around the Citadel.

"Um, You're Zack aren't you?"

Zack turned to see one of Jacob's apprentices. He looked to be in his late teens. He had short black hair and wore blue mechanic's overalls.

"Yeah that's me. You're one of the blacksmiths, right?"

"Um, I'm Charlie. Jacob said to talk to you. Um, Do you have any pointers for me? Um, You know for fighting? Umm, Or whatever."

It was obvious that Charlie was very anxious about the upcoming battle. Zack assumed correctly he had not seen battle before.

"It'll be okay Charlie. I see you have a hammer there. Did you etch that yourself?"

"Yeah I did," Charlie showed Zack his weapon.

"It's beautiful. This will crush those demon punks with ease. Just keep swinging that thing. Watch for the small demons. They like to jump at your face. And keep moving when the big ones come at you."

"Um, Oh. Maybe I'm not cut out for this. Um."

Zack could see his courage was failing.

"I tell you what Charlie. You are about the same size as me. Take my armoured chest plate," Zack unstrapped it and handed it to him.

"Wow, really?"

"Sure. I've killed many demons wearing this. You'll be well protected wearing it."

Zack helped Charlie into the armour.

"What about you?" Charlie asked.

"I'll be okay. I still have this blessed poncho thing. I'm used to fighting without it anyway."

"Wow, thank you. Jacob was right, you are an impressive fighter."

Zack had never thought that about himself, and was stoked to hear that someone else thought so.

"Stay close to the other fighters out there, you'll do great Charlie."

He nodded and walked away.

The fighters assembled at the front gates. Zack could see the few vehicles were driven into gaps in the walls. The fighters helped tip the cars onto their sides to provide a taller obstacle. Many civilians like Charlie had joined the fighters, yet their number was still less than twenty. Zack saw Sandy walking past counting each fighter. She was holding a whip with Rosary beads and wire bound into it.

"Wow, nice weapon Sandy."

"Thanks. I saw it as only fitting as I seemed to have been bossing everyone around here lately," she said smiling.

"So you're joining us in the fighting?"

"Yes, I just have to check the prayer teams first."

Sandy went off to assign teams to each fighter. Zack watched as she pointed a team of seven people towards Zack. He waved back to them. The other fighters waved in turn back to their respective teams.

The Bishop walked into the front of the gates.

"Those who can fire a gun, be ready at the walls," Kephas called out.

Several people picked up assault rifles and got into position.

"Form up," Kephas called.

The fighters lined up and he walked past each one. He then returned with jugs of blessed oil and tipped it over each fighter as he said a prayer.

"May this blessed oil protect you all on the field of battle."

Psalm 91

⁵ You will not fear the terror of night,
nor the arrow that flies by day,
⁶ nor the pestilence that stalks in the darkness,
nor the plague that destroys at midday.
⁷ A thousand may fall at your side,
ten thousand at your right hand,
but it will not come near you.
⁸ You will only observe with your eyes
and see the punishment of the wicked.
⁹ If you say, "The LORD is my refuge,"
and you make the Most High your dwelling,
¹⁰ no harm will overtake you,
no disaster will come near your tent.

¹¹ For he will command his angels concerning you
to guard you in all your ways;

Lastly he poured the remainder over himself. Kephas then rubbed it over himself to ensure he was covered. The fighters upon seeing this did the same. Zack thought it smelt like perfume you'd smell at a funeral. It was ironically appropriate.

"Coat your weapons too," the Bishop directed.

A nervous few moments passed.

"They are coming," someone from the wall called out.

They all looked across the field. In the distance they could see the countless Demons and Husks approaching. Their evil ranks were filled of every sort of horror; Bloodworms, Scarkin, Mortkin, Husks and Summoners. Zack was overwhelmed at their numbers. It was like an entire kingdom was marching against them.

Joel 2

⁶ At the sight of them, nations are in anguish;
every face turns pale.
⁷ They charge like warriors;
they scale walls like soldiers.
They all march in line,
not swerving from their course.
⁸ They do not jostle each other;
each marches straight ahead.
They plunge through defenses
without breaking ranks.
⁹ They rush upon the city;
they run along the wall.
They climb into the houses;
like thieves they enter through the windows.
¹⁰ Before them the earth shakes,
the heavens tremble,

the sun and moon are darkened,
and the stars no longer shine.

Zack heard Mindy groan quietly from beside him.

"It'll be okay," Zack assured her.

She leaned over and kissed him.

"I'm yours," she said, smiling.

"I'm yours too," he replied.

The approaching demon army was getting louder and louder. It sounded like an oncoming tidal wave. The howls and screams they made blended into a horrific droning sound. It was utterly demoralising. They were getting closer and closer.

The Bishop signalled for the prayer teams to begin. The chanting of scared words filled the air. Zack closed his eyes and took a deep breath. He prayed quietly in his own head.

"Thank you God for my life."

Mindy tugged his arm and he opened his eyes.

"Look!" she exclaimed.

She held out her arm. Steam was rising up from her like she was boiling hot. She smiled at him. Then Zack started to feel a surge of Holy power growing inside him. He had a tingling sensation all over his body. He held out his arms and saw steam rising from them too. Zack looked back at his team and gave them a thumbs-up signal. An old lady on the team smiled back and him and kept praying.

Each fighter was now pouring with steam from all over their bodies. Even their breath came out as steam. Zack felt like he could take on the whole demonic army by himself. He felt charged up beyond measure.

The Bishop shouted out in a loud voice. He rallied his army.

Isaiah 40

[29] He gives strength to the weary
and increases the power of the weak.
[30] Even youths grow tired and weary,
and young men stumble and fall;

[31] but those who hope in the LORD
will renew their strength.
They will soar on wings like eagles;
they will run and not grow weary,
they will walk and not be faint.

"We have already witnessed miracles. We are the Lord's chosen. We have endured all they have thrown at us and we are still here. They cannot defeat us. We draw strength from those we protect here; we draw strength from those in Heaven. Draw on every fiber of your mind, body and soul. Hold nothing in reserve. Now channel all that strength into yourself to become God's Holy weapon. You are a sword for the Lord! Who are you?"

The crowd shouted back "A sword for the Lord!"

"Who are you?"

"A sword for the Lord!" they yelled.

"WHO ARE YOU?"

"A SWORD FOR THE LORD!" they roared.

With this battle cry they stormed into the foul demonic ranks. The Demons smashed upon them like bugs on a windscreen of a speeding car. Zack ran ahead with ridiculous speed. He felt as light as a feather. Yet he was smashing aside Demons like they were party balloons.

Zack charged into their lines with his shield up. He drove deep into their ranks, swinging his sword with all his might. Dozens of Demons were blasted backwards from in front of him. His blade moved so quickly it took him a second to understand what had happened. The Holy oil coating and Rite of Battle prayer amplified his every strike. Each swing hit with the force of a heavy truck driving into his foes. He smashed aside large Mortkin and Husks alike. He was unstoppable. Zack and the other fighters fought with the power of magnitudes greater than their number.

Zack could hear automatic gunfire erupt from behind him. Each of the etched and Holy oil coated bullets travelled through multiple Demons. Hundreds of Demons were blown away. Zack knew their stockpile of sanctified bullets was limited. But miraculously they just kept on firing. Swathes of Demons dropped in every direction.

The flood of evil did not relent. Zack was saturated in Demons. He lost sight of his fellow fighters. The evil creatures assaulted him from all sides. Zack jumped to avoid an attack and found himself launch into the air. For a brief moment he was airborne looking down over the battle. He could see large circles of dead Demons cut down around each fighter.

He crashed down into the horde again, smashing aside Demons like a raging toddler with its toys. He was wrath. He was war. He was violence. He cleft limbs and heads. He smashed aside his enemy with a passion.

Zack moved so fast his foe could not keep up. However they had huge numbers on their side. He was submerged in a whirlwind of claws and teeth. He sustained a deep gash on his arm that went down to the bone. But he kept fighting regardless. He was numb to all pain. He glanced at his arm again and saw it healing before his eyes. He fought on with renewed vigour. He cut down Demons like he had been built for this single purpose.

For hours Zack and the others at the citadel fought for their lives. Over time Zack felt his strikes didn't have the impact they did at first. His movements became a little slower. He fought on all the harder. He slayed countless Demons. Slowly Zack started to notice Bloodworms cover the ground beneath the battlefield. He would stomp what he could but prioritised the more dangerous enemies.

Zack was immersed in the battle. He did not hunger, thirst or get tired. Zack lost sight of the grass underneath as it turned to mud then in to a bloody bog. Numerous times he narrowly dodged enemy attacks. He drew upon all the strength and willpower he could muster. Zack kept on fighting.

Hours passed. It began to require more and more effort to inflict the same damage on his foe. His wounds started to heal slowly. He was still killing Demons at a staggering rate but his enemy seemed endless. The Bloodworms were now knee deep and making it increasingly difficult to fight. Zack kept on fighting.

Hours passed. Zack and the other fighters were really struggling now. The prayer teams were nearing exhaustion. Zack had not seen any fellow fighters in a while now. His body was starting to wear out. He was drenched in blood and demonic ooze. He tried to keep his enemies back but was now on the defensive. Zack kept on fighting.

Then Zack saw something he had not seen in such a long time. It was light in the sky. He squinted. A brilliant bright scorching white light slowly started to spread out through the whole sky. The very fabric of reality peeled away and Holy light flooded in. The Demons started to sizzle and cry out in pain. A deafening chorus of Holy Angels permeated the air. It was glorious. Thousands of Angels started to fill the sky.

Zack felt a new sensation surge through his body. It was pain; unrelenting, intense teeth-grinding pain. He looked down to see he had been skewered by a Mortkin. The Demon pulled its arm out of his chest. Zack hacked the Mortkin's head off in a defiant last strike. But it was too late. The Demon had pierced a hole all the way through to his back. The pain was unimaginable. It was like this was the single real feeling he had felt in years. Zack dropped his weapons. Zack lost consciousness and fell backwards.

Chapter 12

Rebirth

Zack opened his eyes. He looked down to see himself dressed in his Gold Star uniform. He had a gunshot wound in his chest. He was bleeding. He looked around. Everything was white. It was like he was inside a cloud.

"Am I dead?" he asked.

"No, you are not dead Zachary Michaels," A deep voice replied.

Zack sat up and spun around. He saw an enormous Angel. It was like the one he saw kill the Magnukin. It was terrifying to behold up close. The Angel had a radiant blue and white glow. Zack cowered in fear.

"Do not be afraid. My name is Gabriel. I have been sent from the Lord God Almighty to explain your vision."

Acts 2

[17] "In the last days, God says,
I will pour out my Spirit on all people.
Your sons and daughters will prophesy,
your young men will see visions,
your old men will dream dreams.
[18] Even on my servants, both men and women,
I will pour out my Spirit in those days,
and they will prophesy.
[19] I will show wonders in the heavens above
and signs on the earth below,

blood and fire and billows of smoke.
²⁰ The sun will be turned to darkness
and the moon to blood
before the coming of the great and glorious day of the Lord.
²¹ And everyone who calls
on the name of the Lord will be saved.'

Zack slowly stood and shielded his eyes.

"What's going on? I don't understand."

"You were injured Zachary. Your body is currently lying on the pavement outside a bank in Brakenside. All you have experienced has been a vision of what is to come. With this knowledge you have been chosen to help the world prepare."

"What? Why me?"

"God loves you and knows you are just right for this task. You have first hand experience of what will be. Use this to bring people to the Lord. Help others repent of their evil ways. Make preparations to fight the evil ones. You know what is at stake. The spiritual world has always been there, but you have seen it manifest physical form. Let the world know of God's love for all humankind."

"How can my body still be on the ground at the bank? That was years ago. Wasn't it?"

"Your entire vision has occurred in less than a moment in the physical world. You will soon return to your body. You will not die from your injuries."

A thousand questions raced through Zack's mind. But he didn't manage to put any into words.

"Go now. God has blessed you," Gabriel said.

Zack blinked his eyes. He was lying on the concrete outside the bank. He looked up and saw the bright blue sky. He remembered his vision and what the Angel had said. Zack jumped to his feet. He saw the gunman and ran over to him smiling.

"It's okay, everything will be okay!" Zack declared with a happy expression on his face.

The gunman didn't know what to do. He pointed the rifle at him again.

"Oh, you can't kill me," Zack said, pointing to his bleeding chest. "Here look, take this." Zack opened up his wallet and pulled out a large wad of the cash that he didn't recall having. He gave it to the gunman.

The gunman just stared at him. Zack could see he was trying to decide whether or not to shoot him again.

"It's okay, Henry Jones. Take this for the deposit you need for Agnes' treatment. The bank will discover their error on your accounts in a few days."

Henry was stunned. He didn't know what to say. He dropped his rifle. Stanley came rushing in with his pistol trained on Henry.

"Don't move!" he yelled.

Zack could see Stanley would fire at any sudden move.

"I got this Stanley," Zack said as he stood between Stanley and Henry.

"You've been shot! Move!" Stanley yelled.

"Oh, this was just an accident. Don't worry about it." Zack lowered Stanley's pistol.

"I'm so sorry, she needs that treatment..." Henry said quietly.

Zack started to feel the pain and the blood loss impact him.

"It'll be alright everyone. I just…"

Zack passed out and slumped to the ground.

…

Zack awoke later in hospital. He could hear hospital sounds around him and Graham and Beth playing a board game. He thought for a moment about all the different people he needed to talk to. He then slowly opened his eyes. He couldn't stop himself gagging on the tubes going into his nose and mouth.

Graham and Beth spun around.

"He's awake!" Graham said.

"I'll get the nurse," said Beth.

"Wait! Did anyone die?" Zack asked.

"No one died. But you came close," Graham explained.

"I'm okay. Let me talk to you both for a minute," Zack pleaded.

"You gave us such a fright. Are you alright Zack?" Beth asked.

"I know I'll be okay. But tell me, do you guys remember anything from before?" Zack was met with confused looks.

"You know the end of the world? The Siege, the Bishop, the Citadel, all the fighting?" As Zack spoke he read their expressions. He decided to leave out the terms 'Demon' and 'Angel'.

"Sorry, I don't know what you're talking about. Maybe it was really vivid dream?" Beth said politely.

"Zack, you hit your head on the concrete really bad. And you got shot and lived to talk about it. Give yourself time to come right," Graham suggested.

Zack realised only he had experienced the vision. He felt overwhelmed and alone.

Zack talked with the nurse briefly. Graham and Beth stayed for a while to chat then they left him to rest.

Zack was left alone with his thoughts. He wasn't sure what to do with all the memories in his head. There was a knock on the door. A policewoman entered.

"Hi, I'm Sergeant Wilson from the Brakenside Police department. I'm here to discuss the events of Tuesday the 15th of March."

Zack nodded.

"Please let me be blunt. I have never seen anyone get shot like you did and live. Let alone someone defend their attacker until they lose consciousness. Are you okay?"

"I'm not crazy, if that's what you mean," Zack said with a smile.

She smiled too.

"I have brought the forms to press charges against Mr Jones for you to fill out when you can."

"I won't need them," Zack replied.

"I'm sorry? You might need some more rest before we discuss this. This man shot you."

"I know. Can you just let him off with a warning?"

"Sorry, no we can't do that. Unless his lawyer works a miracle he'll be locked up for a long time."

"I know a good lawyer that I think will help him out," Zack said as he thought of Salmon.

Sergeant Wilson didn't know what to say for a moment.

"This is going to be an interesting day," she said smiling. She closed her notebook.

"I agree."

"I'm really surprised this whole incident didn't result in loss of life actually. Thank you for your time Mr Michaels. Good day."

"Bye."

She left the room.

Zack dwelled on how he'd best use his knowledge.

"Maybe I'll write a book," he said to himself quietly.

The sound of someone coughing startled Zack. He turned to see a man had been sleeping in a bed on the far side of the hospital room.

"Sorry about the noise, I didn't notice you there," Zack said.

The man rolled over.

"No trouble at all. Sorry, I didn't mean to pry. But it sounds like you've been through a lot."

"Yeah, much stranger times ahead too."

"Oh?"

"Sorry I don't mean to be rude, but I don't think you'd understand."

"Listening is part of my job, I'm here if you feel like talking."

"What's your job?"

"I'm a priest. My name is Douglas Andrews, nice to meet you."

Zack remembered Bishop Kephas mentioning this man as the leading member in the Holy Order of Salt and Light.

Zack beamed.

"Hi, I'm Zack. I've actually met some of your friends. Bishop Kephas, Brother Christopher and an interesting character called Gabriel."

Father Andrews sat up in his bed.

"Oh? I think we'll find plenty to discuss," he said.

Zack smiled.

THE END...?